"There are three authors whose body of work I have re-read more than once over my adult life: Charles Dickens, Jane Austen, and Maud Hart Lovelace."
—Anna Quindlen,
New York Times bestselling author

"Slipping into a Betsy book is like slipping into a favorite pair of well-worn slippers: It's always a pleasure to live in Betsy's world for a little while, to experience her simple joys but also her (thankfully short-lived) sorrows."
—Meg Cabot,
New York Times bestselling author

"I reread these books every year, marveling at how a world so quaint—shirtwaists! Pompadours! Merry Widow hats!—can feature a heroine who is undeniably modern."
—Laura Lippman,
New York Times bestselling author

"I read every one of these Betsy-Tacy-Tib books twice. I loved them as a child, as a young adult, and now, reading them with my daughter, as a mother. What a wonderful world it was!"
—Bette Midler, actor and singer

"Some characters become your friends for life. That's how it was for me with Betsy-Tacy."

—Judy Blume, beloved bestselling author

"The Betsy-Tacy books were among my favorites when I was growing up."   —Nora Ephron, Academy Award–nominated writer-director

"I am fairly certain that my independent, high-spirited grandmother must have had a childhood similar to Betsy Ray's. . . . As I read . . . I felt that I was having an unexpected and welcome peek into Granny's childhood—a gift to me from Maud Hart Lovelace."

—Ann M. Martin, creator and author of the Baby-sitters Club series

"Family loyalty and the devotion of friends to one another . . . for me are the defining characteristics of the Betsy-Tacy stories."

—Esther Hautzig, award-winning author, former director of Children's Book Promotion for Thomas Y. Crowell Co., and publicist for *Betsy's Wedding* in 1955

"I truly consider *Betsy and Tacy Go Downtown* to be the finest novel in the English language! I will never love any other books as much as I love the Betsy-Tacy books."

—Claudia Mills, children's book author, winner of the National Book Award and Golden Kite Award

"I grew up thirty miles north of Mankato, and trips to town were filled with mystery and magic because I was walking the same streets that Betsy and Tacy once walked. The Betsy-Tacy books . . . more than any other books, fed my dream of becoming a writer one day."   —Jill Kalz, Minnesota Book Awards
Readers' Choice Award winner

"At school visits, when kids ask what books I read as a child, I have only one answer: Betsy Tacy—the entire series. . . . Truthfully, I think those were the only books I read as a child. But they were enough to make me know that characters in books had true and honest feelings and that made all the difference."
—Maryann Weidt, author of the Minnesota
Book Award–winning picture book
Daddy Played Music for the Cows

"As a Minnesota girl, I read the Betsy-Tacy books about a thousand times as a kid. I used to go to sleep at night with one of the books under my pillow whispering to myself about the girls, hoping I'd dream I was playing with them."   —Anne Ursu, award-winning author

Emily of
Deep Valley

The Betsy-Tacy Books

Book 1: *Betsy-Tacy*

Book 2: *Betsy-Tacy and Tib*

Book 3: *Betsy and Tacy Go Over the Big Hill*

Book 4: *Betsy and Tacy Go Downtown*

Book 5: *Heaven to Betsy*

Book 6: *Betsy in Spite of Herself*

Book 7: *Betsy Was a Junior*

Book 8: *Betsy and Joe*

Book 9: *Betsy and the Great World*

Book 10: *Betsy's Wedding*

The Deep Valley Books

Winona's Pony Cart

Carney's House Party

Emily of Deep Valley

Emily of Deep Valley

A DEEP VALLEY BOOK

Maud Hart Lovelace

Illustrated by Vera Neville

HARPER**PERENNIAL** ● MODERN**CLASSICS**

NEW YORK ● LONDON ● TORONTO ● SYDNEY ● NEW DELHI ● AUCKLAND

HARPER**PERENNIAL** ● MODERN**CLASSICS**

HarperCollins books may be purchased for educational, business, or
sales promotional use. For information, please e-mail the Special Markets
Department at SPsales@harpercollins.com.

Emily of Deep Valley was first published in 1950 by Thomas Y.
Crowell Company. First Harper Trophy edition published 2000.

FIRST HARPER PERENNIAL MODERN CLASSICS EDITION PUBLISHED
2010.

Library of Congress Cataloging-in-Publication Data is available upon
request.

ISBN 978-0-06-200330-0

HB 09.06.2023

Foreword

One Saturday morning when we were new to America, my sister and I walked to the New York Public Library's Flushing branch, two miles from our apartment. It was my first visit to a library. I wandered through the stacks wide-eyed, fingering spines of unread books like a beggar in a bakery. I could take seven of them home with me! I chose carefully, knowing I'd savor them later on our fire escape, my secret reading sanctuary.

It didn't take long to find Maud Hart Lovelace's concoctions. Her classic novels served as a superb orientation for a newcomer eager to understand the history and heritage of a new world. They took me back to the early 1900s, a time when America shared many of the values that resonated in my old-world home, but they also sparkled with timeless humor that made me laugh out loud on the fire escape.

I was starting to see that the best stories blended three main ingredients: people, place, and plot. Mrs. Lovelace's books had all three, but her characters easily danced off the pages into my friend-hungry heart. I finished the "high school" Betsy-Tacy books first and immediately added Betsy to my growing list of fictional best buddies. She has a fun group of friends, loving parents, and big writing dreams. What was not to like?

Then, in *Emily of Deep Valley*, Mrs. Lovelace introduced me to Emily Webster, a teen who attends the same high school as Betsy. This novel is full of familiar characters—robust Bobby Cobb, stately Miss Bangeter, fun-loving Cab Edwards, and "little, dark-eyed" Miss Fowler, Deep Valley's treasure of an English teacher. Alice, Dennie, Winona, Tacy, Tib, and even Betsy herself make appearances in the book. But even Betsy plays a minor supporting role in what is indisputably Emily's story.

I began rooting for Emily from the get-go. She's treasurer of her class and a master debater—the only girl on an all-guy team who helps her school win the Southern Minnesota Championship two years in a row. Even though she's an orphan, she isn't jealous of her popular, pretty second cousin's doting parents. I admired how Emily sticks to her own classic, simple style when it comes to clothes and doesn't try to imitate Annette's frills and lace. And while other people her age (Don!—more on him later) scoff at tradition, Emily rises early to decorate the graves of her ancestors, dutifully presses her grandfather's uniform, and esteems the old Gettysburg soldiers marching on Decoration Day. When Miss Fowler suggests that a housekeeper take care of her grandfather so that Emily can go to college, Emily's answer is quick: "No. He's eighty-one. I've lived with him all my life." I was impressed by her loyalty and self-sacrifice.

Yes, Emily has many likeable character traits, but unlike Betsy, she isn't best friend material at all. Why not, you might be wondering? Well, because Emily is *me*.

Despite her strengths, she has serious flaws—more serious than any of Betsy's foibles. Emily is shy and socially awkward, and she struggles with resentment. She battles loneliness, weeps in despondency, and wistfully tries to cling to childhood. All of those emotions felt really familiar to the girl reading on the fire escape. In fact, Emily's all-too-human shortcomings and challenges resonate with most girls, even those growing up a century later.

First of all, she's left behind by her friends. As the senior girls in her crowd head off to college, we feel her desolation on the train platform. Depression comes next—a state of mind that Mrs. Lovelace must have understood before doctors began diagnosing it as a treatable condition:

> *"A mood like this has to be fought. It's like an enemy*
> *with a gun," [Emily] told herself. But she couldn't seem*
> *to find a gun with which to fight.*

What young teen hasn't experienced or feared some type of friend-initiated abandonment? In all good young adult Bildungsroman, or coming-of-age stories, the main teen character must confront her own problem. Mrs. Lovelace knew that, and that's why her books are still being read today. Somewhere in the middle of the book, Emily begins to "muster her wits and stand in her own defense." *I can, too*, the reader thinks.

Second, Emily falls in love with a guy who treats her poorly. We discover this in one short, revealing sentence in

Chapter One: "Moreover, Don Walker had danced with her." Don makes his appearance not long after that sentence, making Emily feel "the small tumult which he always created in her heart." By Chapter Two, we know he's a show-off, hypocritical, sullen. He's the one who informs Emily how "stuck" she is in Deep Valley. In short, he's a jerk. Which of us makes it through high school without a crush on a jerk? Readers today still celebrate as Emily discovers (on our behalf, too) that a true lover not only accepts you but also treats you with special care. *Maybe I'll wait for one of those.*

Third, Emily has big dreams to change the world. She admires Jane Addams' Hull House and longs to study sociology so she, too, can help the poor. The good news is that despite the limitations of Emily's life, she finds a way to make that dream come true. *Doesn't that mean I can, too?*

Mrs. Lovelace was adept at creating characters who face challenges we can understand. But *Emily of Deep Valley* also offers the other two intgredients required for a great story: a good sense of place and an intriguing plot.

When it comes to place, we first see the Websters' old-fashioned house with a sagging gate, sloping yard, faded picket fence, and dim, crowded little parlor. By the end of the book, seen through the eyes of love, Emily's home becomes the "Hull House of Deep Valley" and a "treasure of a little house."

Deep Valley's slough in winter provides the perfect metaphor of a desolate, apparently lifeless situation. But it's the slough—the slough Emily loves—which first brings Kalil and Yusef to her with their basket of frogs' legs. Little does she know that this chance meeting is the start of her dream coming true. By the last chapter, the slough in late May is "full of violets and white boughs of blooming wild plum which were dizzily sweet" and "birds singing in the newly leaved trees." Beyond it, Emily can see the ever-present humble rooftops of the Syrians and the lights of the town.

The dilemma of the Syrian families in Deep Valley is intertwined with Emily's internal transformation in the novel's plot. Persecuted in their home country for religious beliefs, these newcomers are struggling to make a living and to become part of the Deep Valley community. For twenty years the townspeople kept them at a distance, but Mrs. Lovelace doesn't allow us to do that. She introduces us to the feisty, outgoing Kalil and his "chunky, square-faced" compatriot, Yusef, and we smile at the closeness of their friendship. She has Kalil remove his cap and say, "Goodbye, my grandpa. I am full of thanks to you. Peace to your age," and our hearts melt. We celebrate Christmas with the shining-eyed Syrian children and visit them at Easter, imagining the taste of Kahik, a sweet cake, and watching their traditional egg-breaking contest.

Maybe that, too, explains why I loved *Emily of Deep Valley* so much. Yes, I was Emily, like every girl, but I also was Yusef, Kalil, and Layla, longing for a warm American welcome. I wanted Deep Valley to give *me* a cup of hot cocoa, a unanimous vote, a joyful babel of hurrahs, a hearty hand-shake, a bottle of violet perfume. I wanted American neighbors to come to *our* house so *my* father could overflow with hospitality: "What a blessed day! You have come to my house! It is yours. You may burn it."

Thanks to the power of Maud Hart Lovelace's pen, I did.

I devoured *Emily of Deep Valley* so often I knew parts by heart. I kept sneak-reading it as an older teen and as a college student, hiding my habit while discussing trendy intellectual novels. On wintry evenings, curled up by the fire in New England, I still turn to my copy as comfort fare, drawing nourishment and inspiration from the pages.

I never grow tired of cheering for Emily, and neither will a new generation of readers. The reissue of this book is especially timely given that hospitality for strangers from South Asia and the Middle East is . . . a bit more shaky. In her 1995 *Horn Book* essay called "Against Borders," Hazel Rochman describes the peacemaking power of authors like Mrs. Lovelace:

A good story lets you know people as individuals in all their particularity and conflict; and once you see someone as a person—their meanness and their courage—then you've reached beyond stereotype.

I know that girls coming of age in our fast-paced, multicultural, high-tech culture will continue to identify with

Emily's struggles and dreams. More of them have faith, care about the poor, and identify with so-called "old-fashioned" values than the media likes to admit. I'm excited that they'll get to meet Emily, come to love the Syrians, and be inspired to "muster their wits and stand in their own defense."

But as this new edition goes soaring out to shelves of libraries and bookstores around the country, forgive me if I like to picture a newcomer to America discovering Emily. I can see her now, turning the pages, as enrapt as I was, with dimples as deep as Layla's in both cheeks. Can't you?

—MITALI PERKINS

Contents

1

The Last Day of High School

"It's the last day of high school . . . ever," Annette said.

She said it gaily, swinging Emily's hand and pulling her about so that they faced the red brick building with its tall arched windows and doors, its elaborate lime-stone trimming, its bulging turrets and the cupola that made an ironical dunce's cap on top of all. Annette threw a kiss at it, then lifted her right hand and opened and shut the fingers in a playful wave.

"Good-by, old jail!" she said.

"Don't you dare call the Deep Valley High School a jail!" Emily's tone was joking but there was warmth in it, too. "Besides, we'll be coming back for Class Day!"

"It won't be the same!" Annette tilted her little dark head on which a complicated structure of puffs and curls was protected by a net and held in place by a ribbon. She smiled up engagingly. "You're sorry, aren't you, Em?"

"Yes, I am."

"I'm not, a bit. That's funny, isn't it? When I've had so much more . . . that is, when I've had so much fun here."

Emily knew what she had started to say . . . "When I've had so much more fun than you have." It was true that Annette had been a belle, and Emily certainly hadn't. But she loved the high school more than Annette possibly could.

"I've been happy here," she said.

It had been a refuge for her. Staring up at the cupola roof, outlined against the blue May sky, she thought affectionately of the hubbub in the Social Room at noon intermission . . . so different from the brooding silence of her home. She thought of the fun she had had with the girls, of the companionship she had known in classrooms, of the joyful challenge she had found in debating on the Assembly Room platform. Emily was on the star debating team which had won the Southern Minnesota Championship for two years running. And there had been parties, too, like last night's Junior-Senior banquet.

"Wasn't the banquet wonderful?" she asked, as she and Annette started down Walnut Street. The high school stood on the corner of Walnut and High. Walnut descended a steep hill, following terraced lawns. There were snowy drifts of bridal wreath around almost all the houses, and birds were as busy as seniors, full of talk and song.

"Marvelous!" answered Annette. "Of course . . ." she laughed contentedly, "I had my hands full. Did you notice how sulky Jim Baxter was because I came with Don?"

"I certainly did."

"Did you really have fun?" Annette looked pleased but puzzled. And Emily knew that she couldn't understand why the Junior-Senior banquet had seemed wonderful to Emily when she hadn't even come with a boy.

But it had. The familiar battered halls transformed by bunting, flags and balloons; the dinner, formally served by excited junior girls; the speeches by Miss

Bangeter, the principal, and by the junior and senior class presidents—Hunter Sibley of the Class of 1912 had done a wonderful job. And the dancing! That had been best of all!

Emily didn't go to many high school dances. It wasn't customary to go unless a boy invited you. But even unattached girls came to the Junior-Senior banquet, and it had been thrilling to hear the music of piano and violin and to join the maze of rhythmically moving figures.

She had danced a number of times—with Hunter, and other class officers; she was treasurer of the class. Moreover, Don Walker had danced with her.

He had done it, probably, because he had come with Annette, who was Emily's second cousin. But it had seemed a breathless boon to Emily that she should dance with Don before high school was over—closed like the covers of a book that could never be read again no matter how much one might wish to do so. They were on the debating team together, and she had a special feeling for him.

Tall and rangy in ankle-length skirts, her curly hair woven into a braid which was turned up with a ribbon, Emily walked smilingly beside her pretty cousin. Annette was so small that she often made Emily feel hulking, and Annette was so pretty—with her sparkling eyes and staccato birdlike movements—that she always made Emily feel plain. Emily wasn't plain, exactly, but her face was serious. She was shy and quiet, although her blue eyes, set in a thicket of lashes under heavy brows, often glinted with fun. Both boys and girls liked her.

"Emily isn't a lemon," she had once overheard Annette say heatedly. Annette and Gladys Dunn had been planning some boy and girl party in the cloakroom and Emily had stumbled in. She had escaped without being seen, but she had never forgotten Annette's blunt defense of her.

It was true, she decided later. She wasn't what the high school called a lemon. But she had never learned to joke and flirt with boys. Or perhaps boys just didn't joke and flirt with a girl who lived with her grandfather in a funny old house across the slough.

Walnut crossed Broad Street and Second and went on to Front, the business thoroughfare, which paralleled the river. The girls were nearing Front when they heard a clatter behind them and the sound of shoe leather sliding along the cement walk.

"Hi, there! Wait!"

They turned to see handsome Hunter Sibley and Ellen, his girl, hand in hand, along with Fred Muller and Scid Edwards and Don. At the sight of Don's tall erect figure Emily felt the small tumult which he always created in her heart.

"How about stopping at Heinz's?" called Scid. "Celebrate the last day of school?"

Annette smiled at Don. "But Em and I have to try on our graduating dresses."

"And Hunter has to practise his oration in the Opera House," put in Ellen, sounding proud.

"Me, too," said Don. "I'm a bright boy, too." He had a deep resonant voice.

"How about you, Em?" asked Hunter.

"I'm practising mine tomorrow."

"You Honor Roll people!" jibed Scid. "You walking encyclopedias! You grinds!"

Hunter grinned. "Don and I could meet you at Heinz's afterward," he said. "Even intellectual giants like us eat ice cream; don't they, Emily?"

Emily laughed, but she didn't know how to respond. It always irritated her, this slowness in repartee, for on the debating platform her tongue was as quick as a bird.

"I've an idea," cried Annette. "Why don't you all come to our house? Em and I have to be there anyway. I know!" she added radiantly, "I'll give a party! Miss Annette Webster cordially invites you to a last-day-of-school party . . . !"

"We'll bring ice cream from Heinz's," Scid yelled. He was a short, merry boy called Scid because he had said in class one day that Columbus "scidovered" America.

"Also Nabisco Wafers!"

"We'll play the phonograph and dance!" And Scid began to dance on the corner of Walnut and Front, circling an imaginary partner.

Don laughed as he always did at other people's antics . . . always, that is, when he was in a good mood.

"We'll expect you then," cried Annette. "But don't come until Em and I are through with our fittings. Mamma will be nervous as a witch."

The crowd broke up and the cousins hurried south along busy Front Street past the Melborn Hotel and the Lion Department Store. Emily felt both pleased and uncomfortable. Every festivity that could be crowded into these last days was a gain. But she well knew she was included in this one only by chance, because she happened to be going home with Annette.

The cousins were excellent friends. They enjoyed each other when family reunions or Annette's mother's assistance to Emily brought them together. But Emily belonged only to the girl part of the crowd. She was seldom included when boys entered in. And even with the girls she was a little apart.

Where Front Street curved to meet the slough, it became briefly residential. There were several blocks of handsome houses standing in large lawns, and Annette lived in one of these, a yellow-painted brick with a bay window, rimmed with colored glass in front.

"Mamma will be furious," giggled Annette, as they approached.

"Aunt Sophie is never furious at you long," said Emily. She called Annette's parents Aunt and Uncle by courtesy. Actually Annette's father was her own dead father's cousin.

"But she's in a state!" answered Annette. "Grandpa and Grandma LaDou are coming for my graduation, and Aunt Lois, and Uncle Edward, and a flock of cousins. And, of course, Miss Mix is there, and presents are just pouring in. And Mamma's a very nervous type . . . ."

"She's wonderful to you."

"I know it. But she has to be handled. Now this crowd coming in won't be a bit of trouble since the boys are bringing the ice cream. But I'm glad you'll be with me, Em, when I break the news."

"Lean on me," said Emily. "I have broad shoulders."

It was obvious at once that Aunt Sophie was indeed in a state. She leaned over the stairs, her black hair wispy about an anxious face.

"What's been keeping you?" she called. "Miss Mix can't do another thing until she tries these on."

"Don't tell her yet," whispered Annette, as they ran up the wide carpeted stairs.

There was a fern in a brass bowl on the newel post, and an Indian head on the wall. Emily loved these bright modern touches. She looked down with pleasure into the parlor with its mission oak furniture, its smart stenciled over-drapes, and dusky blue Maxfield Parrish picture over the mantel. A rim of polished floor surrounded the rug, for Aunt Sophie had long since abolished carpets.

Aunt Sophie hurried them into the front bedroom where Miss Mix sat at a sewing machine. Miss Mix sewed for all the best families of Deep Valley. She came to their houses, and one of Aunt Sophie's kind gestures to Emily had been offering to let Miss Mix make her dresses there, while she was making Annette's. It was inconceivable to think of Miss Mix in the little old-fashioned house across the slough.

Emily liked good clothes, and she dressed well. She spent almost as much money on her clothes as Annette did. In fact, Aunt Sophie was always saying that she wished Annette could spend as freely as Emily spent. Uncle Chester, she said, acted so when the bills came in. Emily's grandfather never told her to spend much or little.

She liked simple clothes, of good materials, well made. She liked sailor suits, and dark pleated skirts, with plenty of soft white waists. They were a contrast to Annette's frills, but they suited her.

Her graduation dress was made of fine white lawn trimmed only with tucks. Emily looked in the tier-glass with pleasure while Miss Mix, her mouth full of pins, squinted critically at the hem.

❧9❧

Aunt Sophie approved it absently. "It's awfully plain, Emily, but you wanted it that way."

"Yes, I did."

Miss Mix took the pins out of her mouth. "It's nice," she said. This was astonishing, for Miss Mix seldom spoke.

"Yes, it really is," Aunt Sophie answered. But her eyes were on Annette's ruffled organdy laid out on the bed. It had tiny white rosebuds along the top of the ruffles and Aunt Sophie was longing to see the effect.

Annette was an only child and Aunt Sophie and Uncle Chester really worshiped her, thought Emily. Uncle Chester might complain about the bills, but he loved to shower his daughter with everything extravagant and lovely. When Annette was in the room they seldom looked at anyone else. They seemed to put everything pertaining to Annette in a special category of supreme importance. The only dress in the room now, so far as Aunt Sophie was concerned, was Annette's dress. But Emily observed this with interest, rather than resentment. Perhaps, she reflected, all mothers were that way. She knew remarkably little about mothers; her own had died when she was born.

Emily finished her fitting and Annette's began. The rosebuds were approved.

"That's fine, Annette. That's all we'll want, so now you can . . ."

But Annette forestalled the instructions, whatever

they might be, by plunging boldly with the news that a crowd was bringing ice cream from Heinz's.

"Annette!" her mother wailed. "When you know how busy we are! Grandpa and Grandma will be coming any minute!"

"We'll clean up, won't we?" Annette prodded Emily. "We'll put all the chairs back."

"The *chairs* back. You're going to *dance?*"

"Of course. But only on the porch."

"And afterward we'll make things as neat as a pin, Aunt Sophie," Emily put in.

"But there are so many presents to open! There were three boxes this morning and two this afternoon." Aunt Sophie was relenting, though. She never could stand out against Annette long.

"We'll open them just as soon as the kids go," said Annette and pulled Emily into her bedroom. Here sunshine poured through white ruffled curtains held back by pink rosettes. There were more white curtains and pink rosettes on the bird's-eye maple furniture, a spread of the same pink and white on the big brass bed. The walls showed high school and college pennants, Harrison Fisher girls, and a fishnet full of photographs.

Annette powdered her nose and adjusted the pins in her elaborate coiffure. Emily retied her hair ribbon and washed her hands. There was time for no more for the door bell was ringing. The girls ran downstairs and the crowd burst in with cartons of ice cream, boxes of cookies and bottles of cherry phosphate.

"How did the orations go?"

"Fine! Fine!" said Don. "Cicero has nothing on me!"

"Hunter was wonderful!" cried Ellen. "How do the dresses look?"

"Beautiful. Mine has little white rosebuds on it."

"If it's as pretty as your Class Day dress . . .!"

"Annette!" called her mother, who was dishing out ice cream. "That reminds me! There's a photographer coming tomorrow to take your pictures."

"Didn't you have your pictures taken when the rest of us did?" asked Fred.

"Yes, in shirt waist and skirt. But Papa and Mamma want me in the Class Day dress and the graduation dress. They never seem to have enough pictures of me. They're silly about me."

Scid kicked Don who gave an appreciative chuckle. "They're not the only ones!"

"And, of course," said Ellen, "next year you'll be away at college."

"Of course."

"All of us will be!"

"All of them but me," thought Emily, and a quick pain seemed to drop down her body like a skyrocket in reverse.

But Scid was cranking the phonograph and music came to her rescue, pouring from the morning-glory horn. They had carried their ice cream through the rich dark dining room to the sunny side porch. The crowd pushed back the rattan chairs and rolled up the green grass rug. Aunt Sophie, forgetting her early annoyance, looked on eagerly.

The boys found partners and started dancing. Don took Annette, of course. Emily danced with Fred Muller, a tall, slender, light-haired boy, who was an exceptional dancer. He and his sister, Tib, danced together at entertainments sometimes.

Emily stumblingly followed his lead. She wasn't a good dancer. But it was such fun!—she felt sure that she could be good if she only had a chance to learn.

The phonograph was playing a popular waltz:

> *"Meet me tonight in dreamland,*
> *Under the silvery moon ... "*

Everyone but Emily was singing.

Emily didn't know the words, but she was happy as Fred piloted her gallantly up and down the porch. Not only her eyes but even her serious mouth was smiling.

If there had to be a last day of high school, she thought, it was wonderful to have it just like this.

2

Emily's Slough

It was sundown when Emily started home. The dance had lasted until the grandparents came, Aunt Sophie's half-French father and mother, from St. Paul. They had driven up from the depot in Mr. Thumbler's hack and alighted with much commotion . . . chattering, embracing, effervescing with pride in Annette. The party had broken up, but Emily had lingered, at

Annette's suggestion, to watch her open presents.

She had begun with a box brought by Grandpa and Grandma LaDou, and it had yielded a gold cross on a chain. From other boxes, with trills of delight, she had pulled silk stockings, a locket set with a half moon of pearls, a princesse slip, a party cap. She had flung the wrappings on the floor, and Aunt Sophie had started to pick them up, but Emily had jumped to do it, folding the papers and winding the bright ribbons neatly around her fingers. She had loved being a part of the family celebration.

The massive round dining table had been laid for supper with a linen cloth and napkins, the best silver, cut glass from the buffet and hand-painted china from the platerail. Savory odors floated from the kitchen where Minnie, the hired girl, a large clean apron tied about her waist, stood over the stove.

"Stay to supper, Emily," Aunt Sophie had urged, but Emily had felt she should go home. To be sure, all her grandfather ate at night was bread and milk. She prepared their main meal at noon. But he was always looking for her at this time of day. So she said goodby and started over the high road across the slough.

The Deep Valley slough, pronounced *sloo,* was the marshy inlet of a river. When Emily had first read *Pilgrim's Progress,* after finding it mentioned in Louisa M. Alcott's *Little Women,* she had pronounced the

Slough of Despond *sloo,* too. She had called it *sloo* until Miss Fowler had told her in English class that Bunyan's Slough rhymed with "how." Miss Fowler had made the correction in a casual unembarrassing way, putting her emphasis on the fact that Emily alone, out of the class, had read *Pilgrim's Progress.*

The difference in pronunciation had seemed suitable to Emily. Slough pronounced like "how" sounded disagreeable, and so did the miry pit in which Christian had wallowed. She loved her own slough, pronounced *sloo,* beside which she had lived all her life.

Now its hummocks of grass, its rushes and cat-tails were moistly green, but she loved it too in the autumn when its aspect was russet, and under winter's pall of snow, and most of all in the spring when it was carpeted with marigolds. It was such a social place—always noisy with frogs and birds. One end deepened to form a pond, and the birds loved it—gulls, sandpipers, red-winged and yellow-headed blackbirds. It sounded like a barnyard sometimes when a gathering of marsh hens was cackling on the water. And the bitterns made a noise like her own dooryard pump. "Thunder pumps," her grandfather called them.

Emily's bedroom looked over the slough, which extended back into the sheltered valley that the town called Little Syria. From her windows she could see the humble rooftops of the Syrians. She could see the sun rise over the marsh and the pond.

She was walking into the west now, toward the sunset, and her grandfather's little white house. She walked rapidly, smiling, for she still felt happy about the party. She felt excited, too, as she always did after she had been with Don. He had danced with her again today, which was most unusual.

When the debating team was off on its trips, he always sought her out. They talked for hours, on trains and in restaurants, about books—poetry, especially. He had a brilliant interesting mind. And although Emily listened at first with humble admiration, she always took fire and talked, too—more than she did with anyone else. They had wonderful times together.

But in Deep Valley he treated her differently. He never took her to Heinz's for a soda. In the Social Room and at parties he paid no attention to her. He was always with lively fashionable girls.

Annette liked him. She was impressed with his intellectual attainments and with an air of worldliness he had. Most of the girls liked him, although he was moody, conceited, and not handsome. There was magnetism in his dark, often sullen, face and his flashing white-toothed smile.

Most of the boys considered him a show-off, but they admired him. And in his good moods he was exuberantly friendly whether he really liked people or not. He slapped them on the back, laughed at their jokes.

"He flatters people," Emily admitted, reluctantly indicting him with a fault that was serious in her eyes. She added at once, "It's because he's so anxious to be liked."

This was true. In spite of his good mind, good family and more money than most, he seemed to have some inner uncertainty, some urgent need of friendship.

Walking home across the slough, she went over everything he had said while they danced. He had jokingly quoted Lord Byron:

"On with the dance! Let joy be unconfined:
No sleep till morn, when Youth and Pleasure meet . . . "

"Which will you be, Emily, Youth or Pleasure? I'll give you your choice. Speak up!"

She had not been able to find a witty answer.

He had asked where she was going to go to college. She had answered calmly but with an inner shrinking that she wasn't going. Gosh, what a shame! he had said. It was a bum world, and he had always known it. To think of her, of all girls, being stuck in Deep Valley!

"I can't imagine a nicer place to be stuck in!"

Emily had exclaimed indignantly. And he had smiled that gleaming smile which so illumined his face.

"Well," he had said then, "it's the State University for me. If I'm a good boy and do my homework, I'll be sent to Yale next year. That's my father's college. How'll you like to know a Yale man?"

The slough was behind her now. Emily followed the faded white picket fence surrounding her grandfather's acre to the sagging gate which was always ajar. The sloping yard wasn't well kept. The grass was filled with dandelions; and the lilacs and snowball bushes needed pruning. The snowballs, though, were in bloom.

The little house huddled against a low hill. It was old and weather-beaten. With its gables trimmed with scroll work and topped by absurd little towers, it looked like a dingy, fussy old lady, shrunken by age.

Emily ran up the steps of the small front porch. No lamps had been lighted, but she knew that her grandfather liked to sit in the dark. The door was closed against the sweet spring evening. Opening it, she was greeted by a familiar musty smell.

"Here I am, Grandpa!" she called.

There was no answer and she went through the dim crowded little parlor to the dining room. His easy chair, upholstered in carpet cloth in a pattern of cabbagelike roses, stood in the bow window which overlooked the slough. He wasn't there. She went on to the kitchen where he ate his evening bread and milk. He wasn't there either. She looked in his bedroom which adjoined the kitchen, and went out to the twilit back stoop. The sky was flushed now. Frogs were croaking in the pond.

"Grandpa! Grandpa!" she cried.

There was still no answer and she felt a small twinge of alarm. Turning she ran back to the parlor and up the stairs. Her own bedroom was empty.

"Grandpa!" she called again, and this time there was an answer. It came from the low garret at the back of the upstairs hall.

"Here I am, Emmy. Here I am."

"But what are you doing?"

"Why, I'm looking for my uniform."

"Your *uniform*!" For a moment she thought that he had lost his mind, that he had gone back to the days of his youth when he served in the Northern Army during the Civil War.

"Of course," answered Grandpa Webster, and his skull cap came through the low door of the garret. His round mild face with arching heavy brows was covered now with dirt and perspiration. A blue bundle dragged from his arms. "You haven't forgotten that day after tomorrow is Decoration Day?"

Decoration Day! It was the most important day in

her grandfather's year, and she hadn't given a thought to it. Penitently she took the uniform out of his arms.

"I'd have gotten it for you, Grandpa," she said. "I want to press it anyway."

"Yes, I suppose so," he said. He chuckled. "It didn't get much pressing, though, when we marched thirty-three miles to get to Gettysburg."

With each passing year her grandfather talked more about Gettysburg. He had served with the First Minnesota there and had reason to be proud.

He followed her to the kitchen where she laid the uniform over a chair while she lit the kerosene lamp and washed her hands.

"You haven't eaten yet, Grandpa?"

"I was hunting for my uniform. Weren't you late, Emmy?"

"Yes, I was. We had a sort of party at Annette's. It was the last day of school."

He looked up quickly. "Your last day of school?"

"Yes, and not just for this year. I'm graduating. Do you remember, Grandpa?"

"That's right," he answered in a pleased tone. "You told me you were. Now you'll be at home all the time."

Emily was silent.

"I wouldn't let you stop until you finished high school," said the old man, sounding proud. "Would I, Emmy?"

"That's right, Grandpa."

He meant to be so generous! In his day there had been no such thing as higher education for women.

He crumbled bread into a bowl and poured milk from a little earthen pitcher. "The snowballs are in bloom."

"I noticed," Emily replied. The snowballs should have reminded her, she thought. The old soldiers always wore snowballs, and every year there was anxiety as the great day approached lest they shouldn't bloom in time. "I'll go up to the cemetery tomorrow. See that our graves are tidy."

"I used to go with you," her grandfather said. He put down his spoon, looking troubled.

"You'll be going day after tomorrow."

"I certainly will!" He smiled radiantly. "The Mayor came out to see me today."

"He did?"

"He wants me to ride in the parade—in an auto. I told him I'd rather walk, the way we did going to Gettysburg. But there aren't more than a dozen of us old fellows left. He says he wants to take good care of us. Let the Spanish-American fellows do the walking, he said. Maybe there's something in it?" The old eyes twinkled under his bushy brows with the same humor Emily's eyes had.

"There's a lot in it," said Emily. "You're eighty-one

years old. I don't want you walking very far."

"Oh, I'll only walk up Front Street. Just to show them I can. That's what Judge Hodges and I have decided. The Judge came over a while today, too."

He usually did. Tall, gaunt, bearded, he was a veteran of the Fifth Minnesota and the two old men loved to argue about the exploits of their respective regiments.

"I don't want you to get so tired you can't come to Commencement," Emily said.

"Commencement?"

"My graduation."

"When is it?"

"Friday night."

"I'll be there," he answered. "Do they make much fuss about it?"

"I told you I'm having flowers—and a new white dress. I tried it on today."

"That's right. I'm glad you got yourself a nice white dress." He put down his spoon again. "Your mother was married in a nice white dress."

She was buried in it, too, thought Emily, remembering the story her grandfather had often told her. The old man's thoughts didn't go on to that sad aftermath. "Yes siree," he said, "the Mayor wants us to ride. But we're going to walk a ways at least. Show 'em we can."

"You'd better get to bed," said Emily. "I'll press your uniform."

The old man went into his little bedroom off the kitchen. He always went to bed before the sunset color was quite out of the sky. Emily washed their bowls and spoons. Then she built up the fire in the range and put the irons to heat and brought out her ironing board.

It was astonishing that she had forgotten about Decoration Day. She hadn't missed a parade in her life. But the dress fitting, the party, Don Walker had put it out of her mind.

"You're going to have good weather for it, Grandpa," she called, testing her iron with a moistened finger.

"What's that? What did you say?"

"You're going to have good weather for Thursday. Nice and cool."

He put his head, in a nightcap now, around the bedroom door.

"It was mighty hot when we marched to Gettysburg," he chuckled. "But we got there just the same."

3
Class Day

BY SIX O'CLOCK THE following morning Emily was on her way to the cemetery.

She had set her alarm clock for five, for she had to practise her oration in the Opera House at one; she must have a final fitting of her graduation dress, and in the evening came the Class Day program. It was a day on which to get a head start.

She walked briskly, dressed for action in an old middy blouse and skirt. Over one arm hung a pail containing a small rake, a trowel, garden shears, and three empty quart jars. The other arm held big bouquets of snowballs and lilacs, tulips and painted daisies, their stems wrapped in newspapers which had been soaked in water.

She had picked them in her own yard while the birds trilled a welcome to their early morning world, and had breakfasted softly, leaving her grandfather's coffee on the stove. Beyond the slough most of the houses were still sleeping, but at Annette's house a curl of smoke suggested that Minnie might be getting breakfast.

A milkman's wagon was rattling from door to door. "Hel-lo," the milkman called in a muted voice. He, too, seemed to feel the camaraderie of the hour and nodded at her flowers. "The missus and I are going up there this afternoon," he said.

It was too bad, Emily reflected, turning east to Broad Street, that she had to go so early, for the cemetery on the afternoon before Decoration Day was a very social place. It was full of people putting their family graves in spic and span order. At the Episcopal Church, she took the curving road up Cemetery Hill and passed through the tall arched gate.

This town of marble and granite monuments was even quieter than the one she had left below. Silvery cobwebs lay unbroken on the grass. Only a callous bob-o-link disturbed the stillness, and Emily made her way with a hushed tread past modest crosses, stately obelisks, and the snowy statue of an angel, to the Webster plot which had a square granite monument with headstones marking the places where her grandmother, father and mother lay. At the foot of the graves her grandfather had placed a small white iron bench.

Ivy covered the headstones, and a moss-rose bush, which her grandmother had planted, stood between the graves of Emily's father and mother. Lilies of the valley on her grandmother's grave had spread untidily.

"I'll have to clear them out," thought Emily. She looked down at the headstone on which a pair of clasped hands was chiseled. The lettering read: "Emily Clarke Webster. Born 1835, died 1904. She hath done what she could."

Emily remembered her well . . . a cheerful, big-bosomed old lady. She was something of a personage in Deep Valley, for she had been its first school teacher. Far back in the fifties, when the town was less than a year old and she was a girl, fresh from New Hampshire, Emily Clarke had opened a little school in her father's parlor. There had been fourteen pupils.

In the last decade of a busy, useful life she had

taken her granddaughter to raise.

"You always *did* do what you could," Emily said affectionately. "Well! I'd better get to work."

Putting down her pail, she thinned out the too lavish lilies of the valley. She raked the dead leaves, clipped the long grass, and dug a hole on each mound, into which she sank an empty jar. Taking her pail, she went to a nearby pump for water. She filled the jars and inserted the still dewy bouquets.

As she worked she continued to think about her grandparents. Cyrus Webster had come out to Minnesota from Ohio, lured by the newly ceded Indian lands. A seminary graduate, he had been attracted to the enterprising young teacher. They were married and staked out a claim over a valuable limestone formation which, after the Civil War, he had quarried with great profit. But his only son had been killed in an accident there.

Emily glanced at her father's dates. "Fred Webster, 1868–1896," said his headstone under a chiseled open book, presumably the Bible.

For all her grandfather's loyal evasiveness, Emily gathered that her father had not been too successful in the quarry—or any place else. Fred Webster had been a changeable, too optimistic young man. He had looked, she understood, like Uncle Chester, who was floridly handsome. But Uncle Chester had had the business ability his cousin lacked. He had taken

Fred's place in the quarry and had risen from foreman to be superintendent and then partner. He ran it alone now.

Emily's slow gaze passed to her mother's headstone. There was a chiseled cherub above "Charlotte Benton Webster, 1873–1894"; 1894 was the year of Emily's birth.

Lottie Benton had been a teacher, too. She had come all the way from Binghamton, New York, to teach in Deep Valley.

"No wonder I want to go to college!" Emily thought. "Two teachers in the family!"

Lottie had married Fred Webster in his parents' home. Her own parents were dead, and she had left no relatives in Binghamton.

"Lottie was a dear, pretty girl," her grandfather always said.

"She was just the one for him. He'd have settled down if she had lived," her grandmother had told her.

"Your father didn't deserve her," Uncle Chester had said bluntly.

But somehow nothing that anyone said ever made her mother real to Emily. The photograph on her bureau of Lottie Benton wearing the frizzed bang, tight basque and looped polonaise of the eighties had never come to life.

Emily sat down on the bench to rest. Her exertions had loosened her hair which broke into curly tendrils around her broad brow and quiet eyes. She sat with her head bent and studied her mother's headstone.

How different her life would have been if her parents had lived! It was strange to think that she might have had brothers and sisters, and girl friends coming for supper or to study and stay all night! She had heard the other girls mention doing this, but she had never done it in her life.

Boys and girls would have come to play the piano or phonograph as they did at Annette's. Boys would have called for her to go to parties, and her mother would have looked her over before she started! Emily had once gone to a party with Annette and she had never forgotten how Aunt Sophie had asked Annette to turn around, watching critically for a hint of petticoat or a hair out of place.

Emily bent down impulsively and touched her mother's grave.

"I wish you could be here to see me graduate. Father, too," she said.

She remembered the tickets she had received for Commencement. Each member of the class had been given six. Emily had use for only one, and she had felt queer when the other girls were discussing how they would manage with so few. She had wanted to offer her extra ones, and she would, of course, before the day came. It occurred to her now with an unexpected stab that if her parents had lived she might have needed every single ticket.

"I'm glad I have Grandpa," she thought, and loving thankfulness swept over her. "I'm glad, even if I can't go to college."

She jumped up. Everything looked fresh and tidy. The graves would be a credit to her and her grandfather when the crowd came up to the cemetery tomorrow.

Going down the hill, her empty pail over her arm, she met Hunter Sibley and his two younger brothers, coming up.

"Doesn't your family come in the afternoon?" she asked.

"Sure," answered Hunter. "But we kids want to decorate Uncle Aaron's grave ourselves."

"What a lovely idea!" Emily warmed with pleasure. The Sibleys' Uncle Aaron had been in the First Minnesota along with her own grandfather. This was a tribute to him, too.

"It was Jerry's idea," said Hunter, and nodded, smiling, at the middle brother, a short boy who still wore knickerbockers although he was a junior in high school. Emily knew him well for he, too, was a debater.

Jerry held up his bouquet. "Look what I found!"

"Lady slippers!" cried Emily. "They're beauties."

"I'm going to put on flags," said Bobby, a ten-year-old with unruly hair, mischievous eyes and big front teeth. "Flags!" he shouted. "And when I put on flags, *I put on flags*."

Both his hands were full of flags of all sizes. Waving them violently, he started to run up the hill.

Emily laughed with the warm enjoyment she always found in children and proceeded on to Front Street and over the slough. Her grandfather was waiting for her at the gate, his round face, beneath the skull cap, sober.

"How did the graves look?"

"Just fine, Grandpa! I took out nice bouquets."

"What did you put on your grandmother's grave?"

"Lilacs."

"She always liked them," the old man said with satisfaction.

"And what do you think the Sibley boys were doing?" She described their pilgrimage and a flush came into his old cheeks.

"When Colonel Colville told us to charge," he said, "nobody ran out on that field any faster than Aaron Sibley."

"You ran fast enough to get a bullet through your arm."

"Only winged, only winged," he answered impatiently. "It might have been death for any one of us."

It was for a good many of them, Emily remembered.

She had heard her grandfather say many times that only forty-seven had come back out of two hundred and sixty-two who had made the gallant charge.

After pumping a pail of fresh water, she went in to get dinner. She put potatoes to boil, fried pork chops and opened a jar of tomatoes she had canned the summer before. She laid a cloth on the dining room table and put on jelly, bread and butter, a pot of tea. They sat down and her grandfather said grace.

Through the bow window in which his easy chair stood, they could see small crooked willows and the slough, still wet from the spring rains. Some Syrian boys had a homemade boat in the pond.

"They killed a snake out there this morning," her grandfather remarked. Presently he asked, "Emmy, did you press my uniform?"

"Yes, Grandpa. I pressed it last night."

"That's fine! That's fine! Judge Hodges was here this morning. He and I don't want to ride in autos, the way the Mayor asks. We want to walk, show 'em we can."

"Well, don't walk too far," Emily answered absently. She was used to hearing him tell the same story, and herself making the same responses, over and over.

"I'm glad those Sibley boys appreciate their uncle, Emmy."

"They're nice boys. Hunter is the president of our class, you know. Grandpa, I have to go to the Opera

House this afternoon. I have to practise my oration."

He looked puzzled. "You told me what that was about, but I've forgotten."

"It's about Jane Addams and Hull House."

"Oh, yes! You said it for me. It was fine."

Gettysburg, Emily Clarke Webster, Fred and Lottie slipped into the past. While she washed the dishes, and her grandfather napped in his chair, Emily recited her oration.

"A woman has awakened the social conscience of this generation . . ."

She enjoyed reciting it, for she liked the story of Jane Addams who had grown up in nearby Illinois, had been graduated from Rockford Seminary there, had traveled abroad and had been so touched by the miseries of the poor that she had decided to devote her life to helping them.

She had done it in such a strange, interesting way, by going to live among them, taking a big house in a poor, crowded foreign section of Chicago and then just being a good neighbor. Hull House had resulted— a "settlement house," it was called—a hospitable center of fun and useful activity for young and old.

"What a wonderful thing to do!" Emily thought, running upstairs to change her clothes. "If I could go to college, I'd train for work like that. I'd love to go to some big city and start another Hull House."

Miss Fowler, the little dark-eyed English teacher, was waiting on the stage of the Opera House. The big front curtain was rolled halfway up to show rows of empty seats.

"I'm going to sit down in the parquet and listen first, and then I'll go up in the balcony," Miss Fowler said. She came from Boston and spoke with an eastern accent. "I'll take your paper although I know it isn't necessary. You won't need prompting."

"I don't think I will," said Emily. She liked to address an audience and was used to it, from debating. Miss Fowler applauded from the gallery, and when she returned to the stage she put her hand on Emily's arm.

"Your oration is very good," she said. "It sounds as though it had sprung from your own thoughts about Jane Addams."

"It did," Emily answered. "Of course, I've done a lot of reading, too."

"But she really interests you."

"Yes, she does. I think I would like social work."

"Emily," said Miss Fowler, looking at her thoughtfully, "I wish you could go to college. You can afford it, I know. It's a matter of leaving your grandfather, isn't it?"

"Yes."

"Wouldn't a housekeeper . . ."

"No. He's eighty-one. I've lived with him all my life."

"The German College has classes in English."

"But he's been waiting for me to get through high school. He doesn't realize . . ." she stopped.

"Oh, well," said Miss Fowler. "It isn't necessary. College would help you to get where you're going but you'll get there just the same."

Emily didn't answer. She ached when she thought about college. So many of the girls in her class were going—to Carleton, or St. Catherine's, or the State University. Mabel Scott, another honor student, was going east to Vassar where Carney Sibley, Hunter's older sister, went.

"No girl in the class would get as much out of college as I would," thought Emily, walking up Front Street. She swallowed hard. "But I mustn't even think about it."

She turned in at the butcher shop and bought a chicken for Decoration Day. She stopped at the shop of Windmiller, the florist, to order flowers for herself for Friday. The other girls would be receiving them from their parents. But her grandfather wouldn't know how to go about buying flowers. He wouldn't mind her buying them, though.

"We have plenty, Emily," he had told her when she was fourteen, and illness had forced him to retire from the quarry. Each month he gave her the money for their modest living, and if she needed more, she had only to ask. She seldom asked, however, for she had been trained in thrift.

She approached Mrs. Windmiller with friendly dignity. "Will you send me a dozen pink roses Friday afternoon? They're for my graduation. I'll pay for them now."

At Annette's, the two dresses were finished, pressed and laid out on the bed. Grandma LaDou came to see Annette in her ruffled organdy and stayed on with kindly interest to admire Emily, too.

"We'll call for you and your grandfather tomorrow night," Aunt Sophie said.

"Oh, thank you!" Emily cried. She had been wondering how they would get to the Opera House.

"Emily," Aunt Sophie added, looking a trifle embarrassed, "are you using all your tickets?"

"My tickets?"

"Yes. For Commencement. I know you each got six. Could you spare us three? We need them desperately."

"Of course. They're in my pocket book."

Aunt Sophie accepted them with fervent gratitude, and after Emily had packed her dress in a box, they went down to the back parlor to see Annette's presents which were spread out on the center table, each one in its bed of tissue paper.

"Thirty-six so far," Grandma LaDou said proudly.

Annette was busy with the photographer, but Emily lingered looking at the dazzling array. When she said good-by, Aunt Sophie and Grandma LaDou each handed her a tissue-wrapped package. Emily flushed with pleasure.

"For me?"

"Of course," said Aunt Sophie. "Graduation presents."

Emily smiled all the way across the slough. It was exciting to have two graduation presents. She had known, of course, that she would receive some, but still it was nice to have them appear. One box was oblong, the other round.

"I'll open them with Grandpa," she thought.

This time he was waiting in his chair in the dining room window. Emily ran in and sat down on a stool beside him.

"Is the sun going to set red?" he asked.

"Why, yes, Grandpa. Look what Aunt Sophie and Uncle Chester have . . ."

"If the sun goes down red, it'll be fair tomorrow."

"It will be fair, all right. Aunt Sophie . . ."

"Judge Hodges and I aren't afraid of the heat," her grandfather said. "Emmy, did you press my uniform?"

"Yes, Grandpa. I pressed it." She was quiet, and her interrupted sentence must have echoed in the silence for her grandfather asked suddenly, "What about Sophie and Chester?"

"They gave me a present. For my graduation. And so did Mrs. LaDou. I brought them home to open with you." She showed him the packages.

Her grandfather beamed with pleasure. "Now that was nice of Sophie and Chester!" he said.

Emily took up Aunt Sophie's box. She untied the ribbons as slowly as possible to draw out the fun.

"What do you suppose it is? A bracelet?"

"Hurry up! Let's have a look at it."

She unfolded the tissue paper and lifted the cover off the box. Twilight was dimming the little dining room but there was still light enough to see.

"Grandpa! Look! It's one of those new fountain pens."

"A fountain pen? What kind's that?"

"You can fill it with ink. You don't need to keep dipping it in the ink pot all the time," Emily explained.

Her grandfather examined it in pleased bewilderment. "Now that was nice of Sophie and Chester!" he said again.

Grandma LaDou had given her a sewing bag made of violet satin, very handsome. Happily, Emily arranged the two presents in their beds of tissue paper on the parlor center table. She took her dress out of its box and put it on a hanger. They went to the kitchen where she set out bread and milk.

"I'll have to eat quickly," she said. "I'm going to the high school tonight for Class Day exercises."

Her grandfather didn't answer, but when he had finished his supper he put down his spoon and looked at her. His head was held low, as she so often held her own, and his eyes, under puzzled brows, glanced up sharply.

"Emmy," he said, "oughtn't I to give you a graduation present?"

"Pshaw!" said Emily. "You're giving me my pretty white dress."

"That's not a present."

"And I'm buying roses for graduation night. They're really a present from you." She jumped up, smiling. "I have to hurry now and change my dress. You get to bed early, on account of Decoration Day tomorrow."

Class Day was a riot of fun. Lights were blazing over the packed Assembly Room. The platform was concealed by a cambric curtain which billowed out grotesquely as concealed figures moved behind its shelter. Now and then Scid Edwards thrust his face, heavily painted and with blackened eyebrows, between the curtains to grimace at the crowd which responded with cheers and laughter.

The senior girls—the ones who weren't in the play—wore their Class Day dresses. Emily's was made of corn-colored silk with long sleeves and a long slim skirt. She sat with Mabel Scott, a tall, dark, fragile girl who, like herself, didn't go with boys. They sat near the front where they wouldn't miss a ripple of the fun.

The play, called "One Night Only," was interrupted continually, not only by forgotten lines but by uproarious laughter. The author's jokes were much less effective than Jim Baxter's difficulties with the monocle he wore as Lord Mulberry—or Hunter on his knees to Nell Hennesy, his wife—or Scid's exaggerated courtship of the maid, Annette, who wore a cap with long floating strings. The audience stamped, clapped and whistled when Scid kissed her.

Between the acts the Class Papers were read to tumultuous applause. The Class Will gave Emily the Carnegie Library. In the Class Prophecy it was predicted that she would debate in the United States Senate.

In the midst of the clapping which followed that, Hunter started a cheer. It had been used all season at the inter-school debates.

> "There's Webster, King and Walker,
> And they can talk a few,
> With such an aggregation,
> We won't do much to you."

Emily had never thought to hear it again. Her surprise and pleasure almost choked her.

The evening ended with the Class Song, written to the tune of "I'd Love to Live in Loveland."

> *"We hate to leave the high school,*
> *To a crowd like you . . . "*

The Class of 1912 was jammed on the stage together, those who had taken part in the play still wearing their makeup, their red cheeks, black eyebrows and fantastic hair. Arms were hooked. Everyone was swaying in unison.

Emily's eyes were shining, but inside she kept remembering that Class Day was the last event before Commencement. The Award Assembly and the Junior-Senior banquet had slipped away. Soon this would be gone, too.

She looked, as she always did, for Don. Annette, hanging on his arm, caught her eyes and winked with roguish affection.

Emily returned to the joyous rhythm of the song.

"We hate . . . to leave . . . the high school," she sang, swaying with the rest.

4
Decoration Day

SHE WAS MAKING COFFEE the next morning when her grandfather's door opened and he came out, dressed in his Civil War uniform. The blue coat was buttoned smartly up to the turned-down collar. A cartridge belt encircled his gently bulging waist. His skull cap was replaced by a jaunty forage cap, and a sheepish smile bathed his face.

"Grandpa!" cried Emily. "How nice you look!"

"Do I?" he asked, trying to sound nonchalant.

"Turn around! You even shined your shoes."

"Of course! In the army you have to shine your shoes or your sergeant gives you Billy Hell. Will you pin on my badge and the medal?"

"I'd be proud to." She fastened the red, white and blue emblem of the Grand Army of the Republic and the Civil War medal on his chest while he stood sternly erect. He inspected them with satisfaction in the wavering kitchen mirror.

"Shall we go out and pick a snowball now?"

"Not yet," she answered. "We want it to be fresh. You don't go to the schools until nine, you know." Deep Valley's "old soldiers" always visited the schools on Decoration Day morning. Then the schools, shops and offices closed, and at one-thirty came the parade.

Emily poured the coffee and dished out bowls of steaming oatmeal while her grandfather, removing the forage cap reluctantly, sat down at the kitchen table. The heat from the range felt comfortable for there was a layer of ice in the air.

"Remember how hot it was last year?" she asked.

"I certainly do. You never can tell about May."

"I'm glad it's going to be cool for the marching. You won't walk very far, though, will you, Grandpa?"

He chuckled. "Just far enough to show the Mayor

there's life in us old boys yet."

When she started to wash the dishes, he said, "Emmy! It's eight o'clock now. Oughtn't we to pick a snowball?"

"In a minute," she answered. But he couldn't wait. While she worked she could see him from a window, walking around the snowball bush in eager anticipation. Smiling, she ran out to join him.

The sun was higher now, glittering on the trees with their small new leaves, on the dewy grass. Emily, too, circled the bush, inspecting the luscious white clumps.

"Snowball is too cold a name for them," she said. Selecting the finest, she cut it carefully. He looked stern again while she pinned it on his chest.

"Now! You look very nice!"

"I'll go to the gate and wait for the auto."

"Tell them about Gettysburg in your very best style."

"By Jingo, I will!" he answered happily.

Emily put the chicken to stew and made a pudding. While she worked she thought about the "old soldiers" coming to the schools when she was a child. Judge Hodges used to tell them about Nashville, and old Cap' Klein about fighting the Sioux. How proud she had been of her grandfather!

Taking a dust cloth she went into the parlor. This

was almost as her grandmother had left it. Emily was a little ashamed of its old-fashioned look, but she thought that her grandfather was too old for change.

Enlarged photographs hung on the walls along with a hair wreath and a picture showing a weeping widow at a tombstone. Wax flowers bloomed under a glass dome. There were a black walnut sofa and chairs, upholstered in horsehair; a secretary with books behind glass; and an old, square, yellow-keyed piano.

She set the table with a linen cloth and her grandmother's Haviland china, and walking down to the slough picked some blue flags with their sword-shaped leaves for the center of the table.

Before the chicken was tender, her grandfather came in, glowing. Loosening his collar, he sank down in his chair and told her about his success at the schools. He went reluctantly, at her urging, to lie down, and when she called him for dinner he bounced up with bright eyes. While they ate he told her about his triumphs again.

His snowball was showering small flowerets now, and Emily went out and picked another. She pinned it on his coat.

"Now you rest while you wait for the Judge."

"Rest! Rest! We didn't get much rest marching to Gettysburg."

"I know. But today you're just marching to Lincoln

Park. And see that you don't go any farther!" They both laughed. "Here's Judge Hodges now," she added, as the doorbell jingled.

In contrast to her grandfather, the Judge was tall and bony with a white beard flowing to his waist. He, too, wore the dapper forage cap and a snowball on his chest.

"I've been telling Grandpa not to walk too far," said Emily.

"Just what my daughter has been nagging me about!"

"I told her we marched thirty-three miles to get to Gettysburg."

"You and your Gettysburg! At Nashville, we didn't waste time walking. We were too busy fighting."

Squabbling and joking, the two old men went out the front door. But halfway down the ragged path, they stopped and came back. Judge Hodges put his hand in his pocket and pulled out a package.

"My daughter picked it out for me," he said.

"Why, Judge Hodges!" Emily unwrapped it, smiling, and drew out a souvenir spoon. There was a replica of the Deep Valley High School on the handle with Class of 1912 engraved below. "I'll keep this always! How kind of you!"

"Well . . . !" He smoothed his long beard affectionately as one might stroke the mane of a favorite horse.

"I've known you since you were knee-high to a grasshopper. And I understand that you're one of the top honor students, have an oration to give."

"I've heard her recite it," Grandpa Webster put in proudly. "It's about . . . what is it about now, Emmy?"

"Jane Addams."

"That's right. Jane Addams. It's fine, too."

"I don't see how Cy Webster could have such a smart granddaughter," said the Judge, giving his old comrade an affectionate whack. They hooked arms and started down the ragged path again, looking somehow younger in their excited gaiety.

Emily put the spoon with her other presents and hurried up to her room. She poured water from a pitcher into a bowl and washed, looking at a splasher that showed two frogs fishing. Except for a Deep Valley High School pennant, everything in the little slant-roofed bedroom was old. There was a black walnut bureau with a marble top. The bed was a towering, heavily carved affair, and her grandmother had embroidered the pillow shams. One showed a setting sun and one showed a rising sun. "Early to Bed" and "Early to Rise," they said.

Emily braided her hair freshly and turned it up with a white ribbon. She put on a white waist and skirt, pinned on a sailor hat and picked up her jacket, pulling a small flag into the buttonhole.

The crowd was three deep along the sidewalks of Front Street. Horses were hitched on the side streets and a mounted policeman was trying to keep the roadway clear. Deep Valley people and country folk alike were dressed in their Sunday best. She saw a group of Syrians; the men in thick black suits, the women with bright scarves over their heads.

Children were waving starchy new flags, and they were all wearing colored caps. There was an epidemic of colored caps, she noticed—some red, some white, some blue.

She stopped in front of Ray's shoe store. (The Ray family had moved away; Mr. Ray's shoe store was someone else's now, but people still called it Ray's.) She was looking for a break in the crowd when Jerry Sibley called her.

"Here, Emily! You can squeeze in with us." He was standing at the curb with Bobby and another boy, about Bobby's age but larger, husky and ruddy blond. After a moment Emily recognized him. He was Bobby Cobb, the nephew of Deep Valley's loved piano teacher.

Both Bobbys were wearing their best suits and ties. Their faces shone from soap and water and their hair was slicked down—under colored caps, of course. Bobby Sibley's was red and Bobby Cobb's was blue.

"What are you all wearing caps for?" Emily asked.

"Don't you know?" answered Bobby Sibley. "We're going to have a Living Flag up at the exercises. Our caps are different colors, and when we all line up, they make a flag. The red is the most important."

"It is not!" yelled Bobby Cobb.

"It is so!"

"It isn't!"

"Who says it isn't?"

"The champion wrestler of the fifth grade!" Bobby Cobb shouted and fell upon his companion.

"Cut it out kids!" Jerry said.

Not only children were getting restless. Anticipation fluttered like the flags. When the policeman went by now, he was greeted with, "When's the parade going to start?" At last, far down the street, "The Stars and Stripes Forever" sounded in brassy exultation.

A decorated automobile led the parade.

"It used to be a white horse, with the head of the G.A.R. riding on it," Emily said. The car was driven by the President of the Automobile Club, and carried the Mayor, the Methodist Minister and a Congressman who kept lifting his high silk hat. Everyone cheered, for the music of the approaching band had already stirred their hearts.

It was the policemen's band. A big flag came at the front, and Jerry snatched off his cap, nudging his brother who snatched off his and nudged Bobby

Cobb. Emily stood very still and straightened her shoulders.

The Drum Major was whirling his baton in deft white-gloved fingers. Behind him came the trombones, sliding in and out. Then came the baritones, the French horns and the tubas, the jubilant trumpets, the field drums and the bass drums, the saxophones and clarinets.

The uniformed policemen marched by, thumping their big feet heavily on the pavement. The firemen followed, clinging to their gleaming trucks. The first band had stopped playing, but another could be heard. No, it wasn't a band! This was the thin ghostly music of the fife and drum.

> *"When Johnny comes marching home again,*
> *Hurrah! Hurrah!*
> *We'll give him a hearty welcome then,*
> *Hurrah! Hurrah!*
> *The men will cheer, the boys will shout . . . "*

A tremendous emotional roar of welcome almost drowned out the sprightly tune. For the "old soldiers" were coming, Deep Valley's survivors of the now historic Civil War, six old men in blue uniforms with badges and bulging snowball clumps.

They were marching in pairs. They didn't keep

time very well. One walked with a cane. But they all held themselves with military stiffness. No beard equaled Judge Hodges' beard. There were flourishing mustaches, though, and a goatee, and old Cap' Klein's chin whiskers. Cyrus Webster was clean shaven but his heavy eyebrows bristled with martial grimness.

Emily's eyes blurred. "They're only marching a few blocks," she said, addressing Jerry, but speaking to reassure herself. She was glad to observe an automobile, ready to receive them, riding slowly just behind.

"Those old fellows get feebler every year . . . and fewer," Jerry said. He stopped, remembering that her grandfather was among the marchers.

Yes, Emily thought, they got feebler and fewer. And so did the old ladies of the Women's Relief Corps who were passing now in another automobile, brave in their new bonnets. Her grandmother used to ride with them! She was gone now. And the white horse of memory was replaced by an automobile. Yet Decoration Day was always the same.

The high school band, playing "The Girl I Left Behind Me," escorted the veterans of the Spanish-American War. They were still youngish and debonair. The National Guard was younger still, marching with zest, greeted with familiar shouts. At the end, boys and girls swarmed into the street.

"Look for us in the Living Flag!" Bobby Sibley called.

Emily hurried up to little pie-shaped Lincoln Park where the statue of a Union soldier surmounted a sparkling fountain. Folding chairs had been set up beneath a giant elm. She was glad to see her grandfather, looking flushed and happy, sitting next to Judge Hodges, and she watched him fondly as the program took its familiar way: "The Star-Spangled Banner"; the invocation; the reading of General Logan's orders; "Tenting Tonight on the Old Camp Ground," which always made her feel lonely; and Lincoln's "Gettysburg Address," which never failed to stir her. The Congressman, in Emily's opinion, said too much about the differences between President Taft and ex-President Roosevelt and not enough about the G.A.R. At the end came "America," and the Bobbys grinned at her out of a Living Flag.

For the long climb up Cemetery Hill, the "old soldiers" accepted the automobile. Emily joined the crowd walking in that direction, and heard herself hailed brusquely.

"Em!"

Turning, she saw Don, tall and square-shouldered. He had a poise, an air of sophistication, which always marked him out. Her welcoming smile did not betray the excitement she felt as he joined her, swinging to the outside of the walk.

He looked gloomy. She sympathized with these moods of dejection for she was subject to them, too. She fought them, but not always with success.

"Mind if I smoke?" he asked.

"Not at all."

He rolled a cigarette. "I certainly need this! Gosh, what a lot of bunk!"

"Bunk? Decoration Day?"

"Don't *you* think it's bunk?"

"Certainly not!" Her surprised indignation swept her into speech. "If I had gone out and gotten killed for my country I'd like to be thanked for it once a year."

"These fellows weren't killed."

"Well, we're all thinking about the ones who were!"

"Oh, are we? How many people are thinking about anything except the impression they are making, or the picnic they are headed for, or how their feet hurt?"

"I imagine that everyone gives a *little* thought to what the day means," she answered slowly. It meant more to her than to most people, she realized. Those young men of the First Minnesota who had charged so bravely to their death were almost as real to her as last year's football team.

She was saturated with her grandfather's joy and

pride in the day, and Don's scornfulness hurt her.

"It's so *nice*," she said in abrupt appeal. "It comes in May when everything's so pretty. And the children are so clean and excited and the old men so happy. And it's always the same. It's—part of growing up in America."

"Emily," said Don, "I'm afraid you're a sentimentalist." He sounded ill-humored and bored.

The blaring horn of an automobile scattered the crowd walking in the road. They looked up to see Annette waving from a Reo driven by Gladys Dunn. Scid and Jim Baxter and Nell were also in the car.

"We've had enough. We're going to Heinz's. Want to come along?" they called, stopping the car.

Emily shook her head. "I have to go to the cemetery."

"Besides," said Don sarcastically, "she likes all this. She's been lecturing me, preaching my duty to flag and country."

"I haven't!" Emily cried in distress.

"Oh, but you have!" said Don, his deep voice scornful, and climbed into the car without even saying good-by.

"I wish you'd come along, Emily," Annette said. But Emily shook her head. She wasn't resentful. She was used to being left out of boy and girl jaunts. The conversation with Don still rankled, though.

"He may think I'm wrong, but I think *he's* wrong. The idea of wanting to deprive the 'old soldiers' of this day! And it doesn't hurt anyone to hear the Gettysburg Address."

Clouds were sailing in a bright blue sky above the hill-top cemetery. More speeches were made, and the graves of the veterans received new flags and wreaths of flowers. Aaron Sibley's grave received its share, but it didn't need them. It looked loved and alive.

"Today means something to the Sibley boys, just as it does to me," Emily thought.

She reached home ahead of her grandfather. He looked tired when the automobile left him at the gate, but he was still happy. Now he wanted to talk about the glories of the afternoon.

"How did we look marching, Emmy? Didn't we cut a dash?"

"You certainly did. Do you know, I think you kept time better than anybody?"

"I always did," he answered. "The Judge doesn't know his right foot from his left."

There were callers—with presents for her. Mrs. MacDonald, the Presbyterian minister's wife, brought a framed copy of the young John the Baptist by Andrea Del Sarto. A neighbor from across the street brought beauty pins. There was quite a nice array on the parlor table now.

After supper Emily said, "Now Grandpa, you get to bed. It's been a long day."

"All right," he answered. "But how about playing me a few tunes first?"

She knew which ones he wanted.

She went to the old piano and played and sang "A Faded Coat of Blue," "Wrap the Flag Around Me, Boys," and "The Vacant Chair." When she started "Tramp, Tramp, Tramp, the Boys Are Marching," her grandfather joined in, in a quavering voice.

"And Don Walker would like to take this away from them!" Emily thought, pressing hard on the pedals.

5
Commencement Day

"We hate to leave the high school
The heck we do . . . !"

AT THE BACK DOOR of the Opera House a wild crowd
was milling around Don, Hunter and Scid, who stood
with their arms spread over each other's shoulders,
bawling a parody of the Class Song to the sky.

Emily, just arrived for the last commencement re-
hearsal, joined in the laughter which rolled down the

narrow alley. Miss Clarke, the history teacher, was pleading distractedly, "Boys and girls! Come in! You *must* come in!"

No one paid any attention to her. She was joined finally by Mr. Stewart—Stewie, the popular coach of debating society and football team. The seniors went inside at last, but they behaved no better.

Laughing and shouting, they roamed and tussled, clambered over the chairs set in ascending rows on the stage, got in the way of a frantic decorating committee.

"Children! Children!" Miss Clarke had stopped calling them "boys and girls" now. Clapping her hands like castanets, she got order at last. The laughter died down, but not out of their eyes. They were all breathing hard. It was only a respite.

Waiting in line on the stage, the boys began to throw their caps, neckties and notebooks into the auditorium. Scid even took off his shoes and threw them. Gladys Dunn dashed down and picked them up and hurled them into the balcony. Bedlam was let loose again.

The Class of 1912 was expressing its excitement, its relaxation, its joy and sorrow and its secret fear in a burst of juvenile hilarity.

Emily leaned against a wall, weak from laughter.

"I hope we're not going to rehearse our orations in

all this," she remarked to Mabel who stood next in line.

"We're not. We just have to be assigned our seats, and practise going down front like we'll do tonight when we get our diplomas."

This was achieved at last. Dismissed, the seniors lingered, exchanging their class pictures. Emily exchanged with Annette, of course, and with dimpled, soft-eyed Nell, and big exuberant Gladys, and Ellen and Mabel. She exchanged with Hunter and Fred and Scid. To her great pleasure, Stewie asked her for a picture. He was leaving Deep Valley—to teach in Chicago.

"And I want to take along autographed pictures of my star debating team. I never expect to have such a team again. Here, Don!" he called. "Your picture!"

"A pleasure, sir!" said Don, saluting. Eyes and teeth shining, he came and stood beside Emily. "How shall I sign it? Walker or Demosthenes?" He wrote with a flourish.

When Stewie had moved on, Don smiled at Emily. "Aren't you going to ask me for a picture? Don't tell me you don't want one!"

As usual, when he teased her, she was at a loss for a reply. He poised his pen above another photograph.

"To the patriot, Emily Webster," he read aloud as he wrote. Handing it to her, he strolled away without even asking for her picture in return.

Back at home Emily found her grandfather's easy chair empty. Adding her booty of photographs to the presents on the center table, she went out of doors, calling him. It was pleasant outside with birds everywhere and white, pink and lavender bushes in bloom. But her grandfather wasn't there, and Emily began to feel a little apprehensive. He seldom went out, and he had been tired this morning.

"Probably he went over to Judge Hodges'," she thought, but as she set the table and creamed chicken for dinner, she kept glancing out the window. Presently, to her great relief, she saw him with the Judge coming up the walk.

She ran out to meet him. "Grandpa! Where have you been?"

He and the Judge smiled slyly. "We've been downtown."

"*Downtown?* But why? You shouldn't get tired today, you know. It's my graduation tonight."

"Oh, is it? I'd forgotten all about it."

"Can't you remember when your own granddaughter graduates?" asked Judge Hodges. He dug his elbow mockingly into his friend's ribs. "Didn't you even remember to buy her a present?"

Grandpa Webster pulled a long face. "Everyone has given her a present but me."

"But you're giving me my flowers, Grandpa." Emily was troubled. "They'll be delivered any time now. Don't you remember? Pink roses."

"Pink roses, eh?" he said, and his hand went to his pocket. Beaming, he brought out a small package and handed it to her while Judge Hodges stroked his beard with satisfaction.

"Grandpa!" cried Emily. "What under the sun is this?"

"It's a present."

"But you . . . I . . . why . . . I didn't expect . . ." She was really confused now, and the two old men roared with laughter.

Her grandfather's face shone like the sun. He nudged Judge Hodges and they both leaned forward as she took off the tissue paper and lifted the cover from a small round box.

"Grandpa!" Her voice was childishly high and excited. Shining from the white satin lining of the box was a round gold watch attached to a dainty bracelet. A watch bracelet! They were the very newest thing. And Emily loved new things.

"Grandpa!" she breathed, unbelieving.

"Do you like it?"

"Oh, yes!" She pushed it over her hand to that point halfway up the arm where it was the custom to wear watch bracelets. "But, Grandpa! I didn't know . . ." she paused.

"You didn't know I knew graduation was a time for presents? Well, I graduated once myself. Got my first watch then. Your grandmother got that big cameo brooch up in the jewel box. And do you know what your mother got?"

"No," said Emily. She was amazed that her grandfather knew.

"She got a locket on a chain. She told me so. That's in the jewel box, too."

"She's wearing it in the picture I have on my bureau!" Emily cried. She felt tears stinging her eyes. After a moment she kissed her grandfather on the cheek. He looked proudly at Judge Hodges.

"I helped pick it out," hinted the Judge, and Emily kissed him, too.

The watch shed its glory over the gifts assembled on the center table. Emily looked at it at intervals during the long afternoon, while her grandfather napped and she practised her oration for a final time, pressed her dress, and watched for the Windmiller delivery boy. He came, and the pink roses were put into the ice box.

After supper she went up to her bedroom to bathe and dress. In embroidered corset cover and petticoat, she brushed out her curly hair. On an impulse she twisted it into a psyche knot and picked up a hand mirror to get the effect. It was becoming, for the modeling of her head was good. But after a moment she took it down.

"I've gone through high school with my hair in a braid, and I'll graduate that way," she decided.

When her hair was turned up with a ribbon as usual and she was dressed in the snowy white lawn, she unlocked the jewel box. The black japanned box, gilded in a swirling pattern and flecked with mother-of-pearl, held her mother's and grandmother's jewelry. Some of it was valuable but Emily had always been indifferent to it. She was surfeited with old-fashioned things.

Now, however, she pulled out the locket which had been her mother's, an oval of chased gold, in a pattern of leaves and flowers, set with garnets. Emily picked up the photograph of her mother and studied it. Sure enough, she was wearing this very locket!

"Probably this was her graduation picture," Emily thought. For the first time the photograph seemed to take on reality. Her mother had been eighteen once, and she had graduated. She had known this strange feeling that something was ending which you had never really expected to end. She had felt excited and relieved, happy and afraid, as Emily and the others had felt this afternoon.

Emily opened the locket, but whatever pictures it

had once contained had been removed. There was only a wisp of dark hair, probably her father's. Slowly she hung the chain around her neck and the locket dropped warmly to her breast.

Downstairs, she took her roses from the ice box and turned before her grandfather. She stood very straight, which added several glorifying inches to her height.

"How do I look?"

"You look like a real young lady. You look nice."

"Grandpa," she said suddenly. "Do I look like my mother?"

"It always seems to me you favor your grandmother," he answered. "And your grandmother used to say you favored me." He added thoughtfully after a moment, "Sometimes, though, you remind me of your mother. It's when you laugh. She was very full of fun."

"She was *full of fun*?" Emily repeated, startled.

"She certainly was. Will you tie this tie for me, Emmy?"

"Yes. And I want to brush your suit."

Uncle Chester called for them late. He had already delivered Annette and the others, he said. He helped Emily into her new opera coat, of satin-smooth tan broadcloth. She threw chiffon over her head and picked up her roses and slipper bag.

They left her at the back door of the Opera House. "I'll be looking for you," Emily said to her grandfather. Although he wasn't used to being up so late, he was smiling and fresh.

The decorating committee had done its work well. And decorum had descended on the class. When the curtain rose, the graduates were seated on the stage against a resplendent back-drop of red, white and blue bunting. Suspended above them—in red, white and blue, also—were the numerals 1912. Ministers and priests of the city, members of the school board and their wives were seated in the boxes. Relatives and friends made an enthusiastic audience.

After the invocation came the stirring "Soldiers' Chorus" from Faust.

"Glory and love to the men of old,
Their sons may copy their virtue bold,
Courage in heart and a sword in hand . . . "

There were no swords present, but courage was being summoned desperately by almost all those scheduled to take part in the program. After a shakily given oration, a tremulous quartette sang "The Lost Chord." Another oration was recited with agonized speed, and Gladys Dunn—subdued, for once—played "Love's Awakening" by Moszkowski on the piano.

Don, who preceded Emily, wasn't nervous. Like herself, he enjoyed command of a stage. In his dark blue suit, with a carnation in his buttonhole, he looked cool and superior; his deep voice rang out impressively.

His subject was "The Need of an Artistic Life in America," and he drew scathing comparisons between the old world and the new. He decried America's dearth of art galleries, museums and symphony orchestras. He scoffed at American architecture and railed especially at middle-western homes, calling them crude and in poor taste. Emily shrank from the memory of her crowded little parlor.

When her turn came she stood up very straight as she always did on the debating platform.

"A woman has awakened the social conscience of this generation," she began in her clear voice. And she told how that conscience had been awakened in Jane Addams during a chance visit to London's east side to watch a Saturday night sale of decaying fruits and vegetables to the poor.

She described the years of travel and thought which led up to Hull House. She outlined Jane Addams' reasons for joining a church: the need to put dependence on some power outside herself, the longing for fellowship, and a growing devotion to the ideals of democracy.

"'When in all history,'" asked Emily, quoting her subject, "'had these ideals been so thrillingly expressed as when the faith of the fisherman and the slave had been boldly opposed to the accepted moral belief that the well-being of a privileged few might justly be built upon the ignorance and sacrifice of the many?'"

Then she discussed Hull House, describing its manifold activities—its kindergartens, its clubs for young and old, and its work for the foreign born.

Down in the parquet her grandfather was looking pleased but sleepy beside Uncle Chester and Aunt Sophie. The LaDous and other relatives filled the row. Her oration was good; there was abundant applause at the end. Emily smiled her slow shy smile.

The president of the school board delivered the address of the evening. Mr. Luther Whitlock was a banker, a short, pompous man with mutton-chop whiskers which he stroked, first to the right side and then to the left, with a commanding finger.

His talk to the graduates seemed to indicate that he would measure their success chiefly in terms of money. Emily didn't care much for him or his speech. But when it was ended he took his place behind a table piled with beribboned parchment cylinders. He called the names of the graduates, and each one crossed the stage to wild applause.

Emily watched them go, one by one. They were going out of her life. They were going out of one another's lives. She herself crossed the stage. It was happening, this climactic event which had always seemed so impossibly remote.

The chorus sang Kipling's "Recessional," and it was over.

At once the class scattered in all directions, and the audience swarmed to the stage. Graduates were surrounded with friends offering congratulations, and with teachers saying good-by. Emily shook hand after hand, feeling happy and tearful.

Groups began to dissolve and disappear. A crowd was going to Annette's, she gathered. Not a real party, or she would have been invited. It was just as well she wasn't, she thought, for her grandfather now looked tired and bewildered. She was glad when Uncle Chester took them home.

After her grandfather had gone to bed, she put her roses back into the ice box and, going to the center table, took up Don's picture. His proud moody face looked out at her. Emily looked back with painful intentness. He was the most wonderful person she knew. And when, now, would she see him again?

She went out to the lawn. The warm dark was full of fireflies. Down in the slough frogs and crickets were singing in melancholy rhythm.

"I'm through high school. I'm finished with something, but I'm not beginning anything. That's wrong. When you finish something, you ought always to begin something new. But I'm just going to go on doing housework, looking after Grandpa."

She felt depression closing in upon her, but she pushed it away. She forced her thoughts back over the day—the delicious fun of the morning, the wonderful unexpected present, the moment of illumination about her mother, the pageantry and beauty of the evening.

She walked slowly up and down, and across the slough the lights of Deep Valley were just a little larger than the fireflies.

6
Under the Locust Tree

THROUGH THE SUMMER she wasn't lonely. She was used to having solitude arrive with the thickening green, the spreading warmth, the long golden days of vacation. When the girls were in town she saw them on picnics or "come and bring your sewing" parties. But those were only occasional ripples in a tranquil sea.

❀ 71 ❀

Contentedly she weeded her flower beds, helped her grandfather with the vegetable garden, and enjoyed the big sprawling lawn. From the front gate at the north and the slough on the east it rose in a tree-lined slope. Nearer the house was a tall honey locust around which, long ago, her grandfather had built a bench. Emily liked this bench with its view of the shore where sandpipers were running and calling, and marsh hens were nesting, not too privately, among the reeds.

She was sewing there one afternoon when she saw two little boys approaching from the slough. Both were bare-legged, wearing tattered straw hats, and the taller one, who strode boldly in the lead, had a basket on his arm. Six feet away, he lifted his hat and swept a bow which Otis Skinner, Emily thought, could not have bettered.

"Hello, ma'am!" he said, coming upright again. He inspected her with round liquid eyes full of joy and curiosity.

He was a Syrian, and a handsome one. His black hair was thick, clean and curly. His black brows were strongly marked, and his olive skin had a rosy bloom.

"Hello," answered Emily, smiling.

He smiled, showing teeth as white as Don's. "Want to buy some frogs' legs, ma'am?"

"Frogs' legs! I've never eaten any."

He turned to his companion with a gesture of astonishment. "The lady has never eaten frogs' legs! But they's dandy," he continued, returning to Emily. "They's deelicious. Um-m-m!" He lifted his head and made the rapturous sound of one tasting Elysian delicacies.

Emily laughed. "Did you catch them yourself?"

"Yusef and I catched them. Yusef and I catch big, big frogs. Great big beautiful frogs. This big!" He put down his basket and indicated a creature of extravagant size.

Emily looked toward the other little boy, a chunky, square-faced child who stared wordlessly.

"He is Yusef?"

"Yes, ma'am. Yusef Tabbit."

"And what is your name?"

"Kalil, ma'am. Kalil Mohanna." He pulled off his hat in another magnificent bow.

"How old are you?"

"My age is ten year. One year in America. Excuse the English, please."

"I'll try your frogs' legs," Emily said, rising.

He extended the basket grandly. "I give you all here for a quarter," he announced, and Emily, smiling, took the basket to the kitchen, emptied the strange-looking mess into a pan and found her purse.

Kalil bowed again over the quarter.

"We are thankful, ma'am. We are full of thanks to you. Good-by ma'am." He ran off lightly, followed by Yusef who, even in flight, turned his head to stare.

Still smiling, Emily went into the house and told her grandfather that they were going to have frogs' legs for supper. She expected him to be surprised but he wasn't.

"They're good," he said. "Your mother used to fix them."

"My *mother*."

"Yes. She learned how back east."

"How did she fix them?"

"It must be written down somewhere," he answered, which sent Emily on a search through old cook books, unfolding yellowed papers on which recipes had been written at long-gone thimble bees, tea parties and Ladies' Aid meetings. At last she found the one she sought, written in a graceful Spencerian hand.

"Frogs' legs, Sauté Meunière."

"Wash the frogs' legs carefully and lay on a clean towel. Season with salt and pepper. Dip in flour and fry in hot butter until golden brown . . ."

A few days later Kalil came back, still accompanied by Yusef. He smiled at her grandfather. They had often talked at the marsh's edge, it seemed.

"Hello, sir. Hello, ma'am. You liked our frogs'

legs?" Kalil's eyes were brightly expectant.

"Yes, we did, very much," Emily replied. "You may bring them again."

He smiled, showing all his white teeth. "Bully!" he cried.

It was a word Teddy Roosevelt had popularized, and it came so oddly from the little Syrian that Emily began to laugh. Her grandfather chuckled, and even Yusef smiled—not understanding the joke but delighted with Kalil's success.

"Bully! Bully!" repeated Kalil, delighted, too.

Roosevelt's name was in the air, for the Republican Convention had just been held in Chicago. Some time before the exuberant ex-president had announced that his "hat was in the ring." He had come to Chicago feeling, he said, "like a Bull Moose," and when, in spite of his popularity, the convention renominated Taft, and Roosevelt formed the Progressive Party, it became at once the Bull Moose Party, and his followers, Bull Moosers.

In Deep Valley, as everywhere, the Roosevelt-Taft feud was tearing friends and families apart. Emily favored Roosevelt, believing, as Jane Addams did, that he spoke for the cause of social justice. The *Deep Valley Sun* was delivered to the house, but Emily was so eager for news that she bought the Twin City papers, too, when she went downtown to the library or the grocer's or butcher's.

She found herself, to her annoyance, always looking for Don. She never went where he might be expected to be. She was contemptuous of girls who wandered in and out of stores or hung around the ice cream parlors looking for boys on whom they had crushes. Yet, in spite of herself, she kept watching for an erect, square-shouldered figure.

She didn't see him in town. But one Sunday in late June he appeared at her home.

She and her grandfather had gone to church, of course. Every Sunday they attended the white stone Presbyterian Church. They had had dinner, and Emily had gone out to the locust tree which was in flower, pouring fragrance into the surrounding air. She was reading the poems of Sidney Lanier when she heard steps and looked up to see Don.

She concealed her emotion behind dignity as usual. "Hello," she said, getting to her feet.

"Hello." He pulled off his hat and gave her the wide white-toothed smile that so transformed his face. "The darned auto stopped right in front of your house, puffing like a steam engine. It knows your kind heart, I suppose. And maybe it knows you have a well."

Emily was quite unable to return his nonsense in kind. "It needs water?" she asked diffidently.

"You've put your finger on it. It needs water, and so do I, if you don't mind."

"Of course not. I'll get a pail and a glass."

She was glad to hurry away, for the glory of his coming almost choked her. She could hardly believe that she was hearing his deep voice, that he was standing in her yard, suave, sophisticated, in a light summer suit with a straw hat.

She stole a look at the kitchen mirror. She had changed after church to an old dress, a faded blue linen. But it was clean, at least, and her hair was neat. She went out to the pump and filled a glass, glad that the water from their well was so marvelously fresh and cold.

Don was looking at her book but he put it down. "What, no cookies?"

"Why should there be cookies?"

"I'm used to having cookies brought out at my approach."

Still she could not respond to his joking, although she responded when her grandfather joked. She knew how to be merry with the girls.

"I'll get you some," she said, turning, and returned with a plate full of sugar cookies she had baked the day before.

He picked up her book again. "Like it?"

"Yes." She began to speak freely when the subject

turned to books. "I like the one about the Marshes of Glynn," she said, turning the pages, and Don read aloud:

"*Ye marshes, how candid and simple and nothing-*
withholding and free
Ye publish yourselves to the sky and offer your-
selves to the sea!"

Emily listened, sitting with her head bent, her eyes grave in their thickets of lashes.

"It makes me think of my slough," she said, when he paused.

"Of the *slough*! 'The wide sea marshes of Glynn'?" He sounded contemptuous but she defended her statement.

"It has the feeling of our slough."

Don rolled a cigarette. He had beautiful hands, dark, with long sensitive fingers.

"It's an interesting rhyme scheme," he observed and launched into a dissertation on Lanier. He was enjoying himself, she could see. The boys would say it was because he was showing off, but Emily knew that he really liked intellectual discussions.

"Of course, he's more the musician than the poet."

"What do you mean by that?"

"He writes for the ear."

"Not always," Emily insisted. "Sometimes he has something to say." And now it was her turn to read aloud:

"As the marsh-hen secretly builds on the
watery sod,
Behold I will build me a nest on the
greatness of God:
I will fly in the greatness of God as the
marsh-hen flies . . . ."

It was just the way they had talked and read and argued off on the debating trips.

He went to the well and refilled his glass, but he seemed in no hurry to draw water for the car. He asked what she thought of the news from Chicago. When he found how ardently she favored Roosevelt he teased her with the familiar insults—that Teddy was crazy—that he wanted to make himself king.

"See here," he said suddenly. His gray-green eyes looked into hers. "I don't know another girl with whom I could talk like this. I think I'll have to come again."

Emily didn't say that she would like to have him. She bent her head and looked away, but she knew that he knew she was glad he had come.

When he was gone she went up to her room. His

picture looked out at her from the top of a chest where it stood with the other class pictures. She had put it in front; that was the only concession she had made to her special feeling for him. She looked at it now with an almost pleading gaze.

She felt sure he had no intention of coming again. Only chance had brought him, and it wouldn't operate a second time.

"He won't come again," she said aloud, firmly. But he did. He came several times in the month of July.

It was very hot that year. There were nights through which it was too hot to sleep and days in which it seemed too hot to live. Almost everyone else was out of town; Annette was in the Twin Cities, shopping. Emily was humbly aware that this was why he favored her. But she realized, too, that he felt a certain comfort and ease in the little house.

He was scornful of it, though, as she had known he would be. She felt an agony of embarrassment the first time he went into the parlor. He strolled about with a superior smile, inspecting the wax flowers.

"It's incredible! Incredible!" he said, half under his breath.

"It's the way Grandpa likes it," Emily answered, flushing. That was as near an apology as she would come.

He sat down at the piano and played "Chop

Sticks," and presently her grandfather came in, his skull cap slightly awry from the nap Don's call had interrupted.

They shook hands.

"I used to hear you talk when you came to the school on Decoration Day, Mr. Webster," Don said. "You fought at Bull Run, didn't you?"

"Bull Run!" exclaimed Grandpa Webster. "It was Gettysburg, young man!"

"Of course! Of course! Gettysburg!"

But Grandpa Webster didn't respond to the charm of the flashing smile.

"That young man thinks he's cock of the walk," the old man grumbled later. After that he usually stayed in his room when Don appeared.

Don did, indeed, have an air of lordly condescension on his visits. Yet he plainly enjoyed them. He enjoyed the pitchers of cold lemonade she made for him, the sugar cookies and molasses cookies which alternated in the jar. He liked the small, clean kitchen and the bench under the honey locust, from which they looked out now at tiger lilies around the house and hollyhocks along the fence and marsh hens down in the slough, noisily busy with their young.

He never suggested taking Emily riding, although the touring car waited in front. He didn't ask her to go to the movies. Coming to see her was favor enough, his manner said. But she was content to sit and listen while he talked, rolling and smoking cigarettes with man-of-the-world nonchalance.

He talked about his plans, and she recognized that he was close to boasting. But that was all right. He knew how interested she was. He liked to talk about himself. Once he asked her to tell him his worst fault.

"How should I know your faults?"

"Well, you do, don't you? Come on, tell me!"

"There's no reason why I should."

"You admit that you know?"

"I don't know what your worst one is."

He began to list them, bitterly, dramatically. He was self-centered, he said, selfish, rude.

He *was* sometimes, Emily admitted to herself. But he was also wonderful—more wonderful than anyone else she knew.

Oftenest they talked about books.

"Emily," he asked one day, "have you read any Browning?"

"I can't make head or tail of him."

"That's nonsense. He comes clear if you study him. He just likes to leave out connectives and relatives. I'll bring him along next time I come."

A reference to his coming again never failed to thrill her. But when this promised visit came, on a hot August day, she was canning peaches, neck to ankle in an apron, her hair pinned away from a burning face. She answered a knock at the kitchen door and there was Don, looking cool and attractive in a white linen suit.

"Why—I thought you were working!" she cried. He had never come on a week day before.

"I've quit. College coming up. The family thinks I need a rest." He held out a book. "I brought you the Browning."

She forgot her chagrin in her pleasure.

"Oh, I'm so glad! Sit down outside, won't you? I'll finish as quickly as I can."

He strolled out to the bench and she filled the jars rapidly, took off her apron and tidied her hair. She didn't take time to change her dress.

"Here I am," she called, running out. "Will you read it to me now? Try to get it through my head?"

"I'm not going to let you off with the ballads," he answered, brightening. He opened the book, but before they began they were interrupted.

"Hello!" called a light voice. Annette in a long white dress with a green and white parasol tilted over her shoulder was coming up the lawn. Don and Emily went to meet her. "I *thought* that was your auto out in front!" she said to Don, and kissed Emily warmly.

"When did you get back?" asked Emily.

"Just this morning."

"I came out to ask Em whether she had any news of you," said Don.

Had he? Emily wondered. What about the Browning then? She felt a painful wrench at her heart.

It evidently didn't occur to Annette that he might have come for any other purpose. She sat down, smiling radiantly. Her dark hair was dressed in curls and puffs with a fillet of green ribbons. Her black eyes sparkled, and perfume drifted out with every flutter of her dress.

Don sat down beside her although Emily was still standing. He began to joke with her, his dark face glowing. Emily felt cast off.

"I think I'll go fix some lemonade," she said.

Back in the kitchen she looked in the mirror as she had on his first visit. Her face was shiny and embarrassed, and that turned-up braid and ribbon were too young. But what did it matter? So far as Don was concerned, the earth might have swallowed her up.

When she took out the lemonade Don and Annette were standing.

"We were just leaving!" Annette cried penitently. "I forgot you said you were going to make lemonade. But we'll stop to drink some; won't we, Don? And, Em, can you come over soon? I want to show you all we bought in the Cities. I'm certainly going to be the well-dressed college girl."

After they were gone, the Browning lay on the bench. Slowly Emily picked it up. It was a small brown and gold volume, *Select Poems of Robert Browning*. It was new, it was unmistakably new.

Holding it tightly, she went into the house. Up in her room, she sat down and began to leaf it through. But she stopped, abruptly, and laid her cheek against it.

It was a present. He had bought it for her!

7
They All Go Away

MISS MIX WAS BACK AGAIN in the big front bedroom at Aunt Sophie's. Annette had bought her tailor-made suit in the Cities—her new hats, too. But Miss Mix was making everything else—school waists and dress-up waists, school dresses and dark silks for dinner, and filmy evening gowns.

As usual Aunt Sophie had offered to let Miss Mix

sew for Emily, too, but Emily had declined.

"No thank you, Aunt Sophie. I shan't bother now while you're so busy with Annette."

"We certainly are busy," Aunt Sophie had replied with obvious relief. And Emily was glad that she didn't press the point. Emily took no interest in clothes this fall. What use would clothes be when she wasn't going away?

Not everyone was going away to college, of course. But the girls who were staying home were registering at Teachers' College or business college or the German Catholic College on the hill—all except one or two who were getting ready to be married.

"Married! Someone from our class!" the girls exclaimed to each other in amazement.

Everyone was busy with new enterprises—except Emily. She busied herself with the enterprises of the others. She clung to the girls, sharing their fevers of shopping and sewing, their trips to the doctor and dentist, the excitement which possessed them. She came closer to Annette than she had ever been. When the Epsilon Iotas wrote asking Annette for dates for rushing parties, Annette actually crossed the slough to tell her cousin.

"Why don't you get a telephone!" she scolded. "But I just had to come. I can't talk to Gladys, for no sorority has asked *her* for dates—and it's so terribly important. Sororities are the most important thing in college, Em."

Emily laughed at that.

"Well, for me they are!" insisted Annette, laughing too. "After I'm in a sorority and have gone to a few formals, I'd just as soon quit and get married."

"Who to?" asked Emily, too interested to be grammatical.

"Why, I don't know! Maybe Don, if I can make him ask me." Annette gave her little merry laugh. "Come on back with me, and see the negligee Mamma found at the Lion. Gee, with all these clothes I feel as though I were getting married now!"

There was a round of luncheons, teas, and card parties for the girls who were going away. Even Emily gave one—for Annette. She was too sensitive about her home to entertain often. But the giddiness got into her blood.

Telling her grandfather about the plan with elation, she started house-cleaning. She took up the carpets and pounded them out on the lawn. She took down the lace curtains and washed and starched and stretched them. She scoured the windows, and wiped the picture frames, and carefully bathed the knick-knacks in the what-not, and polished all the heavy old furniture, poking zealous fingers into carved bunches of grapes atop the sofa and side chairs.

Washing the yellow keys of the piano she thought, "I'll buy some sheet music to make this look more up to date."

She longed, as always, for new furniture and modern innovations—a furnace, a sleeping porch, and especially a bathroom! But she tried to shake such ideas out of her mind.

"I'll fill the house with flowers. It really will look sweet. Now, if I could only think what to give them to eat!"

The other girls served such novel refreshments—cheese fondue, shrimp wiggle, rice pilaff, and marvelous concoctions of marshmallow, pineapple and whipped cream mixed together. They learned about them from their mothers who served such things at luncheons. Emily was bewildered by them.

"What's the best thing I cook, Grandpa?" she asked.

"New England boiled dinner," he answered promptly.

"But, Grandpa! I'm thinking of my party. The girls are going to stay to supper. I want to give them something nice."

"Roast chicken?" he asked hopefully. "And that giblet gravy your grandmother taught you to make? There's nothing wrong with your apple pie either."

"I'd like something new."

"How about frogs' legs?"

"Grandpa!" She jumped up eagerly. "That's just

the thing! If you see Kalil, call him in, so I can order some."

"I see him every day. He comes to get minnows for fishing," her grandfather answered. And sure enough, the following morning he appeared with Kalil, trailed by Yusef as usual.

Kalil was delighted with the enormous order.

"We will bring an army, a big, big army of frogs' legs!" he cried. "There not be any frogs left in the slough."

The idea of a party seemed to enchant him. "You give them sweets? You play music?"

"Is that what you do at your parties?"

"Yes, ma'am. The Syrians like flutes. And they like drums." He blew an imaginary flute and beat an imaginary drum, his round eyes sparkling.

Emily laughed. "Well, we'll play the piano! Now be here early with the frogs' legs, please."

When the great day came the little house looked its shining best. The windows were open, framing the green lawn, and the garden still full of summer flowers, and the slough where sumac was reddening and red-winged blackbirds were gathering in flocks. Her grandfather had retired to his room.

"I'll fix my own supper. Don't pay any attention to me. Just have a good time," he had said. And Emily knew they would have a good time as soon as she saw the girls spilling out of Gladys' Reo.

All of them, except Emily, had their hair up now . . . in pompadours thrust forward with combs in front, in side pompadours well padded with rats, in puffs and curls and psyche knots, often banded with ribbon. In their long tight dresses they looked like young ladies, but they were behaving like children.

"They're on a tear," Mabel called. Like Emily, Mabel enjoyed, rather than participated in, such moods of silliness.

"It's our last chance before college gets us," shouted Nell.

"We can feel its awful clutch!"

Up in Emily's bedroom where they went to lay their wraps, Gladys discovered the class pictures. She seized a photograph.

> *"My heart leaps up when I behold,*
> *Scid's picture in my hand . . . "*

Emily's shy smile widened and she broke into a laugh.

They ran downstairs and out to the lawn to play children's games—leadman, and statues, and in-and-out-the-windows.

They noticed Emily wearing the Progressive Party pin and shouted, "Sock 'em, Teddy!"

"Emily's a Bull Mooser!"

"She's a New Woman!"

"That reminds me of my recitation," cried Annette, and pushing them to the grass, she delivered Rudyard Kipling's new poem about the female of the species.

Inside again, Gladys rushed to the piano. They sang loudly "When the Midnight Choo-choo Leaves for Alabam" and "Oh, You Beautiful Doll" and a song about two little love bees buzzing in a bower. When they sang that one Gladys, impersonating Hunter, dropped to her knees at Ellen's feet.

They stopped singing and talked about boys.

Mabel said Annette should favor Jim Baxter over Don. Jim Baxter! thought Emily. He was nice enough; and a football star, of course; but just a big hulking— pumpkin head! How could Mabel mention him in the same breath with Don?

But others agreed. "That Don Walker is conceited."

"He certainly is. He has the most superior air."

Emily flashed out, "That's because he *is* superior." After she had spoken she flushed, but nobody noticed.

"Em's right," said Annette. "He's very intellectual. He admitted to me that he found high school pretty childish . . ."

She was silenced by a thrown cushion.

Although they ate early, the September twilight had already fallen. Emily didn't have place mats—which were the stylish thing, of course—but candlelight shone graciously on her grandmother's gleaming damask, the heavy silver, the thin pale dishes. And the frogs' legs were highly successful. They not only caused excitement and merriment but they were delicious as well, and so were the scalloped potatoes, and the garden vegetables, the hot biscuits with home-made gooseberry preserves and the fresh peach pie.

Emily sat at the top of the table, a quiet little smile on her mouth. It delighted her that the girls had had such fun. She would remember for a long time, when they were all away, Gladys at the piano, Annette reciting with her ridiculous gestures:

"The Female of the Species,
Is more deadly than the male . . ."

There was only one moment when she felt anything but happy. That came when the girls were leaving and Gladys, sitting down at the piano again, struck up the University of Minnesota hymn:

"Minnesota, hail to thee,
Hail to thee, our college dear . . ."

In leaving, Annette put her arm around her. "It was a wonderful party, Em. You ought to give them oftener! I'm glad I'm going to college if it makes you entertain."

Ellen said soberly, "I wish you were going, too, Em."

Mabel added, "So do I."

Emily didn't know what to answer, but fortunately Gladys broke in, "Let's go up to the high school tomorrow and show off! What do you say? Watch the poor kids toiling!"

"Let's wear our new fall clothes!"

"Oh, let's! Let's!"

So when they started out next morning, Emily, in a Peter Thompson suit with a red hair ribbon, was the only one who looked like a school girl. The others were impressive in gigantic velvet hats and long slim suits; Gladys Dunn's was slit to the knee.

Hilariously they climbed Walnut Hill and passed through the big front doors of the high school. Inside was the familiar smell of chalk dust and healthy perspiration. The stairs were crowded, but the students seemed younger than they had seemed last year. They seemed to belong to a different world.

When the others went into the Social Room, Emily lingered in the upper hall, looking in the trophy case at the debating cup she and Don had helped to win.

"I wish Stewie was here," she thought. "I wonder who's coaching the debating team this year."

She hailed Jerry Sibley and asked him.

"The new civics teacher."

"What's his name?"

"Mr. Wakeman."

"I'll bet he isn't as nice as Stewie," Emily said.

Then the bell rang and the visiting alumnae marched self-consciously into the Assembly Room where the faculty sat on the platform—Miss Clarke, Miss Fowler and the rest—ranged behind Miss Bangeter, the queenly principal.

Annette nudged Emily. "Good looking!" she whispered, indicating a newcomer among the teachers, a large young man with an air of easy self-possession.

"It must be Mr. Wakeman, the new civics teacher," Emily said. "He's coaching the debating team."

After the exercises they scattered to the various classrooms, speaking in new familiarity with the teachers. Several of them asked, "What are *you* going to do, Emily?"

"Just take care of Grandpa," she always answered cheerfully. She was consistently cheerful and matter-of-fact.

It was hard to maintain this attitude, however, during the next few days. One by one her friends went away, and there was a train party for each. Mabel Scott left first; Vassar was so remote. Then Hunter and Ellen departed for Carleton, and Nell for St.

Catherine's. Last of all went the large gay group headed for the State University at Minneapolis.

Walking to the four forty-five, Emily saw a line of birds weaving through the sky. Even the birds were going away!

The seekers after knowledge were waiting on the station platform, rimmed with parents. Jim Baxter looked glum. Fred Muller's face was shining under well-brushed blond hair. He was going to study to be an architect.

"Wish me luck, Emily," he said.

Scid, a flower in his buttonhole, was making jokes about Gladys' slit skirt. Gladys chased him down the platform. Don, in a new ulster and new snap-brim gray hat, smoked cigarettes and acted old and worldly.

He didn't say a private word to Emily. He was busy teasing Annette. "Everyone will know *you're* a freshie!" he told her, for her new tailored suit was green, and her big hat was green, and she wore a flat green bow at the neck of her waist.

At last, with expectantly swinging bell, the train pulled in. They all piled into the parlor car, and Emily looked around with interest at the big easy chairs, the large well-polished windows, the racks for luggage, the white-coated porter. She had never traveled—not even to the Cities.

"All aboard!" shouted the conductor, and everyone climbed off except the travelers, who came out to the observation platform. Still jokes were shouted, and messages, and admonitions, but a whistle blew, and slowly, inexorably, the train pulled away.

Aunt Sophie was dabbing at her eyes.

"Don't be silly!" Uncle Chester said. "You can go up to see her next week."

"But we're going to *miss* her so! You'll have to come to see us often, Emily."

"I will."

She refused a ride and walked briskly up Front Street, trying not to feel as though a trap door had shut.

Dusk was chilling the air but it smelled of September, of beginnings. September was a month of beginnings—or ought to be. She checked that thought.

"Now, I'm not going to let this get me down. I'm not made that way. Thank God, I have a backbone, and a good stiff one, too . . ."

She started over the slough.

"I'm sorry not to be going to college, of course. But you can't have everything. I have my home—and Grandpa. There must be lots I can do."

The slough was noisy with birds and frogs as it always was at twilight. Above her grandfather's house, pink was fading from the sky. She turned in at the sagging gate and walked up the path under the shadows.

At the porch she stopped to wink violently. She lingered, breaking off some withered lily stalks, and strolled around the side of the house.

"Now, I'm not going to be a cry baby," she said.

But out of sight of any window, she dropped down on the cellar door, put her face into her hands, and cried.

8
The Slough of Despond

AFTER THE FIRST FEW DAYS things didn't seem quite
so bad. The blow had fallen. It was automatic to pick
up courage and go on.

The apples on their gnarled apple trees were red.

"Let's get those apples picked," Emily suggested.
"I'll make some into apple butter—colored with elder
berries like I did last year."

"It was good," Grandpa Webster remembered.

They raked and burned the fallen leaves, talking sociably.

"Hunting season must be on," said Emily, hearing a shot in the slough.

"There didn't use to be any hunting season," her grandfather chuckled. "We used to take a dog and go out whenever we liked."

"Aunt Sophie will be asking us over for dinner," remarked Emily. Uncle Chester was a hunter, and a wild duck dinner was an annual family event.

Her grandfather brushed away a flying piece of soot and smiled at her across the fire.

"It's certainly nice to have you home, Emmy. You're not going to be lonesome, are you?"

"Of course not," she lied.

They set the hard-coal heater up in the parlor. September was still golden sweet but the mornings and evenings were cool. The heater kept the downstairs stuffily warm. Her grandfather and Judge Hodges played chess there.

Emily saw children going past to school, carrying books, lagging and laughing, and she envied them. Oh, to be going back to school!

"But I'm not and that's that!" she told herself sternly. "Grandpa, I'm going out and wash storm windows."

"All right, Emmy. You're certainly a go-ahead," he said.

Letters and cards had begun to come back from the departed ones. Emily answered them the same day they arrived. Mabel wrote, describing the big college on the Hudson. A letter from Ellen told of Hunter's opening achievements at Carleton. There were letters from Nell and Gladys and Annette. Annette was being rushed by several sororities.

"The fraternities are putting up a battle for Don, too," she wrote. "He hasn't decided which one he's going to join."

There was no letter from Don. Somehow, after those summer calls, Emily had really expected one, and it hurt that he didn't write.

She read in the paper that Woodrow Wilson, the scholarly Democratic nominee for the presidency, had addressed the university. Don knew how interested she would be in this event. But he didn't write.

An attempt was made on the life of Theodore Roosevelt. The three-cornered campaign was putting on frantic speed. She longed to talk it over with someone, but her grandfather always branched off into a discussion of Abraham Lincoln.

"Don might write! He might!" she thought, holding back tears as she bundled the newspapers out of the way with furious energy.

Depression settled down upon her, and although she tried to brush it away it thickened like a fog.

"Why, the kids will be home for Thanksgiving! That will be here in no time. I mustn't get this way," she thought. But she felt lonely and deserted and futile.

"A mood like this has to be fought. It's like an enemy with a gun," she told herself. But she couldn't seem to find a gun with which to fight.

One day at dinner her grandfather had a story about Kalil. He had been bitten by a snake.

"Just a harmless water snake. I was near by and saw the critter. But Kalil hit the sky. While I washed him off and put on iodine he was wagging his hands and describing the snake to Yusef. You'd have thought it was a prehistoric monster." He chuckled, but Emily didn't smile. She had stopped listening after he said the snake was harmless.

Her grandfather's tone changed. "I believe you're lonesome, Emmy."

"Why, of course not!" she answered hastily. "How—how's Kalil now?"

"Pretty well. But he runs into trouble in school. It's his English, he thinks. The boys tease him."

"It's a good thing there's a big group from Little Syria. They're company for each other," Emily answered listlessly.

Her grandfather studied her from under his bushy brows.

"Emmy," he said. "Maybe you'd like to take music lessons again?" He loved music, and she hadn't touched the piano since the crowd went away.

"Perhaps later," she evaded. She wasn't in a mood for music somehow. "I'm planning to do a lot of reading this winter."

"Maybe you'd read out loud to me, like you did when I was sick?" he suggested hopefully. "You remember how we liked *Kenilworth,* and you said we were going on to *The Talisman,* but we never did?"

"That's a good idea. We'll have to do it."

But she put it off. The books she longed for weren't the old-fashioned novels in the glass-enclosed shelves of the secretary; they were the books her friends at college would be reading under Richard Burton and Maria Sanford and the other famous professors whose names she knew, or the works on sociology she would have liked to study for Jane Addams' sake.

She did bring home books from the library, in armloads, replenishing them every two or three days. She read avidly, indiscriminately, using them as an antidote for the pain in her heart. But they didn't help much. There was no one to talk them over with. They were almost as useless as the newspapers.

"I know what I'll do," she decided. "I'll go up to

the high school. We had such fun that day we went before."

But the visit was not a success. It was not at all like the merry expedition with the girls. The seniors were chattering about class pins and caps. The Philomathians and Zetamathians were having their annual fight for members. And none of it concerned Emily any more—not even the debating club.

"Wakeman will be good, I think," said Jerry Sibley. "You know he's coaching football, too; like Stewie. I've been elected cheer leader," he added, grinning.

"You have?" She was surprised. Jerry didn't seem the type, somehow.

"I'm too small for football, but Wake said he wanted to put me to work," Jerry replied. "Come out to a game sometime. See what a good comedian I am."

"I will."

After that, when the team was playing at home, she went to the games, walking alone down Front Street and out to the athletic field, joining—but never being part of—the cheering crowd around the sidelines.

Jerry had developed into a comedian indeed. He brought a student's zeal to the business of leading the calls and cheers. His glasses laid aside, he jumped and leaped and even turned somersaults.

"He's marvelous! He's wonderful! He's as good as

Rathbun up at the U," Emily heard the girls saying.

"That was a good idea of Mr. Wakeman's," she thought, observing the pride on Jerry's gleaming face when he ran off the field. It was good for Jerry to be in a place of importance. He had been too much the student, in the shadow of his handsome older brother. How had Mr. Wakeman known? She looked with interest at the big new coach.

After the games the high school boys and girls drifted down Front Street into the drugstores and Heinz's ice cream parlor. Emily went into Heinz's. The big mirrored room was jammed with rooters, yelling and screaming, rushing from table to table.

"This is childish. I'll never come again," she thought, but after the next game she drifted in, a wistful, lonely figure.

No one except her was alone. "Oh, well," she consoled herself, "Thanksgiving will soon be here, and I'll have some friends again!"

She didn't let herself think how swiftly the brief vacation would fly.

October had turned the world into a bowl of brightness. The distant hills were clothed with colored trees. The locust tree was yellow among red and golden and russet companions. And down in the slough boys jumped from hummock to hummock, gathering cat-tails.

The slough was still teeming with ducks. She and her grandfather were invited to the expected dinner—duck with apple dressing, baked by Minnie to a queen's taste.

Aunt Sophie was full of news of Annette. She had been rushed by five sororities and had joined the Epsilon Iotas.

"Don sent her the most beautiful corsage bouquet when she pledged."

"Has Don pledged?"

"Certainly. Didn't you know? He's joined the Sigma Thetas—I think that's the name. I can't help mixing them up and it makes Annette furious," Aunt Sophie said, wrinkling her brow.

He might have written, Emily thought!

In her room that night she took up the volume of Browning. She kept it on her bureau and never saw its brown and gold cover without a quiver of her heart. She turned the pages, trying to bring back some of last summer's happy intimacy. It was like a dream now that he had ever come, that they had talked and joked and eaten cookies, watching the marsh hens with their babies.

"He's forgotten I ever existed. I'd better forget about him," she declared aloud.

There was wind and rain, and the leaves fell faster. Soon almost all the trees were bald. Wilson, the tall professor, was elected President. Dejectedly, Emily took off her Bull Moose pin.

It grew colder and the vines and flowers froze. The last migrating birds hurried away. The little shore birds she had loved to watch were gone; the frogs and snakes were hibernating. Winter was hovering, ready to pounce.

The heater kept the downstairs cozy. The two old chess players reveled in its warmth. But the upstairs, heated only through registers in the floor, was cold. Emily's room was too cold to read in, but it didn't matter. Her grandfather went to bed right after supper, and the parlor then was hers alone.

Drawing her favorite, stenciled rocker close to the lamp, she worked on her High School Memory Book. She lingered over every page—the programs of Philomathian rhetoricals, the announcements of debates, the place cards of parties with the girls. She unscrewed her graduation fountain pen and wrote countless letters.

She wrote more letters than she received.

"They certainly are slow in answering," she thought, beginning a letter to Nell who already owed her a letter. "But then," she admitted to herself, "they're not living in my life the way I'm living in theirs."

That was exactly what she was doing, she realized. It was wrong, but what else was she to do?

She bent her head to her arms in real despair.

What did the future hold for her, she thought? Not marriage and a family, for she was not attractive to boys. (Not getting a letter from Don had settled that.) If she were to have a career, she should be preparing for it now.

She thought of Jane Addams going through Rockford Seminary and on to her rewarding travels.

"Grandpa will die some day, and then what will I do?"

She was eighteen—that should be such a wonderful time!—and she was doing nothing. Life was passing without love or work. Tears began to flow and she jumped up, crumpling the letter. She walked to the window and looked out.

The sky was covered with low-hanging clouds but she could see the slough, frozen into a sea of hard brown billows. Except for a line of untidy muskrat houses, there wasn't a sign of life in that desolate place.

"It isn't my slough. It's a Slough of Despond," she thought bitterly. "Oh, what shall I do? What shall I do?"

In the morning it was snowing. A slow stream of flakes was dropping past her window, and the slough was covered with a thin white film through which dead rushes, quills and cat-tails poked.

She felt heavy and lifeless, and her mind reached out despairingly for something to fill the day.

"There's the St. John game." St. John was Deep Valley's traditional rival. "I'll go to that. And there's a pep rally up at the high school this morning."

Her grandfather was standing at the kitchen door, throwing out crumbs. He always fed the loyal blue jays, nuthatches and chickadees which stayed the winter. He looked around with a timid half-smile on his face and she knew he wanted to discover whether her dark mood still held. The look cut her.

"Good morning, Grandpa!" she said, trying to make her tone cheerful. "I'm going up to the high school. There's a football rally this morning."

"Good! It will do you good!" he said, and after breakfast, when she was finishing the morning work, he approached her.

"Emmy, I've been kind of worried about you. All your friends are gone away. Maybe you ought to go, too?"

Her eyes blurred. "Why, that's ridiculous!" she said. "I wouldn't leave you for the world. Besides, I like it here. I just love Deep Valley."

"Do you?" The old eyes looked anxious. "Really?"

"Of course." She'd have to do better or he would see how she felt, thought Emily as she put on her heavy coat, buckled her overshoes, and tied a scarf over last year's round felt hat.

The snow was still coming down, soft as feathers, brushing her cheek. She had always loved the first snow. But today it made her unhappy. And she entered the high school uneasily. The rally was open to the public, of course, but very few people, except students, attended.

The teachers all greeted her kindly, but there was something disturbing in Miss Fowler's manner—pity or disappointment, Emily didn't know exactly what. She went into the crowded Assembly Room and took the only vacant seat, which happened to be up front.

The team sat on the platform and the meeting opened with the school song. Jerry led the crowd through a few preliminary cheers, and Miss Bangeter made a speech.

It wasn't a very good speech. Miss Bangeter didn't really consider football important, although she tried to, and everyone understood. Then "Wake" was introduced and a roar of affectionate approval rose. Plainly, the school liked the big, casual young man who stood smiling on the platform.

But Mr. Wakeman's speech wasn't right either, although he had a most engaging manner and a likable southern voice. He didn't say the right things. He knew football, but he didn't really understand about the rivalry between Deep Valley and St. John. He didn't know how long it had lasted nor how deep it went.

Emily could see that Jerry wasn't satisfied. His eyes behind the big glasses kept roving over the room. He evidently found the help he was seeking, for when Mr. Wakeman ended Jerry sprang to his feet.

"We have a distinguished visitor today, someone who can tell us about the last four games with St. John. I want to introduce a star debater from the class of 1912, and a great Deep Valley football fan, Emily Webster!"

Emily was astounded and acutely embarrassed, but Jerry started last year's cheer:

*"There's Walker, King and Webster
And they can talk a few . . . "*

The school caught it up and it did sound wonderful, laden as it was with the memories of previous triumphs and of Don. Urged forward by cheers and clapping, she got to the platform, and she was never embarrassed there. When she began to speak all her debating skill came back.

She described the long rivalry amusingly, calling the teams Minnesota's Hatfields and McCoys. She told dramatic anecdotes from games of other years. She pointed up the times Deep Valley had won to prove what the team would do today. And she made the times Deep Valley had lost supply as strong a motive for winning. She worked up such enthusiasm that Jerry had to end the applause by calling for the school song again. The team marched off the stage but he motioned to Emily to stay, saying eagerly, "I want you to meet Wake."

Flushed and smiling shyly, she found herself shaking Mr. Wakeman's hand. The young coach was regarding her with friendly observant brown eyes.

"That was a wonderful speech, Miss Emily."

"Thank you."

"It's lucky for us you were here today. I'd heard about you from Stewie."

"You had?"

"He thought very highly of your debating. In fact," he added, "everyone around here does. I've heard so much about Emily Webster that I've been wanting to meet you." He smiled. "The joke is that I've seen you a number of times but I thought you were a high school girl. It was the hair ribbon, I reckon. Well, you're still a high school girl at heart."

His tone was laughing. The remark was innocent, but suddenly all Emily's happiness in her triumph fell away. She wasn't still a high school girl. And she couldn't keep on pretending to be one forever. She didn't belong here. She was a ghost.

She went soberly down the stairs and out into the snow. The more she thought about Mr. Wakeman's statement, the clearer the pattern of her behavior grew. Humiliation choked her. Anger rose, a furious anger at herself, and she walked faster.

"I was wondering last night what I could do. Well, there's one thing I can do, and I'll do it as soon as I get home. I can put up my hair!"

9
Hair Up

SHE WAITED UNTIL DINNER was over and the dishes done, and then she went up to her room. Standing at the mirror, she stared at her angry, determined face, with the big taffeta bow behind. She snatched off the ribbon, unbraided her hair and brushed it out vigorously. It rebounded in curly spirals.

"The reason I didn't put up my hair was that I was

clinging to high school," she thought. "There doesn't seem to be anything in my future, so I'm clinging to the past.

"But I can't stop living. I can't tie up my life like Chinese women do their feet. I've got to go on somehow.

"I don't know just what I can do, stuck here in Deep Valley." It was, she remembered, Don's disparaging word. She had never forgotten it. "But I know I'm going to do something, and I'm *not* going to go to the game this afternoon!"

Working swiftly, she parted her hair in the middle, pomped it softly on the sides and pinned it in a psyche knot. The new arrangement was becoming but she didn't care. She gave her image a wrathful glance.

Her grandfather was taking a nap, and her mind was still churning.

"I'll go downtown. Get a soda or something."

She put on her coat again. But when she put on her hat, she was forced to smile. The round school-girl felt, which had been perfect with her hair ribbon, perched absurdly on top of the psyche knot. She took it off.

"I'll have to buy a new hat. A good thing, too. It was wrong, not getting any new clothes this fall, just because I'm not going to school."

The snow had stopped falling and the sun had

come out, shining on the tender whiteness. Her head bare, her cheeks still burning, her hands deep in the pockets of her coat, she strode across the slough.

"I'm ashamed of myself. I'm just plain ashamed. I've been mean to Grandpa. I've been self-centered and selfish and rude . . ."

The words sounded familiar. They were the same, she realized, that Don had applied so dramatically to himself, and she laughed aloud.

"Well, they're true in my case!" she thought, chagrined.

She passed Heinz's Restaurant, and shuddered. It was empty now, but soon, when the game was over, it would be filled with screaming boys and girls. How ridiculous she must have looked sitting in there alone!

She walked on to Roxey's drugstore. "A soda will cool me off, maybe, and then I'll go shopping for a hat."

Climbing to a stool at the soda fountain, she caught a glimpse of an attractive-looking girl and smiled, and the girl smiled, too, looking more attractive than ever. Emily saw, with amazement, that it was herself. The new headdress gave her a winning air of maturity.

"My hair is really nice that way," she thought.

"Hello, Emily! Why aren't you at the football game like a loyal alumna of Deep Valley High?"

Turning, she saw Cab Edwards, Scid's older brother.

"Why aren't you there yourself?"

"I'd like to be. But I'm a businessman. Didn't you know?" He ran the family furniture store next door to Roxey's.

"Well, I'm grown up myself," she answered, not intending to be flippant. The words came rushing out because her mind was so full of her new resolve.

Cab laughed. "Oh, you are? Think you're pretty big, don't you, just because you're graduated?"

"Well, didn't you, after you graduated?" she asked, speaking quickly to cover confusion.

"I never did graduate." Cab hailed the clerk. "Hey, there! A little attention, please! What will you have, Emily? A banana split, or are you too grown up for that?"

"I'll have a strawberry soda."

"A strawberry soda for the lady. Bring me a chocolate nut." Cab swung to a stool beside her. He looked like Scid, slim and sprightly. His suit was freshly pressed, his shoes freshly shined, and his black hair shone like patent leather.

Annette, Emily knew, would ask whether he had been kicked out. But she had never learned that form of repartee. She was quiet and Cab went on: "Never graduated. Never went to college. But I'm glad Scid could go. Have you heard from him?"

"No. But Annette mentions him in her letters sometimes. They all seem to be having an awful lot of fun."

"Fun! Fun! It isn't for fun we're handing out what it costs to keep him at the U." But Cab didn't look as severe as he sounded. He was eating his chocolate nut sundae with relish, and he had a gay light in his eyes.

"What are you doing with yourself?" he asked.

She answered hurriedly, "Buying a new hat." And again she found that she had been unintentionally humorous.

"Whew! There's a winter's work for you!"

"I have to buy a hat that will go over a psyche knot."

At that he roared with laughter, and Emily laughed, too. She felt no constraint with him. He was only Scid's big brother. Although he couldn't be more than twenty or twenty-one, to her eighteen, he belonged in the adult world.

But then he said an astonishing thing, which revealed in a flash that he believed she belonged in the adult world, too.

"Say, Emily! There's an Elks dance a week from tonight. I was just wondering who to ask, and here I run into you. It's providential. Want to come?"

Her long training in calmness enabled her to restrain

most of her surprise. "Why, I'd love it! I don't dance very well, though."

"Well, I'm just the one who can teach you." He winked. "I'm awfully glad you can make it. I'll stop by around eight-thirty. Have to get back to the old grind now." He paid for his sundae, and her soda, picked up his hat, and was gone.

Emily sat for a long thoughtful time, looking at her empty glass. This was astonishing! She knew she would be exhilarated later, but now she was only thankful, deeply thankful.

She knew that Cab's gesture was extremely casual. She didn't overestimate the importance of his invitation. Cab Edwards took out first one girl and then another; she remembered having heard that about him. The astonishing thing was that he had put her in the category of girls whom men invited.

Had it happened just because she had put her hair up? Had it happened because her angry mood gave her a light and sparkle which she usually lacked? She didn't know.

But she did know that even though she thought so much of Don—"I'm really in love with him, I suppose"—it did her boundless good to be invited to a dance.

She got up at last and walked to the millinery shop. Mrs. Murdock brought out half a dozen beautiful hats. Emily selected a broad-brimmed brown velvet with one rose underneath, and a small fox cap which matched her furs.

"It will be nice for walking, and skating," she thought, all her normal interest in clothes aroused by Cab's invitation.

She would wear her Class Day dress to the dance, she decided, but she went to the Lion Department Store and bought a party cap. The frivolous little caps, made of tulle, net or lace, were much in fashion.

Emerging from the Lion she heard a blare of music. The high school band was coming up Front Street. It actually took her a moment to remember that it must be returning from the St. John game.

"Cheer, cheer, the gang's all here!"

The rooters were marching and singing with their arms around each other's shoulders. Excited children ran along beside them.

"Who won?" Emily called.

"We did!"

"What was the score?"

"Ten to nothing."

She was pleased, but it didn't seem important.

That night after supper she sat down at the piano. She played Paderewski's "Minuet," which she had been studying when she stopped taking lessons in her busy senior year, and some of the hymns her grandfather loved.

"It seems good, Emmy," he said, "to hear a little music again."

"I'm going to play every night after supper like I used to. That is, when I'm not going out. I'm going to a party next Saturday."

"That's nice," he answered, beaming.

She went to the bookcase and took out *The Talisman*. "And we must get at this! I think Scott belongs to the winter, don't you, Grandpa? He's so long-winded, and winter evenings are so long."

"You're exactly right," he answered.

The next day at church, while the minister prayed, Emily said her own prayer, a prayer of thankfulness.

Monday afternoon she took her skates and went over to the pond. The pond was so shallow that it froze quickly, and it was already covered with boys. They had built a fire; orange flames were leaping. It was good to be on the ice again, she thought, sailing down the pond with her hands in her muff.

During the week she pressed the corn-colored silk. She cleaned her long white gloves and hung them to air and shook out her opera cape.

On the night of the party she dressed her hair with care.

"This psyche knot brought me luck," she thought, inspecting it in a hand mirror. She put on the party cap but after a long thoughtful scrutiny she took it off.

"It doesn't belong to me. It isn't my type," she decided.

But she had to wear something in her hair; headdresses were elaborate now. She rummaged through the jewel box and found a square gold comb. That might be good. It was! It looked well with her mother's locket, too.

She put on her opera cape and gazed into the mirror, into glowing eyes, unlike her own. She felt excited and strange and uncertain, but happy. She was going to a dance!

Waiting in the little parlor, she felt a familiar twinge. It did look so old fashioned! But probably she could manage it so Cab wouldn't come in.

She kissed her grandfather. "Leave the lamp lighted for me; won't you, Grandpa?"

"I will, Emmy. Have a good time."

She stood by the door and slipped out when she saw Cab coming up the walk.

Two other couples were waiting in the automobile—Dennis Farisy, Winona Root, Lloyd Harrington and Alice Morrison. They had all been in high school with Cab. Lloyd had gone on to the U but had dropped out last year. The girls had finished Teachers' College and were teaching near Deep Valley.

Cab presented her breezily. "See what I found when I robbed the cradle?"

"You want to watch out for these graybeards, Emily," said Winona. She was a tall angular brunette, very full of fun.

"I'll take care of you," said blond Alice Morrison, tucking her hand under Emily's arm.

At the Elks Club the three girls left their wraps in the dressing room, touched up their hair, put on powder and came out into the parlors together.

It was a distinctly mixed group so far as age was concerned. There were a few girls from Emily's class, men and girls from graduating classes of several years previous and married couples—young, middle-aged and old.

Cab introduced a number of men. "Miss Webster" sounded agreeably odd. They wrote their names on her dancing card and he scrawled his own in the vacant places.

Lamm's Orchestra, Deep Valley's best, was seated on a platform at one end of the room. The music of the opening waltz soared across the floor:

"To you, beautiful lady,
I raise my eyes . . . "

Emily wished ardently that she were a better dancer.

"I ought to take some lessons," she thought, after getting out of step for the third time. But Cab was good natured about her mistakes.

She felt exhilarated by the music and the crowded room with its rhythmically revolving couples. The women looked so fashionable and gay in their tube-like skirts, some slit to the knee. Those who didn't wear party caps wore feathers or bands of tulle in their hair. Emily was glad she had found the comb.

She was quiet at first, but Cab brought out her laughter. She found herself having a very good time. A buffet supper was served at midnight, and for this they joined a group which made a wide half-circle in one of the parlors. Wilson's election was being discussed.

After supper, she felt more at ease. These people liked her. It didn't matter to them that she hadn't been popular with boys in high school. No one even knew it, and if they did they wouldn't care. High school wasn't important to them.

She fitted in well with a crowd like this—better than she had with a high school crowd. They weren't so silly, and her dignity—a disadvantage in high school—really helped. They were interested, too, in more of the things she was interested in. She had thoroughly enjoyed that talk about the election.

"We're glad Cab robbed the cradle," said Winona when they parted.

"Let's get together again," Alice suggested. "You know, Emily, after you're out of school you don't stick to your own high school class. You mix up with all the other crowds."

"Even graybeards like us," said Dennie, poking Lloyd.

The others were going home, but Cab took Emily to the Moorish Café where they had rarebit and coffee.

Emily had never been there before. The long room with its oriental hangings was lighted dimly from brass lamps and an orchestra was playing softly. He told her that he was going to Minneapolis for the Wisconsin game.

"Scid wants me to come."

"How did it happen," Emily asked, "that you didn't go to college?"

Cab's face sobered. "Why, I had to pitch in and support the family. My father died just after I finished my junior year in high school. Old Mr. Loring ran the store in father's place, but he needed a helper and there wasn't money to pay for one. I learned the business, and when Mr. Loring died I took over."

"How did you—feel about it?" Emily asked diffidently. "About giving up college, I mean?"

"Badly," Cab answered. "I thought I wanted to be an engineer. But do you know, Emily, I'd have made a darn poor engineer. And I'm a good businessman. I really like the store. What's more, I've got a head start on a lot of other boys who'll go into business eventually."

Emily was silent.

"It was a satisfaction to be able to send Scid to the U, but it wouldn't surprise me if he didn't stay more than a year or so. I've a hunch he's a businessman, too. Now the next in line, my little sister, she's different. She'll profit by college."

"Yes," Emily broke in passionately. "And so would I." She stopped in flooding embarrassment, for they hadn't been discussing her. She had had no intention of talking about herself. The exclamation had burst out because of the fullness of her heart.

Cab asked quietly, "What do you mean?"

"I mean . . ." she floundered, blushing deeply, "I'm like your sister. I'm a student, too. I want more education terribly."

"And you can't go to college on account of your grandfather, I suppose." Cab looked troubled. "Well, I found education here. Old Mr. Loring educated me. The U would have been just four years of play."

"It wouldn't be for me," said Emily, but she stopped abruptly. She knew that Cab was sympathetic and interested, but she was ashamed of her outburst. It was so unlike her. She never confided. Besides, in the Moorish Café, after a dance, she ought to keep the conversation light.

Summoning all her poise she smiled and changed the subject. "I remember your class," she said. "I remember Betsy Ray and Tib Muller . . ."

"We had a lot of fun," Cab replied, sounding relieved. "Did you ever hear how Betsy Ray taught me *Ivanhoe?*"

He told her the story, which was so funny that Emily began to laugh. Cab ordered more coffee and went on to other tales of his crowd. To her infinite relief Emily saw that he hadn't been too much disturbed by her impetuous confidences.

He took her home in Mr. Thumbler's hack and told her at the door that it had been swell. They must do it again sometime. He sounded as though he meant it, too.

"Maybe this is the answer," Emily thought, back in her own little room, undressing. "Maybe social life is the answer, going around with an older crowd."

10

Emily Musters Her Wits

AT CHURCH NEXT DAY Dr. MacDonald said something that helped her. Emily's mind kept drifting away from the sermon to last night's fun. But suddenly this sentence flashed out—it was a quotation from Shakespeare, she thought:

"Muster your wits: stand in your own defense."

She had no idea in what sense he had used it, but it

seemed to be a message aimed directly at her.

"Muster your wits: stand in your own defense," she kept repeating to herself on the long walk home. After dinner she sat down in her rocker, looked out at the snow and proceeded to muster her wits.

"I'm going to fill my winter and I'm going to fill it with something worth while," she resolved. "I'm not going to neglect Grandpa, either."

One thing she could do, beside housekeeping and cooking: she could practise the piano. She enjoyed playing, and it would be a satisfaction to try to master the instrument.

"I'll start taking lessons again," she planned. "Another thing I can do, of course, is read—not the way I've been doing, but to some purpose." She knit her brows.

"I'll read Scott to Grandpa, but perhaps there's something else he'd enjoy that I'd enjoy, too—something we could study together." She smiled broadly. "Abraham Lincoln! Grandpa would like anything about Lincoln, and I've never read a good biography of him. I'll ask Miss Fowler which one would be best."

And then an idea swept across her mind like a wind sweeping away gray clouds to show a sky of sparkling promise.

"I wonder whether I could get a group together to

study something under Miss Fowler. We could study Browning!"

She still hadn't got past the ballads. In fact, she seldom opened the little brown and gold book. But it was more precious than anything she owned. "Except my mother's locket, maybe," she thought.

She knew that she wanted Browning for Don's sake. But there could be nothing wrong in seeking the same pleasures he was enjoying.

"The first thing to do is ask Miss Fowler whether she would take such a group. If she will, then I'll go to Alice Morrison." She remembered what Alice had said about getting together. "Perhaps she'd like to join and would help me find others."

She jumped to her feet. "I'll go and ask Miss Fowler right now. And while I'm about it, I'll go to Miss Cobb's, too."

She went to Miss Cobb's first. She was more than a little in awe of Miss Fowler who, although so small and cordial, had a definitely regal air. Miss Cobb was an old friend.

She was a large, gentle woman with blue eyes and white skin and reddish-gold hair, now growing gray.

"She must have been really beautiful when she was young," Emily thought as they sat talking in the warm little parlor which held two pianos—a grand and an upright—for four-piano arrangements at recitals.

She thought of Miss Cobb's story. She had known it all her life, but it had never seemed real until this afternoon. It struck her poignantly now that Miss Cobb had been just a little older than she was when she broke her engagement to marry because her sister had died of tuberculosis, leaving four children.

Miss Cobb had started teaching the piano and had made a home for them. But the first three had died of their mother's disease, one by one, when they came to adolescence. Only Bobby remained—the champion wrestler of the fifth grade—making a snowman now on the front lawn. What struggle and suffering and sacrifice Miss Cobb had known, Emily thought, and yet she was always cheerful! She was smiling now with real affection.

"I'm so glad you have time for your music again. I remember how well you played Paderewski's 'Minuet.'"

"I was studying that when I stopped my lessons," Emily replied.

"Well, we'll begin with it! When would you like to start?"

"After Thanksgiving," Emily answered. The return of the crowd seemed such an epochal event that she couldn't get her mind on music until it was over.

Miss Fowler lived in a small apartment in a big private house on Broad Street. The little Bostonian answered Emily's ring herself.

"I was just going to make myself some tea. Now you can join me," she said, taking Emily's furs and coat.

When Miss Fowler went to the kitchen, Emily looked around the living room with pleasure. There were oriental rugs on the polished floor. The walls were lined with bookcases, and the table bore a new *Atlantic Monthly*, an *Outlook*, a *Theatre Magazine*, and several books still in their paper jackets.

Emily picked one up—*How to Live on Twenty-four Hours a Day*, by Arnold Bennett.

Over the mantel, beneath which a fire was crackling, hung a brown sepia picture of the Church of Notre Dame in Paris. On another wall was a pinkish-colored picture of St. Mark's Square in Venice. Emily recognized copies of a Greuze girl, Whistler's Mother, Raphael's Madonna of the Chair.

"Maybe Miss Fowler has been abroad. Maybe she's seen the originals of some of these pictures," Emily thought.

The teatray held a fat silver pot, a silver cream pitcher and sugar bowl with tongs, a plate of sliced lemon and two flowered cups.

"I love to talk over tea," Miss Fowler said. She looked at Emily closely with her black, very penetrating eyes, and Emily felt sure Miss Fowler knew that she had come with some project in mind.

Emily asked the question about Lincoln first.

"Herndon is still the best," Miss Fowler answered promptly. "*The True Story of a Great Life*. It's a collaboration with Weik." She put down her cup. "You've discovered, I see, that we have to build our lives out of what materials we have. It's as though we were given a heap of blocks and told to build a house . . ." She paused, and smiled. "You and your grandfather will have a wonderful time with Lincoln."

This made it easy for Emily to suggest the Browning Club.

"I'd love it!" Miss Fowler responded. Her dark eyes gleamed.

"Would you have time to take us?"

"Of course. I'd never refuse one evening a week to Browning."

"I thought I'd ask Alice Morrison."

"She'd be interested, I think. And there are several girls from her class in town." They planned eagerly. "Do you own a copy of Browning?"

"Yes, I do."

"I'd like to use Richard Burton's edition in the Belles Lettres Series."

"That's the very one I have!"

"Well, get yourself a notebook and some pencils then," Miss Fowler said gaily. "We'll meet here,

Tuesday evenings. When would you like to begin?"

"Right after Thanksgiving," Emily replied.

She rose, warmed not only by the tea but by the prospect of buying a notebook for study. She stopped at a drugstore and called Alice Morrison who fell in at once with the idea.

"I know several girls who would like to join."

"I think we ought to make Miss Fowler accept a fee," said Emily.

"Oh, of course."

"I'll call you again, and we'll work it all out."

The next day, walking on air, she went to the library for the book on Lincoln, and to Cook's Book Store for two small fat notebooks. She bought a box of pencils and a pencil sharpener. It was like getting ready for the first day of school.

"It's amazing," she thought, "what you can do when you muster your wits."

A few days later she went to the Lion Department Store and bought a new dress. It was quite unnecessary to bother Aunt Sophie with Miss Mix. There were very nice ready-made dresses. Emily found a rose-colored wool trimmed with brown velvet, buttoned up one side with a long row of brown velvet buttons. (Side fastenings and up and down rows of buttons were the newest thing.)

That night she brought the jewel box down to the

fire and laid out the old-fashioned earrings, the bracelets, the gold chains, the lockets and brooches. She had realized on the night of the party that these gracious old things were becoming to her. She tried on pearl earrings and looked at herself in the mirror.

She wished Cab would invite her to another party. Her old moody self tried to say that she had been a failure, but she knew better.

"He's been up to the Wisconsin game. Besides, Cab Edwards changes around. I wish I could improve my dancing, though." Just possibly he might have asked her sooner if she had danced better.

There was a dancing school in town but the classes were only for children. At first thought she felt foolish going for private lessons, but she laughed herself down.

"Pooh! It's nobody's business but my own. I'm studying everything else. I might as well study dancing, too."

And she walked down Front Street to Mrs. Anderson's Select Dancing Academy.

Mrs. Anderson was a large woman, with a hard, tired face. She was lame. How had a lame woman undertaken to teach dancing, Emily wondered? Probably the training in dancing had come first, and Mrs. Anderson had not been deterred from her chosen career, although it must be difficult and tiring to lead children as she was doing now through so endlessly many steps.

> *"Everybody's doing it, doing it, doing it,*
> *Everybody's doing it . . . "*

The pianist, whose red hair was pomped all around like a halo, thumped out the same tune over and over again.

Emily took her first lesson on the spot. Mrs. Anderson called for a waltz and, oddly enough, the red-haired pianist chose the very tune which had opened the Elks dance.

> *"To you, beautiful lady . . . "*

Only now Emily didn't dance with a partner. She went through the steps alone, over and over, while Mrs. Anderson, in front of her, demonstrated as she called, *"One,* two, three. *One,* two, three."

It was fun to move about the polished floor with no qualms about her lack of skill.

"I'll learn some of the new things, too . . . the Gaby Glide and the Turkey Trot," Emily thought.

Thanksgiving was near now. Emily and Aunt Sophie were drawn together by their mutual eagerness.

"You and your grandfather are coming for

Thanksgiving dinner," Aunt Sophie reminded.

"Oh, of course!"

"But Annette gets in Wednesday night. Won't you come to the train with us?"

"I certainly will."

It was a cold night with wind racing down the station platform, but the parents and Emily waited with warming joy. At last came the whistle and the tolling bell, and the great light of the engine.

The home-coming students rushed to their waiting families, but all, even Don, paused to greet Emily.

"You look just like the Deep Valley High School," he said with his wide smile, shaking her hand.

Annette threw her arms around her and kissed her. Emily smelled a new delicious perfume.

"Em! You old darling! I hope you're coming home with us?"

"I'm coming tomorrow for Thanksgiving dinner. Grandpa and I are."

"I want you with me every minute. I want you to just follow me around. Hear?"

"She's going to be too busy following me," said Nell, hugging her.

"No! No! Me!" cried Gladys.

"I'll follow you all everywhere," said Emily happily.

It was like a breath of heaven.

For three days she really lived. She and her grandfather went to the Thanksgiving dinner. But even Minnie's turkey was nothing compared to the joy of sitting in Annette's room after dinner, hearing her tell about the university.

She showed Emily her Epsilon Iota pledge pin. "The girls are adorable! Just adorable!"

She told her all about the rushing parties and pledge day. When Gladys came in, Annette turned the talk away from sororities, for Gladys had not been asked to join one and it had been hard on her, Annette had confided to Emily. They talked about fraternity dances and college football games—which were very different from high school football games—held in great arenas. Jim Baxter was going out for football; he had made the second team.

They told her about the Oak Tree where everyone went for sundaes and coffee. "It's the Heinz's of the university," Annette explained.

They described the crush in the post office when you went before chapel to look for notes, or blue slips, or invitations.

"Or corsages," Gladys put in mischievously.

"Don really did put one there for me when I pledged," Annette explained.

They talked about "fussing" and "dates" and "river banking." That meant walking with a man along the path which followed the Mississippi. When indignant parents called them downstairs they went to the piano and sang a song about river banking:

> *"When we go strolling, river banking,*
> *Wandering along,*
> *Strolling through the dusky shadows*
> *All the world's a song."*

Don and Scid and Jim came in.

Don was very collegiate—more so than any of them, Emily thought. The padded shoulders of a new striped suit made him look even bigger than he was. And he kept his coat open to show the pledge pin on his vest. He was in a very good mood, flashing his shiny smile and laughing uproariously at all of Scid's jokes. But he paid a minimum of attention to Emily.

Scid noticed that her hair was up. The girls had noticed it earlier, saying that they liked it that way. They said so again and Don turned and looked at her indifferently, but he didn't speak.

She had thought she would tell him about the Browning Club, but that was impossible. It seemed impossible that they had ever been friends.

Gladys played "Minnesota, Hail to Thee" and "Ski-U-Mah." They were all singing, their arms around each other's shoulders. Emily was singing with them, but she felt uncomfortable. She did not have the sense of belonging she had felt at the Elks dance. Even though there was an extra boy she decided to leave, and when she suggested that she take her grandfather home, no one protested. Jim Baxter even looked relieved, she thought.

Uncle Chester drove them in the auto.

All day Saturday and Sunday she stayed with the girls, drinking in their words. She didn't tell them, as she had intended to, about the party with Cab. It didn't seem as important as it had. Maybe Gladys would call him a graybeard.

She didn't mention her several projects either. She felt sensitive about the dancing lessons, and she knew that Miss Cobb and a Browning Club would only sound dull. But on Sunday night when the train carried them away, Emily was glad for her "program of self-improvement." She wouldn't, she resolved, let herself be downed another time.

"I've learned, at least, to muster my wits in my own defense," she thought and telephoned Alice.

11
Crack the Whip

ON MONDAY EMILY STAYED at home, doing house-work furiously, baking cookies and a cake. Her grandfather, sitting in the bay window, called out that the skating must be good.

"There's quite a crowd on the pond."

A little later he observed that he had seen Kalil go past . . . without Yusef. And when Emily came to sit beside him, after frosting her cake, he remarked thoughtfully, "I like to see Kalil playing with American boys for a change."

"But do you suppose he has skates?" Emily went to the window. Through the bare trees she could see the fire at the edge of the pond and the graceful figures of skaters, but she could not recognize Kalil. She jumped up.

"I believe I'll go out myself," she said. She bundled into her short jacket and furs and caught up her skates.

It was growing late; the snow was a cold pale blue, and the crowd was thinning out. Only a handful of boys remained, shouting at the far end of the pond. Skating near them, she saw Kalil with a red muffler flying above his shabby coat. He didn't have skates, but he was pleased, she saw, to be one of the group. He was laughing, and struggling to stand up on the ice. He waved at her excitedly.

She turned and skated slowly to the other end of the pond, looking beyond the yellow willows to her little white house, grimy-gray against the snow. The locust tree rose ghostlike above its forsaken bench. And the bare trees on her hillside blurred against the sky where the sun hung like a red Japanese lantern.

When she turned again, the boys were playing crack the whip. Hands locked, they were skating in

Indian file. They gained speed, and the leader—a burly overgrown boy—stopped suddenly with a warning yell and pulled the line around. It broke, and the skaters went whirling over the ice. Good fun, no doubt, but pretty violent, Emily thought, skating peacefully with her hands in her muff.

The line formed again, and this time at the perilous end a red muffler flamed. But Kalil didn't have skates—and he was much smaller than the others! She pushed forward.

Seeing her coming, the leader started skating. Kalil ran frantically behind the last skater, who held Kalil's hand firmly. He lost his footing but his companion would not release him. The leader yelled, "Hold on!" and cracked the whip with savage vigor. Kalil went rolling and tumbling over the ice.

The boys skated away, whooping, "Dago! Dago!" Emily cried after them but they would not stop. At the fire they tore off their skates and went scrambling over the slough.

"Barbarians!" she exclaimed as she helped Kalil to his feet.

He was shouting a stream of unintelligible—something. What did the Syrians speak? Arabic? Emily wondered. He was trying to wave his arms, but whenever he waved the right one he yelped with pain and pulled it back against his breast.

A little English broke into his talk. Emily gathered that his tormentors were dogs and that God would punish them in a number of dramatic ways. Tears of rage were running down his cheeks.

"Never mind them!" she said, putting her arm around him. "How do you feel?"

"I'm killed, ma'am. I'm going to die, God save!" he sobbed.

"Oh, no, Kalil! It isn't that bad."

"My arm, she hurts terrible." He was cradling his right forearm in his left hand.

"Come over to the house," said Emily. She skated slowly while he hobbled beside her. Reaching land, she took her skates off quickly.

Grandpa Webster was waiting at the front door. "What's the matter?"

"I'm killed, sir, God save! I'm going to die," said Kalil.

"Light the lamp, Grandpa. It's his arm."

"What happened?"

"They were playing crack the whip and Kalil was at the end—without skates! Those horrible boys!"

Kalil's fists brushed away the last of his tears. "It's because I'm a foreigner, ma'am," he explained. "It's because I speak the English funny."

"That's no reason for them being so mean." Emily took off his worn overcoat gently but he winced. She took off his jacket, rolled up his right sleeve and ran her fingers cautiously over the forearm.

"It's swelling. But it's just a simple sprain, I think. You look at it, Grandpa."

He took the small arm in knowing fingers while Kalil waited with anxiously dilated eyes.

"Just a sprain," Grandpa Webster agreed. "Make a cold compress, Emmy. Some cookies might help, too. Did you know, Kalil, that cookies were good for sprains?"

"Cookies? Sweets?"

"That's it." They sat down beside the stove and, while Emily applied cold compresses, Kalil munched cookies and her grandfather talked.

"I saw plenty of sprains in the Civil War."

"The Civil War?"

"Abe Lincoln's war."

"Were you a soldier, sir?"

"Call me Grandpa Webster. Yep! I was a soldier. And you must be a good soldier now till this stops hurting. It won't hurt long. It may turn black and blue but that just gives you something to show Yusef. Where was he today?"

"He has a sickness. He sneezes."

"Too bad. Bring me a towel, Emmy."

"What are you making, my grandpa?" Kalil asked curiously.

"A sling."

"Did you make things like that when you were a soldier?"

"Yep! Made 'em by the dozen." The shirt was rolled down, the jacket and shabby overcoat replaced, the sling hung about Kalil's neck and his arm was placed carefully within it.

"I'll walk home with him," Emily said to her grandfather.

Kalil looked up quickly. "You'll walk home with me, ma'am?"

"Why, yes! You wouldn't mind, would you?"

"Oh, no! I am full of thanks to you."

"It's a good idea," Grandpa Webster said. "She can explain to your mother what happened. I'm ashamed of those boys."

"It was because I speak the English funny," Kalil said again in a confidential tone. He took up his cap. "Good-by, my grandpa. I am full of thanks to you. Peace to your age!"

"Peace to your age!" Kalil always pronounced his *p*'s like *b*'s, but "beace" could only mean "peace." "Peace to your age!" What a beautiful wish! Emily thought.

They went out the kitchen door. It was not yet six o'clock, but darkness had fallen. The snow gleamed with ghostly pallor and a few early stars were caught in the nets of the trees.

Kalil took her to a path that followed the edge of the slough.

"Is this the path you use when you come to see us?" Emily asked.

"Yes, ma'am. Yusef and I come often by this path. Here's where I got bitten by that big, big, great big— Ouch!" He stopped measuring off the snake and settled his right arm cautiously in the sling.

"Kalil!" said Emily, laughing. "How can you talk, now that your arm is hurt?"

"But, ma'am! I talk with my mouth!" He started to bring his right hand up in illustration, stopped with another "Ouch!" and joined in her laughter, his eyes sparkling upward.

The tiny lights of Little Syria were now pricking through the gloom.

"You've lived here a year?" Emily asked.

"Yes, ma'am! My father was here first. Then he sent for my mother and me and Layla, my sister."

"How do you like it?"

"Oh, very much! America, she's a dandy country."

Emily had not visited Little Syria in several years, and night veiled it now, but she remembered it as a dirty dilapidated place. The humble little houses stood side by side, facing an eastern hill on which rose the ramshackle mansion of old Mr. Meecham.

He had come from the east years ago and bought all the land in this valley. Then he had cut it into building lots and had built himself a fine house. When he had failed, because of the distance from the center of town, to sell lots to his fellow citizens, he had sold to the Syrian colony and had stayed on in his mansion, cutting himself off angrily from the rest of Deep Valley. He still had money. His team of white horses was the finest in the county and it was driven by a coachman, too.

Kalil turned in near the end of the row. As they mounted the narrow porch the door flew open and a small dark face poked out—a little girl's face, although she was wearing earrings. Long black braids with red rags woven into them swung on either side.

At sight of Kalil she let out a welcoming cry, but when she saw Emily she darted away. Her place in the doorway was taken by a tall man with a huge flowing mustache. Behind him peeped a small woman in a full-skirted, faded, purple dress. She also wore earrings.

They were all talking at once, with vehement gestures, in whatever language it was that Syrians spoke. Layla wore glass bracelets which jangled as though they, too, were eager to have their say. The father, presently, broke off into English.

"Welcome, Miss! Come into my house. My house is honored . . ." Emily made out the stately words in spite of the stumbling pronunciation.

She found herself inside, and seated. The small parlor was lighted by a kerosene lamp, hung from the ceiling. A cast-iron stove in one corner quivered with heat. There were several cheap wooden chairs, a low table; and a low bench ran around all four walls. The room was carpeted cheerfully in red.

Kalil continued talking in the foreign tongue, gesticulating madly with his good left arm. The little sister took Emily's muff, laid it carefully on a chair. She looked at her with Kalil's round liquid eyes, and when she met Emily's gaze big dimples popped out. The little mother tripped out to the kitchen and Layla reluctantly followed.

The mustached father continued to overwhelm Emily with his welcome.

"What a blessed day! You have come to my house! It is yours. You may burn it."

"Burn it! I can't be understanding properly," Emily thought.

"Peace to your feet for bringing my son home!" he continued. He examined Kalil's sling. "Peace to your hands for making this . . ."

"It's a sling, my father," Kalil interrupted proudly.

"Peace to your hands for making this sling . . ."

"No, my father! Her honored grandfather made it."

"Peace to his age!" the big man said with dignity.

There it was again! That beautiful phrase!

Emily felt ashamed to have their small services so extravagantly praised.

"Why, we didn't do anything! I came home with Kalil because I wanted to explain about his arm. My grandfather examined it, and it isn't broken. It will be all right soon."

The mother returned bearing a dish of dried figs and one of raisins. The little sister carried a saucer full of nuts. She was trying not to smile but she wasn't succeeding. Her dimples, Emily thought, were big enough to poke your finger in.

Everything was deposited on the table, which was now drawn close to Emily's chair. The mother went to the kitchen again and Layla trailed after, her face turned to look at Emily until she was out of sight.

The father kept on talking grandiloquently, urging Emily to eat the figs and the raisins and the nuts, and shortly the mother came back with a small, long-handled, copper pot. Layla, close on her heels, brought a tiny cup which her mother filled with strange-looking coffee, very black with froth on top.

"You mustn't be so good to me! I've done nothing at all!" Emily protested, but her words went unheeded. They all looked on radiantly while she nibbled and sipped.

The coffee was thick and sweet.

"You like our coffee? That's Damascus coffee."

"These nuts—they're named pistachio."

"Please honor us, Miss, by taking another fig."

When she got to her feet at last, all four started chattering. Layla, running to an inner room, returned in a coat with a yellow scarf over her braids, and Kalil replaced on his curly head the cap he had taken off.

"But you're not coming with me!" Emily cried.

"Of course, ma'am!"

"It's not at all necessary. And it must be time for your supper."

"They are honored to go."

With Kalil and Layla holding her hands on either side, Emily went down the steps.

"God preserve you and your blessed grandfather!" The big man smiled.

"God bless!" cried the little mother. They were the first English words she had used.

Emily smiled, delighted and bewildered. "I must come again," she thought.

They went back to the little path. There were myriads of stars now, and the slough slept beneath a silver counterpane.

"What language do Syrians speak?" Emily asked.

"Arabic, ma'am. But we wish to speak the English."

"Does Layla speak any English?"

"Sure," said Layla, dancing at her side. "I speak the dandy English."

"And she sings," said Kalil. "My sister sings like a—like a—sparrow."

"No, sparrows don't sing! You must mean like a thrush."

"Sure. She sings like a thrush."

"I wish you'd come to my house and sing for me some day. Does your mother speak English?"

"No. She's a woman. Women," Kalil explained grandly, "don't speak the English much."

"Your father," remarked Emily, "speaks wonderful English." She paused for a tactful approach. "But I was puzzled by something."

"What was that, ma'am?"

"He said I could burn your house."

"Oh," answered Kalil, shrugging, "he said that to be polite. Of course, ma'am, he knows you won't do it."

"But she could—if she wanted to—my brother," Layla reproved him gently.

12

Poetry, Music, and Dance

"How good is man's life, the mere living!
how fit to employ
All the heart and the soul and the senses
forever in joy!"

EMILY WAS COMING HOME from the Browning class. It was a boisterous night; snow blew into her face as she walked across the slough, her body bent and braced to meet the wind. She didn't feel cold. She felt exhilarated to the ends of her mittened fingers. The richness of "Saul" warmed her like a fire.

"No wonder Don loves Browning!" But she amended that thought. "No, it's surprising! Don hasn't the joy in life, and the faith in people, and the—the love of God that Browning has. Or has he? Maybe I don't understand Don."

She struggled up the snowy path to her door.

"I'm going to talk with him when he comes home for Christmas," she resolved, stamping her feet at the threshold. It was silly to let him ignore her when they had so much in common.

Going into the silent house, she laughed suddenly. "I'm not so humble as I used to be. But who *could* be humble, studying Browning? He makes you feel important just because you're a human being."

The Browning class had met only twice, but it had already changed the color of Emily's winter. Miss Fowler had stressed her conviction that Browning was not "a poet for the cultured few." It was true, she said, that he wasn't easy reading. You had to keep your dictionaries and reference books handy. But he was vital, red-blooded, with a deep interest in all human problems. He gave supreme importance to the battle between right and wrong.

"I count life just a stuff
To try the soul's strength on . . . "

Miss Fowler quoted, and Emily felt it a tonic.

She was braced, too, by the reference, in Dr. Richard Burton's introduction, to Browning's schooling, which had been irregular, ending with a single term at London University, but ". . . his education then was just beginning and was to last through a long lifetime of eager, wide and absorptive culture until death itself."

Emily wrote down that phrase, "eager, wide and absorptive culture."

"That's what I'm going to try for," she thought.

She was absorbing culture in Miss Fowler's apartment, absorbing it with every pore. Miss Fowler had, indeed, seen the originals of the pictures on her walls. When they discussed the life of Browning and his invalid poetess wife in Florence, Italy, she brought out a great stack of postcards collected during a European sojourn. There were pictures not only of Italy but of Switzerland, the German cities, Paris, the British Isles.

And even more important than Browning and the postcards was the talk beside Miss Fowler's fire. The group of women included, besides Emily and Alice, Miss Sparrow, the librarian, two young teachers and a young married woman named Mrs. Jack Delaney who was a graduate of Smith.

Their talk ranged over a wide field: Woman Suffrage—Mrs. Pankhurst and Christobel were both in prison that winter. President-elect Woodrow Wilson.

Henry George. Ibsen. Tolstoy. George Bernard Shaw —Miss Fowler loaned Emily *Man and Superman*. They talked about the New York plays. Mrs. Delaney went to New York often. They talked about music, about opera. Miss Fowler had heard Wagner's *Ring* in Bayreuth, Germany.

Emily found she had much to think about as she shoveled high-walled paths through December snows, chopped wood for the kitchen range and tended the coal stove. This sat on its zinc pad like a fat insatiable monster. She shared with her grandfather the work of shaking it down and filling it with coal and taking out the ashes. The red glow behind its isinglass windows was pleasant, but it spread dust unmercifully, making housework harder. Ruefully Emily rubbed cream into her chapped hands at night.

She was extremely busy. Planted seeds produce a garden that requires tending. And all her desperate efforts to find self-expression were sprouting into demanding growths. Dancing lessons took only an hour a week. But piano lessons must be practised, and Browning and Lincoln took time.

Mrs. Delaney entertained the group at Sunday night supper, and they made a pleasant plan to go to plays at the Opera House together. Deep Valley was conveniently located between the Twin Cities and Omaha; and a good theatrical production stopped there now and then.

Moreover, quite unexpectedly, in mid-December, Cab invited her to another dance.

"Why the dickens don't you have a phone put in?" he accosted her when they met on Front Street. "It's a long way across your slough. Do your beaus write notes of invitation and wait for an answer? You've got a lot of confidence, girl."

Emily laughed, shy but pleased, and Cab proceeded, "It's the Elks Club again. Same crowd as before. If you had fun the last time——"

"I did."

"Will you come then? Next Saturday night?"

She wore the corn-colored silk again, and again she had a very good time. In the first place, her dancing had improved.

"Gee whiz! I must be quite a teacher," Cab exclaimed after they had circled the room.

She danced with zestful accuracy through a program of waltzes, two-steps, schottisches, polkas. There was no chance to try out her Gaby Glide; the Elks Club was too conservative for that.

"No wonder the girls are so crazy about dances!" Emily thought. "They're fun!"

She had just finished a lively polka with Jack Delaney when she saw Mr. Wakeman. The big young man was standing alone, his hands thrust casually into his pockets, surveying the room with a smile. His gaze reached her just as Jack Delaney took her to her chair, where Cab was waiting. She saw him look at her with a puzzled expression and then he came forward.

"Good evening, Miss—Emily," he said in his soft southern voice. "I didn't recognize you for a moment. I've been wanting to see you, to hear what you thought of the St. John game."

"I didn't go," Emily replied.

"You didn't go? After the way you pumped for it? Whatever happened?"

"Say you sprained your ankle," Cab joked.

But Emily only smiled.

"Can't I have a dance and get at the truth of the matter?" He took her card, but it was full.

"Next time, then!" he said. "Remember, I'm going to find out." His brown eyes smiled down at her; he bowed and turned away.

"He's a nice guy," remarked Cab.

"The team certainly likes him," Emily answered. Her own feelings were mixed; he was associated in her mind with that awful "high school girl in a hair ribbon" remark! But if he hadn't made her angry that day she wouldn't have put up her hair! She wouldn't be here!

Cab laughed. "The team's crazy about him. It took

them a while to figure him out, though. He's so easy-going, and speaks so soft. The team thought at first that maybe he *was* soft. At practise one day he was saying, 'Get down, when you charge! Keep low! *Hit hard!*' and the right guard on the first team, a big strong smart alec, said, 'Maybe you'd play guard on the scrubs, and give me the idea, Mr. Wakeman.'

"Wake looked them all over, and smiled that slow easy smile of his and said, 'Sure, if you think that'd help.' And he got down in the scrub line, but before he did he told the quarterback to send the next play through him.

"I doubt if he put out more than half his strength. But he certainly hit hard enough to knock Mr. Smart Alec flat. The scrubs picked up twenty yards.

"When Wake came back the first-team guard was just getting up. 'Did that give you the idea?' Wake asked with that easy smile, 'or shall we try it again?'

"The big kid grinned and said, 'Nope. We won't try that again. Not ever, Mr. Wakeman. I got the idea—*completely.*'"

Emily laughed, well able to visualize the scene.

The next day she bought a new party dress—just in case she should be invited to the Christmas dances. She didn't want to have Miss Mix make it, for then Aunt Sophie would know that she had hoped to be invited—and, of course, she never had been in the past. But things were getting to be so different!

She found a beautiful gown: a patterned white tunic over pale blue silk with a spray of blue silk corn flowers embroidered on the bodice.

"You ought to wear blue corn flowers in your hair," said the saleswoman. "It would be good because your eyes are so blue."

"I will," Emily thought. "And I'll wear those old pearl earrings from the jewel box." They were just the lustrous shade of her tunic.

It was almost time for the Christmas college visitation. Front Street was putting on evergreens and holly; the store windows were glowing with gifts and the sleighbells, ringing along snow-packed roads, had a holiday chime.

In the little house across the slough there were holidayish things to be done. Emily picked greens from her own hillside and wove them into wreaths for the windows and made a decoration for the table of hemlock boughs and pine cones. She had long since baked her fruit cake. Now she baked Christmas cookies and a mince pie, too, for although they always went to Aunt Sophie's for dinner, she liked to have a mince pie in the house.

She had bought gifts for Aunt Sophie, Uncle Chester and Annette, and a copy of Herndon's *Lincoln* for her grandfather. Library copies were all very well, but when you loved a book as much as he loved that one, you ought to own it. She was working slippers for him, too.

He had taken cold and sat at the big window in the dining room with a shawl over his shoulders. He wasn't allowed to go out. But he sent Judge Hodges on a mysterious errand which meant, Emily knew, presents for herself. And shortly before Christmas he said, "Emmy, I want you to do some shopping for me."

"Of course, Grandpa. What is it?"

"I want you to take some money out of the bank and buy skates for Kalil and Yusef."

"Grandpa! What a nice idea!"

"Buy good ones," he adjured her. "There's nothing worse than a poor pair of skates."

"I certainly will," said Emily. "And *I'll* buy presents for them, too." She would also, she thought, buy a doll for Layla. She felt a little ashamed that her grandfather had been the one to think of the Syrian children.

"It's because my mind's on the crowd coming," she thought. That great event was expanding in her thoughts like a soap bubble—and was just as iridescent.

They would be home for two weeks and a half.

"Two whole weeks and a half!" Emily exclaimed often.

Although she had lost some of her dependence on the crowd, she longed for them even more than she had at Thanksgiving. For this return would have a peculiar quality, she felt. During this vacation she might cease to be an outsider in man-and-girl affairs; she might really come to belong.

She had changed. It wasn't just that she had put her hair up and bought some pretty clothes. She was growing up, just as they were. She was changing inside. For the first time, she felt herself their equal.

"I wish," she thought more than once, glancing at the new white and blue dress hanging in her closet, "I wish I would be invited to the New Year's Eve dance." That was held every year at the Melborn Hotel and was the climax of the holiday season.

She counted the days of that last week. Before it ended Hunter and Ellen had arrived. Mabel, rumor said, would be on the train with the University group when it came in Friday night.

She was! Hunter and Ellen and Emily, waiting with the parents on the platform, saw her first of all when the train rolled steaming into the station. She had been standing with her wraps on since the last town, she cried to them, jumping down the steps. She was followed by them all—Don, Annette, Jim Baxter, Fred, Nell, Gladys, and college students from other classes—but they didn't count.

There was a melee of bags and satchels, willow plumes and new fur caps, Christmas bundles, flung arms and cries of rejoicing.

The home-coming freshmen gathered in a yelling circle.

"Cheer, cheer, the gang's all here," they sang revolving, their arms on one another's shoulders. They opened the circle to let Emily in. She sang with them, blurry-eyed.

13

"The Sweetheart of Sigma Chi"

EMILY WAS THANKFUL next morning for Judge Hodges and the interminable chess. The Judge came in early, stroking his beard, his eyes twinkling. He had a new opening, he said—Cy Webster could never figure this one out.

"By Jingo, I can!" Grandpa Webster knotted the shawl closer around his shoulders and began to set up the chessmen. Content that they were settled for the morning, Emily hurried into her wraps and ran out, her face glowing with anticipation.

She went first to Mabel's, and they went together to Ellen's who was said to be at Annette's. On the Webster steps they met Nell and Gladys. Aunt Sophie, in high spirits, welcomed them all.

"This is like old times," she said, as they pulled off snowy overshoes. "Now don't go up to Annette's room! I want to hear, too."

While they talked and laughed on the sun porch, which had a miraculous summerlike warmth, Aunt Sophie came in and out happily, bringing apples and fudge. Once she stopped to put her hand on Annette's dark head.

"We're glad; aren't we, Emily?"

"Are we! Aunt Sophie and I have certainly missed you."

The merits of the University, Carleton, St. Catherine's and Vassar were argued in every conceivable combination. Mabel told of a trip to New York. She had seen Otis Skinner in *Kismet*. Nell told of a Christmas pageant in which she had played an angel and lost a wing. Annette and Gladys told of sunlight dances, of the freshman-sophomore debate.

"Is Don on the team?" Emily asked.

"He isn't going out for debating."

Why not? Emily wondered.

"Are there any girls on the team?"

She did not mean to sound wistful, but Gladys suddenly enveloped her in a bear hug. "There would be if you were there!"

"Emily!" Nell cried penitently. "We're doing all the talking!"

"That's what I want you to do!" Emily said. But it wasn't quite true. She was rather anxious to tell them about the Browning Club, and the dances with Cab, and even her dancing lessons. She had learned to do the Gaby Glide. But the girls were accustomed to her listening rather than talking. The conversational tide swept on without her.

Mabel asked Emily to go home with her, but she shook her head. The chess game couldn't last forever; she had to get her grandfather's dinner.

"Why don't you all come to my house this afternoon?"

"I have to wash my hair," said Annette. "And Mamma won't let me go out afterward. Come here!"

"But so do I have to wash my hair!" cried Gladys.

"I'm going for a marcel wave," said Nell, and Ellen added, "I have to press a dress and do my nails."

"What is all the beautifying for?" asked Mabel. "Oh, I see! Dates! Men! Then, Em, you come up to my house tonight and we'll talk them over."

"We'll pick them to pieces," Emily agreed, and everyone laughed.

Annette broke in, "Before we part—I'm giving a sleighing party Monday night. Papa's hiring the Bluejay, and you're all invited."

"I want you for a luncheon after Christmas."

"I'm planning an evening party."

"Well, don't make it Sunday!" Annette said. "We're busy then, you know."

"I'm not busy," Emily thought quickly. She felt a twinge that she had not been invited to what was plainly a man-and-girl party.

"But it doesn't matter," she thought, walking home. "Nobody realizes that I've started going out. There'll be men at Annette's on Monday. And there are more than two weeks left."

She went to Mabel's that night, and they talked about Vassar. She heard about Mabel's roommate who came from Rhode Island. Mabel had visited her at Thanksgiving, and she liked the roommate's brother, and he liked her.

"He's a science major at Princeton," said Mabel demurely. She, too, was planning to major in science.

Emily heard about the marvelous courses, the step sings, the bacon bats. Back in her room she thought with satisfaction how wonderful it was to have the crowd back.

She *did* wish she were invited to that Sunday night affair—whatever it was! But there were two weeks left!

She took a quick look at the white and blue dress. "I'd like to do the Gaby Glide in *you*," she said, and knelt down, smiling, to say her prayers.

She was pleased, emerging from church the next day, to see Don in the crowd. Her grandfather's cold had kept him at home, so Emily was alone, and she knew that she looked well. The brown velvet hat with the rose underneath was becoming and harmonized with her brown, fur-collared coat. She was wearing white gloves.

He came up to her smiling. "Well, well, little Em'ly!"

"I wouldn't call myself exactly little."

"Did you think you were tall and queenly?"

"I know I'm tall." She was taller than ever this winter, she thought, because she now held herself straight, due to skating—or Browning—or something!

But he was still taller, and his shoulders had that proud masterful squareness. He had taken off his hat, and the sun shone on his smooth dark hair. He looked well groomed, like the city—

He fell into step beside her and walked with her all the way home. She had thought he would drop off at Annette's, but he didn't. He went on across the slough.

She had forgotten how much she liked his voice. It was deep and full of melody. You forgot he wasn't handsome—and he wasn't—when he smiled and when he spoke.

She told him eagerly that she had come to love Browning, and he looked indulgently amused.

"He's a little too optimistic for me."

"But you have to be optimistic in this world, Don."

"I'm not, and I get along fine."

She saw that he preferred to talk about himself, so she asked why he hadn't gone out for debating.

"I got fed up with it in high school," he answered contemptuously, which made her shrink. He couldn't suspect how much that would hurt her or he wouldn't have said it, she thought.

"I tried out for Masquers, the dramatic club, and made it. We're going to put on Shaw's *Arms and the Man*. I know I'm not another John Drew, but the fellows want us all to go out for something—the fellows in the fraternity, I mean."

He talked on and on in a mellow-toned flood. She knew he felt he was impressing her. But she loved it. She *was* impressed. There was no one, no one like Don!

At the gate he stopped and pulled out a pipe. "To solace my homeward walk," he said.

"When did you take to a pipe?" Her eyes were on

his long, dark, sensitive fingers as he tamped tobacco into the bowl of the pipe.

"Oh, gosh! Months ago! We're all pipe smokers at the house . . ." He took the pipe between his teeth and lighted it.

Emily did not ask him in; it was Deep Valley's dinner hour. But he did not hurry away. He leaned on the gate post, and his gray-green eyes studied her. He could see, she felt sure, that she had changed.

"Emily, have you read any Shaw?"

"Why, I'm reading *Man and Superman* right now."

"*Man and* . . ." He threw back his head and laughed. "Well, don't let it give you any ideas!" To her intense annoyance Emily colored.

"I'd like to see a Shaw play performed," she said quickly.

"So would I. There's pretty good theatre up in the Cities. Annette and I take in everything that comes along. We're planning to see Maude Adams in *Peter Pan.*"

"I believe that's coming here, too," Emily said, and he looked faintly annoyed.

He took off his hat again. "Good-by. I'll be seeing you around."

"Oh, of course!" She put out her hand. "We're all going up to school tomorrow."

"Not I! Oh Lord, when will the rest of you grow up!"

Emily went slowly into the house and up to her room. When she had taken off her hat, she looked in the mirror. This was a different Emily from the one she had looked at that August afternoon when Don had left with Annette. The upsweep of hair was becoming, it emphasized the broad serenity of her brow. The texture of her skin had always been rough, but it looked rich and peachy this winter. She smiled into her earnest blue eyes.

"I don't want to take Don away from Annette!" she thought. "And, of course, I couldn't! I only want him for a friend. But oh, how I want that!"

Nothing, she thought, could give her more needed confidence than to have Don accept her as one of the desirable girls.

The morning at the high school was a carefree revel. It was tradition for the old grads to come for the Christmas tree at which joke presents for faculty and students were dispensed with much hilarity.

Emily looked around for Mr. Wakeman but he wasn't there.

"Miss Bangeter let him off early so he could get home in time for Christmas. He lives way down south somewhere," Jerry Sibley explained.

There was a gay crowd out—not only from the class of 1912. Carney Sibley was there, talking with Mabel. Emily saw Cab, who shook his hands over his head jovially in her direction. He was with a large group of 1910-ers.

"Betsy Ray and Tacy Kelly are visiting my sister," Fred Muller said. "Gee, I didn't know folks acted like that after they got to be twenty! A party every day!"

That was why she had had no invitation from Cab, Emily thought, and her heart sank a little. But only for a moment. She was interested to see Fred's pretty blond sister who went to school in Milwaukee, and Tacy Kelly who used to sing at rhetoricals, and Betsy Ray—especially Betsy, because she had written short stories which had been published. She was practically an author.

Betsy looked much as Emily remembered her from high school, tall and slim with red cheeks, always laughing. She was wearing a plaid dress with a plaid ribbon tied around her head. Meeting Emily's eyes, she waved, and so did Alice and Winona who were with her.

Annette touched Emily's arm. "I'm leaving to meet Don. He wouldn't come up. He thinks all this is infantile." As she spoke, a pair of sophomores dashed past, the pursued screaming, the pursuer waving mistletoe.

Emily laughed. "I get his point."

She was glad to note that she no longer felt any nostalgic longings. But, unlike Don, she enjoyed being back.

"I'll see you tonight at my party. And by the way, Em—" Annette paused and put her hand on Emily's arm. "Jim Baxter will stop by for you."

"Jim Baxter! But he hasn't asked me."

"No, he—asked me to ask you. You haven't a telephone, you know." But that was ridiculous! Emily thought. He had been right here in the Assembly Room a few moments ago.

Annette seemed embarrassed. "I have to hurry. Bye-bye!" she said, and was gone.

Emily looked after her with a sobering face. Annette had asked Jim to call for her, of course. She had thought no one else would do so! Emily turned away to the cloak room slowly.

She wouldn't have minded walking over to Annette's alone. She was used to going to parties alone. But she minded Jim calling for her when he didn't want to. He hadn't even gone through the formality of asking her!

Injured pride stung her as she found her wraps and went downstairs. At first she thought she wouldn't go to the party. But that would hurt Annette, who had meant well, she knew, and Aunt Sophie who was always so kind. Besides—she had counted on this evening. She was besieged with invitations to girls' afternoon affairs, but this was the only one she had for a man-and-girl party.

"No. I won't let this spoil things for me. I'll go and have a good time. Muster you wits! Muster your wits!" she told herself, trying to smile as she tramped across the slough.

At home she laid out her sweaters and warm waists, selecting the most becoming one, a red flannel trimmed with gold buttons. "And I'll wear a red ribbon—and my new fur hat!"

She was sorry it wasn't a more glamorous type of party to which she could wear a pretty dress. But clothes didn't matter, really.

"It's inside I've changed most. Don saw it when we walked home from church, and he will tonight," she thought.

She waited for Jim that evening with a resolute smile on her face. She had not put on her wraps ahead of time tonight. She would risk his thinking the parlor was queer, she had decided. She looked nice, and he might as well see it before she buried herself in the clumsy sweaters and coats and shawls one wore to a sleighing party.

"Cab had a good time with me. He asked me a second time. Probably the U has improved Jim Baxter and we'll have something in common," she encouraged herself. But when the old doorbell chimed, and she let him in, she saw that he had changed very little. He was the same big, hulking, stolid boy.

And moreover, he looked mad.

"It isn't because he has to take me. It's because he can't be with Annette," Emily told herself with desperate insistence. But logic did not help. The moment she saw his sullen face all her self-confidence died like a fire under a thrown pail of water.

Her calmness as they shook hands was the stiff aloofness she had had in high school, not the easy dignity she had felt with Cab's crowd. She tried to joke about the piles of wraps but he did not respond. He buckled her overshoes grimly.

They went out and she asked him how he liked the U. He said, "Fine!" and relapsed into silence. When she said she understood he was on the second football team, he said, "That's right!" and let the subject drop.

It was a cold bitter night and the slough seemed endless. Emily felt guilty about every step. What a walk to take with a girl you did not wish to walk with!

As soon as they reached Annette's house—while she was greeting Aunt Sophie—Jim Baxter disappeared into a group of boys. He did not come near Emily again.

The crowd milled about the Webster parlor in the highest spirits. They all looked ridiculous in their unwieldy garments. It was an atmosphere, Emily thought, in which anyone should be able to have fun. But she felt painfully awkward. She was almost in a panic.

She forced herself to conversational overtures but they sounded hollow. No one seemed to respond.

"I shouldn't be trying so hard. No one else is trying," she thought. Scid and Fred were teasing Gladys about the stocking cap she had borrowed from her little brother. Emily laughed with the others but she thought her laughter sounded too loud.

Don was avoiding her. Now there was none of the half-admiring friendliness he had shown on the walk home from church.

"He can see that I don't fit in, and he doesn't like being associated with a girl who doesn't fit in," she thought wretchedly.

Aunt Sophie was distributing horns and candy.

"Can't I do that, Aunt Sophie?"

"Why yes! Thank you, dear."

It helped to have something to do.

Don and Annette were dancing now, clowning in their cumbrous clothes.

"Do the Gaby Glide!" Nell called.

"Go ahead! Do the Gaby Glide like you did Sunday night at Don's!"

At *Don's!* *Don* had given the party! And he had not invited her even though he had seen her Sunday morning before she had—collapsed like this. She must have been mistaken when she thought he had found her attractive.

Despair swept her. She felt crushed, unable to go on. But fortunately at that moment sleighbells jingled merrily outside.

"It's the Bluejay!" everyone cried and they rushed out into the icy night blowing horns and shouting. They piled in, not without scuffling. Every man seemed determined to sit beside a particular girl. But Emily wasn't one of the girls.

She found herself with Don on her right and Scid on her left but it was by chance. Don's concern had been to be beside Annette. Scid had been striving to sit with Gladys. In the midst of the noisy jubilant crowd Emily sat marooned. But she didn't care. She was too heartsick to care.

The night was as cold as her despair. It was ten below, somebody said, but there was hay in the bottom of the bobsleigh and there were plenty of buffalo robes. Now and then a rider hopped out and ran to warm his feet, throwing snowballs at the company.

The sweet jingling of the sleighbells was drowned out soon by singing. Emily had always loved it when the crowd sang, but tonight the music seemed to pierce her heart. "Moonlight Bay." "Shine on Harvest Moon." "Down by the Old Mill Stream." She tried to join in but her throat was dry.

There was one song they sang over and over again. It was new, a dreamy waltz, "The Sweetheart of Sigma Chi." It seemed to typify for Emily all the talk about fraternities and sororities, fussing and dating, in which she had no part, everything to which she didn't belong, everything she was being left out of.

"The girl of my dreams is the sweetest girl
Of all the girls I know . . . "

Don sang it to Annette, looking down into her face, his arm around her shoulder. Scid sang it to Gladys.

"As long as I live I can never bear to hear that song!" Emily thought, sitting rigidly between them.

After an hour or so they went back to the Websters' for oyster stew.

"There's just one thing to do in a situation like this," Emily decided. "It's to go home!"

She found Aunt Sophie in the kitchen. "I'm going to slip out, Aunt Sophie. I want to get home. Grandpa has that bad cold, you know."

"But can't you wait for some oyster stew?"

"I'd rather not. I'm worried about him. It's been a wonderful party."

Aunt Sophie went to the dining room door. "That

boy who brought you, Jim. He'll take you home. I'll call him."

"Please, Aunt Sophie, don't!" Emily seized her aunt's arm, then quieted her voice. "I don't want to break up the party, and I'm so used to walking home alone. Please! Let me just slip out!"

"All right," Aunt Sophie said reluctantly. "But you're coming for Christmas dinner."

"If Grandpa is able . . ."

Aunt Sophie was not listening now. "Minnie, I tasted the stew. Just a little more salt, I would say, and a big lump of butter . . ."

Emily ran out the back door.

Suddenly she was glad that her grandfather had a cold. They wouldn't have to go to Annette's for Christmas!

"We won't go," she thought angrily. "I'm not going to put up with this situation any longer!"

The wind on the slough was cutting. Tears froze on her cheeks. Halfway across she started to run. She found herself longing for the shelter of her little room and even more for its solacing solitude.

14
A Christmas Party

BEFORE SHE WAS QUITE awake next morning, Emily remembered that something dreadful had happened. She pressed her arm across her eyes to hold it back, but it came—the detestable memory of the sleighing party!

She sat up. "Look here!" she thought. "I've got to see this thing in the right proportions!"

The room was frigid, and she reached out for her bathrobe and pulled it over her shoulders. As she sat staring into the murky darkness, she was still bitterly resolved not to go to Annette's for Christmas.

"Not that I'd behave again the way I did last night! I don't know what came over me! Annette's asking Jim to call for me started it, I guess. But it would be just the way it was at Thanksgiving. The kids would drop in after dinner . . ."

Talk would be about their colleges, their new experiences. She had had new experiences, too, she thought with proud resentment, but when she was with the crowd they seemed to become of no importance. It was true even with the girls.

"I tag them around, but I'm like a shadow. Well, I won't do it any more!"

She wasn't tired of her friends, but she was tired of pursuing them as though her own life were worthless.

"I'll make another plan for Christmas," she decided. "A good, definite one! And I'll make it before I tell Aunt Sophie we're not coming, so she can't talk me down."

She jumped out of bed and dressed quickly, groping for ideas. It wasn't easy, she discovered, to make a spur-of-the-moment plan for Christmas. So many people were tied up with family affairs.

She searched among her winter's associates. Miss

Cobb went to relatives, she knew. Miss Fowler was going to the Cities. Mrs. Anderson? She had come to like the courageous lame dancer. But her grandfather didn't know Mrs. Anderson. He would be disappointed at not going to Aunt Sophie's unless she made a plan he would enjoy.

She went to the window, rubbed away a patch of frost, and stared out thoughtfully. The east was a mass of small fiery-red clouds. Her eyes fell on the Syrian rooftops, and she smiled suddenly.

Kalil and Yusef! Her grandfather loved them; he had asked her a dozen times whether she had remembered to buy the skates. And she had been wanting to see Layla again. Maybe they could come Christmas afternoon for a party!

"We could trim a tree for them!" she thought.

She ran downstairs and shook the coal heater and dumped in a scuttle of coal. Her grandfather came in and she turned around, smiling.

"Grandpa," she said. "I've been thinking. You have such a cold and the weather is so bad—let's stay home for Christmas!" His face fell and she rushed on. "Let's ask Kalil and Yusef to come here for a party! And that cute little Layla I told you about."

His eyes beneath their bushy brows kindled. "Why, I believe I'd like that, Emmy! I'm sorry not to go to Chester's, but—could you get us a turkey?"

"Of course! We'd have turkey sandwiches for the children. And I'd get a tree. It would be fun to trim a tree again."

"By Jingo, it would!"

"Maybe you could pop some corn this morning—for stringing."

"I can! I can!" He grinned. "If I can only keep the Judge from gobbling it all up!"

"We'll string cranberries too. But first I must ask the children . . ."

It would be too awful, she thought, if they couldn't come! She raced through breakfast. Before nine o'clock her feet were on the path to Little Syria.

The weather was still piercingly cold, but a great golden sun made a difference. Nuthatches were running nimbly up and down the trees; chickadees were calling; squirrels were frolicking. On the slough side there were muskrat houses and small mysterious-looking tracks—rabbits, probably.

But even morning sunshine could not make Little Syria attractive as she approached it from the rear. Woodpiles, chicken houses, dump heaps were desolate mounds of snow. The little houses seemed half buried in it, and they needed paint. So did Mr. Meecham's mansion. Ascending the street, along an Indian trail which had been shoveled through the snow, she saw Christmas wreaths and red paper bells in the windows. They went to her heart, and suddenly she wanted the children for their own sakes as well as her own.

"I'd like to do something for them! Oh, I hope they can come!"

In front of the Mohanna house Kalil and Yusef were tusseling with such vigor that Emily thought at first they were fighting. But when she came close she saw from their smiling faces that there was no break in the Damon-Pythias relationship. Kalil snatched off his cap, his eyes beaming.

"Hello, ma'am! You come to see us?"

"Yes, Kalil! Merry Christmas!"

"Merry Christmas!" he shouted, pumping her hand.

"What were you doing?"

"We were practising. How are you, ma'am? How is my grandpa?"

As usual Yusef let Kalil do the talking, but when Kalil released her hand he took it and pumped, too, a joyful, astonished—affectionate look on his round prosaic face. Emily put her arms across their shoulders.

"I want to see your mothers," she said, and they climbed to the porch, and Kalil opened the door.

Mr. Mohanna was sitting on the floor, cross-legged, a red tasseled cap on his head. He was smoking a strange sort of pipe which stood on the floor beside him, a ropelike tube leading to his mouth. He rose in dignified welcome, and behind him the little wife fluttered and Layla danced, her long braids swinging.

"You have come again to my house, Miss! It is yours. You may burn it!"

"Merry Christmas!" said Emily to stem the tide of eloquence.

"I hope you will live to see many more holidays, Miss."

"I came . . ." Emily began. She saw Mrs. Mohanna dart toward the kitchen and sought to restrain her from producing another feast. "Mrs. Mohanna, please, come back! Mr. Mohanna, I wish to talk with your wife."

"But certainly! Honor us by taking a seat!"

"Won't you please call her back? I can only stay a moment."

It was useless! She found herself seated and relieved of her muff as before. The figs came out and the raisins and the nuts, and today there were pastries, too—round ones with a hole in the center, and glassy ones with big nuts inside, and a crusty brown one which seemed to be made in layers and was, she discovered, oozing honey.

"They are for Christmas!" Kalil explained excitedly.

"That's *baklawa*."

"It's perfectly delicious."

"You like it? Have another then!"

They were all looking on in delight.

"My father," cried Layla. "May we show her the donkey?"

"You have a donkey?" asked Emily in surprise.

The children began to laugh. "It is the donkey on which the Blessed Virgin rides. See?" They led her to the small clay figure of a woman on a donkey. It stood about a foot away from a home-constructed cave holding a manger with toy sheep and cows around.

"When it comes near Christmas, ma'am, we make the cave. But we put the donkey way, way over there by the kitchen door. Every day we move it a little, just a little. And on the Night of the Birth it reaches the cave."

"And that's tonight!" cried Layla.

"Tonight!"

Even Yusef shouted, "Tonight!" and the parents turned radiant faces. Emily was suddenly swept with fear that the children might prefer to be at home for Christmas.

"What do you do on Christmas Day?" she asked.

Kalil shrugged. "Oh, we have dinner. The Night of the Birth is the important time. Then we move the donkey into the stable. And we all go to Mass. And when we come home we have sweets."

"Then on Christmas afternoon," said Emily timidly, looking at the father, "could the children come to my house for a party? Kalil and Layla, and I want Yusef, too, of course."

"A party?" repeated the big man. He stared at her in bewilderment.

"Yes. A Christmas party."

Kalil grasped his father's hand. "Oh, please, my father! The boys at school went to a party once, but the Syrians weren't invited. It was a birthday party."

Layla had grasped her father's other hand. She was imploring him in Arabic. The mother stared at her husband with bright pleading eyes.

Yusef turned and bolted out the door, plainly in search of his own parental permission.

"We're going to have a Christmas tree," said Emily.

"My father! You hear? A Christmas tree!"

"Yusef has a Christmas tree. His father has a store of his own. I carry the peddler's pack. But you could look at Yusef's tree."

"Please, my father! We want to go to a party."

Mr. Mohanna brushed at his eyes, but then he smiled, his teeth shining beneath the enormous mustache. He bowed to Emily.

"They may come. My thanks to you and your honored grandfather. Peace to his age!"

Yusef returned, shouting in Arabic. He could come, too.

The parents stood on the porch again as Emily departed, accompanied by Kalil and Yusef—and Layla, who put on her coat and scarf as before to join the guard of honor. This time Emily went up the hill to the corner where the shabbiness of Little Syria met the gentility of the town. The children left her there calling out "Merry Christmas!" and "Three o'clock!" That was the hour decided upon for the party.

Walking on down Pleasant Street she met Alice Morrison who lived near by in an old-fashioned house at the top of a sloping lawn. She was returning from town, her yellow hair blowing, her arms full of bundles.

They both sang out, "Merry Christmas!" and Alice cried, "I was just going to send you a note. Can you come to my house Friday afternoon? I'm giving a party."

"The Browning Club?"

"No. Girls from my class, mostly. You know Betsy Ray and Tacy Kelly are in town. I want you to get better acquainted with them—and them with you."

"I'd love it!" Emily went on in a glow. She was glad to be bolstered by Alice's friendship, as well as by Little Syria's devotion, before going to Aunt Sophie's—her next stop. She dreaded going back into the yellow brick house after last night, which seemed now like a horrible dream.

But it wasn't too difficult. Annette wasn't at home. And Uncle Chester and Aunt Sophie, who were trimming their Christmas tree, did not protest too much.

"I know how you feel," Aunt Sophie said. "Grandpa *is* getting pretty old. But won't you be lonesome?"

"We're giving a little party," Emily said, smiling. "I didn't want Grandpa to be too disappointed about not coming here, so I asked some Syrian children to come in."

"Syrian?" Aunt Sophie's tone expressed utter mystification.

"We got acquainted with them last summer. They used to sell us frogs' legs. Grandpa's very fond of them."

Aunt Sophie knitted her brows. "Are they clean?"

"As clean as I'd be if I lived in Little Syria. They're very nice and have beautiful manners."

Uncle Chester smiled down. "Do you know, Emily," he said, "you remind me of your mother sometimes."

"I do?"

"Yes. Lottie was always taking an interest in foreigners. She used to tell me about the Poles in Binghamton."

Emily looked up at him, her blue eyes luminous. Somehow her mother came to be more of a companion all the time!

She went on down Front Street and bought a tall hemlock. The grocer promised to deliver it at once. She bought a few ornaments to add to the old ones stored in the attic at home, and some gifts to supplement the skates and the doll.

"Let's see! What did I want most when I was eight? A bottle of perfume! I longed for it!" she remembered, and bought some violet perfume and some red embroidered mittens—and picture books and games for the boys—and candy canes for them all.

"It's fun to be getting Christmas ready for children," she thought.

When she reached home her grandfather and the Judge were setting the tree up in the parlor.

"Here's where your grandmother always put it."

"I remember."

"I've been invited to the party," said the Judge. "I had to be asked after all the work I did, popping corn."

"By Jingo, you ate more than you popped!" cried Grandpa Webster. He was more excited by the party than Emily had dreamed he would be.

That afternoon they strung the popcorn and made some of it into sticky balls. They strung cranberries, too, and garlanded the tree, and put on small white candles. Emily brought down the ornaments. During the years since her grandmother's death they had always gone for Christmas to Aunt Sophie's. The box was just as her grandmother had packed it last, each ball and star and angel folded in tissue paper.

"I remember some of these from when I was a little girl," Emily said to Uncle Chester who had come in laden with packages for them only to be loaded with others to take home.

He inspected a rubicund Santa. "I remember that fellow from when I was a little boy."

After supper, Emily and her grandfather wrapped the perfume and mittens, games and books. But they put the doll and skates in plain sight at the bottom of the tree.

When the fire was fixed for the night, Emily sat down at the piano.

> *"It came upon the midnight clear*
> *That glorious song of old . . . "*

Carols were like no other songs, she thought. They sounded so pure and sweet, as though they came from heaven. She sang "O Little Town of Bethlehem" and "Holy Night," her grandfather joining in.

He was sitting in his easy chair and when she rose he called out, "Look, Emmy! It's snowing! Just the thing for Christmas Eve!"

She went to the bay window. Out in the darkness big flakes like pieces of cotton were coming slowly down. She watched them, smiling, her hand on his shoulder.

He reached up and patted it. "I'm lucky to have you, Emmy. Christmas wouldn't be much fun alone."

"I'm lucky to have *you*," she answered, a lump coming into her throat.

The party was a noteworthy success. The presents Emily and her grandfather opened in the morning, although much appreciated, and the turkey dinner at noon, were as nothing compared to the afternoon's festivity. The snow had cleared and the sun shone brightly in a sky of flawless blue. Emily had shoveled the walks both front and back. Kalil and Yusef always came the back way, but maybe, she thought, for a party . . . ! She was right. At three o'clock exactly three small figures came formally through the old front gate.

Feet stamped with care on the porch. The ancient doorbell gave out its gentle chime. Emily opened the door to see three shining faces. They all carried packages, and even before their wraps were removed they presented them with a graciousness at which Emily marveled.

"My mother hopes you will take this poor piece of lace. She made it herself."

"These sweets are for you, my grandpa! Peace to your age!"

Even Yusef made his speech, and Layla was presented to Grandpa Webster, smiling.

"Bless my soul, what dimples! They're like potholes!" he said.

They were all scrubbed and shining. The hair of the boys was plastered down with oil. Layla's braids were tied with real ribbon. She wore the usual earrings and bracelets, and her eyes were rimmed with sooty black. But they were bright enough without it—especially when she saw the doll!

"Look, my brother! Look!" she cried when Emily pointed out the yellow-haired baby which had real lashes, eyes that opened and shut, and a pink dress. She snatched it to her bosom.

But Kalil was too busy to look. He and Yusef were shouting over their skates, and Grandpa Webster was chuckling. "You can play crack the whip on them, my lads! I'm going to watch you right out of my window."

"And a book! A book in the English!"

"Smell me, my brother! Perfume! Flowers! Umm!"

There was such a clamor as the little house had not heard in years. Judge Hodges came in the midst of it, with more packages, and it started all over again.

They were fascinated by the piano. One by one they touched the keys. Emily played Christmas carols, and they listened with awed admiration. Layla knew "Holy Night," and she sang it alone. She did, indeed, sing like a thrush.

"Layla has a talent for music. Maybe I could give her piano lessons," Emily thought.

At last they trouped out to the Christmas table. Grandpa Webster said the blessing as usual, and Kalil, Layla and Yusef all crossed themselves and murmured. There were turkey sandwiches, dill pickles, Christmas cookies and cakes, and cups of hot cocoa with marshmallows floating on top.

When they rose the children murmured something again. It sounded like, "May your table last . . . forever."

After supper the candles on the tree were lighted. Judge Hodges went home, Layla sat down with her doll and Yusef with a puzzle, and Kalil took his book and went to Grandpa Webster. He leaned against the old man.

"Won't you read to me, my grandpa? I don't know the English very well."

"Emmy," said her grandfather, opening the book, "we ought to help these children with their English."

Emily was clearing the table, but she put down the plate she held in her hand. Of course, they could help them with their English!

"*There's* something I can do with Grandpa," she thought. "I'll have them come here regularly. Maybe I ought to have some American children, too. That's what they need most of all, to mix with Americans."

She interrupted the reading. "Grandpa, I have a wonderful idea! Let's get up a Boys' Club—Kalil and Yusef and some American boys. They could meet here."

Her grandfather stared admiringly. "Emmy, you're a smart girl!"

She smiled at Kalil and Yusef. "Wouldn't you like to belong to a club with some other boys?" she asked.

To her surprise they did not answer. Kalil looked at Yusef with a troubled face.

"Do you know what a club is?" she persisted.

"Yes," said Kalil. "We know about clubs. But ma'am! American boys don't like to play with us Syrians. Do they, Yusef?"

Yusef shook a sober head.

"Pooh!" said Emily. She knew he had a point, but she would handle it somehow. "Not all American boys are like the ones who teased you on the pond.

We'll get up a fine club if you'd like to join."

"Oh yes!" cried Kalil. His eyes began to sparkle. "That would be dandy. Wouldn't it, Yusef?"

Layla dropped her doll and came running. "Can I come too? Can I come to the Boys' Club?"

"Of course," Emily replied.

"But ma'am," protested Kalil, looking anxious, "she's only a girl."

"Pooh!" said Emily again. "In America, Kalil, girls are important."

"Are they?" he asked, staring.

"I'm going to give Layla piano lessons."

"Piano—lessons?"

"I'm going to teach her to play the piano—if she wants to learn. Do you, Layla?"

Layla nodded dumbly.

"She can come whenever the club meets. She can be an honorary member."

Layla jumped so that her braids swung, her bracelets tinkled, and the air was suddenly full of violet perfume.

"I'm an *honorable* member of the Boys' Club!" she sang. "I'm an *honorable* boy!"

15
Old Year into New

"GRANDPA," EMILY REMARKED at breakfast, "I couldn't handle this Boys' Club without you. I love children, but I don't know boys."

"Well, I do!" he answered confidently, pouring maple syrup over three well-buttered pancakes. "I was a boy myself, and I had a boy of my own, and your grandmother and I practically raised your Uncle

Chester. I'll help you to keep them in order."

"But what do you suppose they would like to do? Study something?"

"Not on your tintype! Not if they knew they were studying, that is! But Emmy, they'll decide for themselves what they want to do. That part won't be hard. The hard part will be, like Kalil said, to get some Americans to join."

"I believe you're right," she answered soberly. People looked down on the Syrians—because they were poor, or because they spoke broken English, or because they lived by themselves and kept their foreign customs. She didn't know why, exactly.

"Why do you think people feel so superior to the Syrians?"

"Just because the Syrians are different!" Grandpa Webster answered. "It's human nature, I guess. Most of the folks who make fun of them don't mean any harm. A few, though, are downright spiteful."

"Like those boys who teased Kalil."

"Yes. And Luther Whitlock down at the bank. The old bonehead! I told him a cute story about Kalil and he started running the Syrians down. Said this country was too full already, and they ought to have stayed where they belonged."

"And he's the president of our school board!" Emily exclaimed indignantly.

"That's right. Now old Meecham who's their neighbor speaks well of the Syrians. He says they're honest and don't make trouble. And do you know why they came to this country?"

"I don't believe I do."

"To get religious freedom. Just like our Pilgrim fathers! They're Christians, the ones who live in Deep Valley, and Syria is mostly Moslem, I guess."

"Well, there's an argument for me!" Emily said. Gathering up the dishes, she felt the same mental stimulation she used to feel when preparing for a debate. She must muster all the reasons why Syrian and American children ought to be friends. "And the best one I know," she thought with a smile, "is that the Syrians are so nice."

"Who are you going to tackle first?" her grandfather called out.

"The ten-year-olds I know best are Bobbys Sibley and Cobb."

"They'd be good ones. Sibley is a very public-spirited man. And, of course, Jessie Cobb is the salt of the earth."

"And four children—five, counting Layla—are enough for this size house. So I guess I won't have any trouble after all," Emily replied.

But even when the club was formed, she wouldn't be through with this matter, she resolved. It was time

Deep Valley took some interest in the Syrians.

She decided to call on the Sibleys and Miss Cobb that afternoon. Dressing, she caught a glimpse of the white and blue party gown hanging in her closet, and it gave her a pang, but she said to herself briskly, "None of that!" and closed the door.

She walked over the slough with her head high, and when she was passing the Webster house the door flew open and Annette beckoned. "Come on in!"

"I can't," Emily called. "I'm on an errand."

"Oh, dear! I want you to see my Christmas presents. And Nell asked me to let you know that she's having the girls tomorrow."

"I'm awfully sorry," Emily replied. "But I'm going to Alice Morrison's."

"You *are*? That ought to be fun! Well, stop by for me Saturday for Ellen's luncheon then."

"I will," Emily answered and waved her muff in glad relief. She was thankful not to have to see the girls for two days. They weren't to blame for her difficulties. Even Don wasn't to blame. People didn't need to have other people at their parties unless they wanted to, she told herself, wincing. But she had to break away somehow from her old out-grown self.

Miss Cobb seemed surprised by the idea of the Club, but she offered no objections.

"Bobby isn't at home. I think he'd like to join,

though. Especially if Bobby Sibley does."

"I'm going to invite him next," Emily replied. She told Miss Cobb about Layla and the plan to teach her music, and Miss Cobb's face lighted with interest.

"I think it's awfully nice of you to do that, Emily. Do you have a beginner's book? Here, let me loan you one! And bring her to see me some day. Won't you?"

Emily proceeded to the Sibleys' house on Broad Street. Bobby himself answered the door, grinning, and took her to the library where his father and Carney were sitting by the fire. Tall, handsome Mr. Sibley rose to greet her, smiling. Emily knew him well; she had been in his Sunday School class. Carney passed popcorn and candy. She was a pretty fresh-faced girl who wore an enormous diamond on her engagement finger—the biggest diamond, Emily thought, that she had ever seen.

Since Bobby was present Emily stated her errand briefly. She did not go into her reasons for forming the club. But Mr. Sibley must have sensed them. He looked at her thoughtfully.

"It's a very sensible beginning, Emily," he said. He turned to Bobby. "I think you would like to join; wouldn't you, son?"

"Sure," said Bobby amiably. "Will there be refreshments?"

"Yes. At every meeting. And I make good cookies."

Emily smiled at him. "Bobby, do you know any Syrian boys?"

"Naw! They're . . ." he stopped, and looked cautiously at his father.

"What were you going to say, son?"

"You told me not to say it."

"Then I'm glad you didn't."

"They're not dagos; are they, Dad?" asked Bobby, and grinned broadly to have outwitted his parent.

"Kalil and Yusef," said Emily, "sold me frogs' legs last summer."

"Did they?" asked Bobby, looking interested.

"Yes. They're fine frog catchers."

"I catch pollywogs," said Bobby, "and they turn into frogs. It's easier."

Carney accompanied Emily to the door. "I'm interested in what you're doing," she said. "I'm taking sociology in college. And I've often thought about this foreign group in Deep Valley, how little was being done for them—nothing, actually, except what America offers to anyone."

"I've just begun to think about them," Emily replied.

Carney smiled, showing a lone dimple. "I have an idea you haven't stopped," she said. "I'll be seeing you at Alice's tomorrow. Maybe we can talk about it there."

But for a rollicking hour Alice's party, the next afternoon, offered no chance for serious talk. Like Fred, Emily was amazed at the youthful high spirits of the ancients of 1910. Winona, she knew, was as exuberant as Gladys, but she had not expected to see Betsy Ray and Tacy Kelly, visitors from the Cities, acting so wildly absurd.

Betsy was wearing the same plaid dress, but not the ribbon. Her hair was high atop her head in long sausagelike rolls with curls tucked here and there.

"Don't I look distinguished?" she demanded, parading. "Don't I look like a lady authoress? Tib did it! To think that I have to go through the U with my hair in a bun while Tib is wasted in Milwaukee."

"Not exactly wasted," said Tib, preening like a little yellow bird.

"Ye Gods!" cried Winona. "Can I believe my eyes?"

The girls were bringing out tatting, crocheting and embroidery work and Betsy also had whipped out something white. Emily gathered from the uproar that Betsy never sewed.

"It's a dish towel," she said complacently.

"A *dish towel*?" cried Irma Biscay.

"Isn't it lovely? I'm hemming it for Tacy, the future Mrs. Harry Kerr. Everyone is making her luncheon sets and dresser scarves. I can't let her go to the altar without some of my handiwork; can I?"

"Be Gorrah!" cried Tacy. "I'm not going to wear a dish towel to the altar!"

"You're going to wear a Paris creation; aren't you, Tacy?"

"White satin with a fine long train!"

"Betsy will step on it!" warned Tib. "I'd never trust Betsy to be *my* bridesmaid. She'd start composing a poem or something at just the wrong moment."

"Tib Muller!" Betsy lunged at her. "If I'm not your bridesmaid, the marriage won't be legal!"

Tacy wiped her eyes. "Let's stop acting like imbeciles!" she said. "I'm ashamed of us, Emily."

"It's because we're so glad to be back," Betsy explained, releasing Tib. "And I am *so* going to be your bridesmaid!"

"Of course you are, *liebchen*. But I'm not going to get married for a long, long time. I'm going to see the world," said Tib.

Emily, like the rest, was laughing, but suddenly she yearned for her own crowd. A crowd was pretty nice, she thought. You went through school with them; you were one another's bridesmaids, maybe; even your children got to be friends sometimes.

But then the girls started talking about the New Year's Eve ball, and that brought back her bitterness. With this group, when Winona asked, "Going, Emily?"

and she had to shake her head, Alice put in, "Oh, you probably will! Not all their royal highnesses have made up their minds on whom to bestow their unutterable boons."

Over sandwiches and coffee, and a highly acclaimed bisque of macaroons, the talk grew more serious. Carney asked Emily about the Boys' Club, and there was a lively interest in it. Alice lived near Little Syria and knew a good deal about the settlement. Betsy, Tacy and Tib had played with a little Syrian girl when they were children.

"She was a princess."

"Betsy! Don't fib!"

"But she was, really! A Syrian emeera! I've never forgotten her." Betsy's eyes grew dark.

Betsy wasn't exactly pretty, Emily thought, in spite of her warm hazel eyes and fair skin. She had irregular features, widely spaced teeth. But you liked to look at her, somehow. Emily was pleased, when the party broke up, to find Betsy sociably hooking her arm.

"Cab Edwards has been talking to me about you."

"He has?" asked Emily.

"He seems to feel badly because you couldn't go to college—although usually Cab says college isn't important."

"He knows I felt badly about it," Emily replied.

"But I find . . . I mind it less all the time. There's lots to do right here in Deep Valley." She heard herself telling eagerly about her music and dancing and the Browning Club.

"It's been a—surprising year," she ended.

"I think I know." Betsy frowned to find the right words. "I'm a year behind my class in college, Emily. I had to stop in the middle of my freshman year and go out to California. I wasn't well, and my grandmother needed company—

"I didn't want to go. I hated to get behind in school. I hated to leave my friends, and Joe—Joe Willard, the boy I was going with. But Emily, I had a wonderful year! I had expected it to be a lost year. That was what I kept calling it sadly to myself, 'a lost year!' Lost!"

In spite of her earnestness Betsy began to laugh.

"It was just about the most wonderful year of my life! While I was living so quietly with Grandma I had time to write, which is what I like to do best in the world. And I met an uncle who knew about professional writing, and he gave me a lot of good advice, and I started selling stories. But that wasn't the most important thing . . ."

They were nearing the Mullers' house where Carney, Tacy and Tib were waiting. Betsy slowed her pace.

"That 'lost year' gave me a chance to do some thinking. I got acquainted with myself, I *found* myself, out there in California. It's hard to explain. I was going with Joe before, and I still go with Joe. At least, I like him best; but he's gone off to Harvard. I wanted to write before, and I still want to write. But I changed. I—I began to see the pattern. It did me good to get away from my friends. Do you see what I mean?"

"Yes, I do," said Emily slowly.

While she was taking off her coat at home her grandfather said, "That Cab Edwards was here."

"Cab? What did he want?"

"He hung around a while. We talked about the Civil War. We had a real nice time."

"Did he—did he leave a message?"

"Yes," said Grandpa Webster. "He left a note." He dipped into his vest pocket, but his fingers came out empty. He tried his coat pockets, his trouser pockets. "What did I do with the dinged thing! Oh, I remember!" He trotted to the clock shelf. "Here it is! I knew I put it somewhere."

Emily opened it.

"Anything important?" her grandfather asked.

"Pretty important." She looked up, smiling tremulously. "It's an invitation to a dance. To the big New Year's Eve ball at the Melborn."

She flew upstairs to her closet and took the white and blue gown into a tearful embrace.

When she called for Annette next day, Annette took her joyously up to her room. She, too, went to her closet and brought out a new evening gown—a pink marquisette trimmed with multiple tiny pink bows.

"And a slit skirt, Em! To the knee!"

"It's darling!"

"I'm going to wear it to the Melborn—the New Year's Eve ball, you know."

"I know," said Emily, smiling. "I'm going."

"*You're* going?" Annette's astonishment was so great that they both laughed. "Who with?"

"Cab Edwards."

"Has he been taking you out?"

"Just to a couple of dances!"

Annette kissed her rapturously. "He's very nice! And so terribly old! Mamma! Mamma! Guess what!"

Aunt Sophie came hurrying in, and she was as pleased as Annette.

"But do you know what they say about the Edwards boy, Emily? He changes girls a lot. He doesn't want to get serious because he's head of the family."

"Well, that suits me!" said Emily, laughing. "We're just *friends*, Aunt Sophie!"

Aunt Sophie looked dubious.

"Wait till the girls hear! Let me tell them," Annette urged, and during the salad course she dropped her bomb. The surprise was unflattering but the unfeigned rejoicing warmed Emily's heart.

"She's been going around with an older crowd," Annette explained importantly.

"See that you don't get to like them as well as you do us!" cried Nell, hugging her.

Emily could feel her stature rising—like Jack's beanstalk! It was astonishing, but not so astonishing as the way her own feelings had changed. "And all because of a dance!" she marveled.

The corn flowers in her hair, and on the white and blue gown, were as becoming as the clerk had said they would be. And she wore the pearl earrings—although earrings weren't in style.

"But they suit you!" Alice said turning her around when they met at the Sibleys' where Cab took her first, to join his crowd. Emily met Sam Hutchinson who had put the big diamond on Carney's finger, and the man who had come down from the Cities to take Betsy to the dance. Bob Barhydt was his name.

Tib Muller looked angelic in a white dress trimmed with swansdown. "I made it myself," she said when Emily admired it. "I have so many talents. I can sew and cook and draw and do Betsy's hair."

"And dance," said Emily. "I hope you and Fred are going to dance together tonight."

Tib gave her light laugh. "Oh, naturally! He's engaged me for the Gaby Glide."

Automobiles left the party at the brightly lighted Melborn. They swept across the lobby and up the grand staircase, and music rushed down to greet them, for Lamm's Orchestra was already playing.

> *"Oh-h-h-h-h every evening hear him sing,*
> *It's the cutest little thing,*
> *Got the cutest little swing . . ."*

"*Hitchy coo, hitchy coo, hitchy coo,*" everyone sang, and Cab jigged at the entrance to the ballroom which was glowing with poinsettias and holly. He handed Emily her slipper bag.

"Don't take too long to powder your nose."

"I won't."

There was a frantic belated scribbling of names. Bob Barhydt asked her for a dance, and so did Sam Hutchinson, and Lloyd, of course, and Dennie, and Tom Slade in his West Point uniform who had come with Irma Biscay. Some boys from her own class slid across the room. Were they, too, impressed, she wondered, by her going around with an older crowd? Hunter came, and Fred, and Scid—but he was Cab's brother; he didn't count.

Jim Baxter didn't come. "Why should he?" Emily thought blithely. "Jim Baxter and I will never in this world have anything in common." Why, she wondered, had it seemed so tragic to be unable to charm him at the sleighing party?

Don was the length of the room away. She recognized him at once by his proud square shoulders. She saw him dancing with Annette—and with Gladys, Nell, Ellen. He looked moody and contemptuous.

She kept hoping he would ask her for a dance. But he didn't. He didn't even look her way. And yet she was sure not only that he had seen her but that he knew she was having a wonderful time.

"He doesn't like it," she thought. "He likes me always to feel inferior."

She recognized his faults more plainly than she used to. But the feeling that swept her when she saw him was deeper than it used to be; it was frighteningly deep.

"I'm growing up. I'm capable of feeling more. And I'm in love with him!" she acknowledged in her heart.

She felt depressed. The orchestra was playing "The Sweetheart of Sigma Chi."

But that gave way to "Everybody's Doing It," and Fred Muller made her try the Turkey Trot. Everyone praised her dancing. "I must tell Mrs. Anderson,"

Emily thought. "She'll be so pleased!"

She met Annette in the dressing room. "Having a good time?" Emily asked.

"I'm trying to," said Annette. "But Don is in the vilest mood! Sometimes I think I'll ditch him for Jim. Jim is sure to be a football star."

Out on the streets an eloquent whistle blew. Inside a cheer went up and horns and rattles made a joyful din. The orchestra started "Auld Lang Syne," and everyone joined hands and danced in a great revolving circle.

Nineteen thirteen was coming in! She had dreaded it so! But it found her, Emily Webster, dancing at the Melborn.

"Maybe my 'lost year' is going to be like Betsy's, wonderful!" she thought.

Cab shouted over the racket, "Making a New Year's resolution?"

"Yes, I am," Emily called back.

"What is it?"

"I'm going to put in a telephone!"

"Hooray!" he cried, as the circle broke, and whirled her into a waltz.

16
The Wrestling Champs

THE DAY AFTER NEW YEAR'S was memorable on two counts. First, Emily ordered a telephone. She told her grandfather hesitantly at breakfast that she wished to put one in.

"Why not? Why not?" he answered. "We have plenty of money in the bank."

"You don't think it would bother you?" she asked.

"Not a bit. I kind of like the things."

The second event was, of course, the formation of the Boys' Club.

The three Syrians arrived first, coming in the front gate as before, stamping their feet carefully on the porch, and showing brightly expectant faces at the door. As before, too, they were scrubbed and shining and carried gifts.

"You mustn't do this!" Emily protested, unwrapping a package which proved to contain a *baklawa* cake, criss-crossed like a checkerboard. "You don't bring presents to a club."

"But it's the New Year's, ma'am! Happy New Year!" cried Kalil.

"Happy New Year!" "Happy New Year!" echoed Layla and Yusef.

They ran to shake hands with Grandpa Webster, and Kalil started to tell him about their adventures with the skates, gliding in long strokes around the dining room and falling with an exaggerated bump. He sat laughing with his curly hair tousled while Grandpa Webster shook with mirth, Layla squealed and an appreciative grin spread across Yusef's broad face.

Emily took Layla to the piano and showed her the beginner's book. "We won't have time for much today," she said. "But we'll do what we can. Next week, come half an hour early and we'll have a real lesson. Climb up on the piano stool now."

Layla jumped up like a squirrel and waited, bright-eyed. Emily drew up a chair alongside. She thought back down a corridor of years to her first lesson from Miss Cobb and struck a note.

"That's middle C," she said. "We always begin with middle C."

Shortly she saw the two American boys turning in at the gate in their heavy overcoats, knitted caps and shiny new rubbers. They looked big and rosy. They were in no hurry to come inside but scuffled in the snow and threw snowballs. They climbed the steps with a suggestion of reluctance.

"They're the ones I'll have to work hard with," Emily thought.

Introductions were stiff. Kalil and Yusef started to shake hands as they did with grown people. The two Bobbys looked sheepish, and Bobby Cobb said roughly, "We know these kids!"

"And this is Layla!" said Emily.

"Pleased to meet you," they muttered in unison, staring with mixed curiosity and admiration. The earrings, the bracelets, the red-tied braids looked odd, but she was certainly pretty.

"Draw up and get warm," urged Grandpa Webster hospitably, and they all took chairs near the glowing heater. Bobby Sibley kicked Bobby Cobb who kicked him back, and Bobby Sibley grinned. The Syrians looked at them with bright vigilant eyes.

Emily passed fudge, and Grandpa Webster asked, "Have you thought of a name for your club?"

"I don't think we ought to name it until we elect officers," answered Bobby Cobb.

"You can't elect officers until you know what you're electing them to," objected the other Bobby.

"Oh yes you can! You just go ahead and elect them!" Bobby Cobb looked at the Syrians. "I think an American boy ought to be president," he said.

No one replied and Emily passed the fudge again. "Do any of you have any ideas about a name?" she asked.

"It might be just the Boys' Club," said Bobby Sibley lamely.

"But it isn't a Boys' Club! We've got a girl in it; haven't we?" Bobby Cobb looked belligerently at Layla who gazed demurely at the tips of her worn shoes.

"Not exactly," said Emily. "But she'll be coming to take a music lesson on your club day, and she'd like to be an honorary member, if you don't mind."

"Naw, I don't mind!" said Bobby Cobb.

"She could be here for refreshments," said Bobby Sibley, and grinned at her.

Neither Kalil nor Yusef spoke. They had not spoken since the Americans came in.

"Better get going then," Grandpa Webster said briskly. "Pass the fudge again, Layla. We'll call it the Boys' Club till you think of something better. And now you'll want to elect officers, I suppose. They'll need some paper and pencils, Emmy."

"Here they are."

"President first," said Bobby Cobb. "And I think—" But Emily interrupted.

"Before you vote," she said, "I'd better repeat all your names. This is Kalil, and this is Yusef—" To her distress, the two Bobbys giggled.

Bobby Sibley tried to sober his face. "Those are funny names," he remarked in half apology.

Kalil spoke eagerly. "Mine means Charles," he said. He pronounced the "ch" oddly. "And Yusef's name means Joseph."

The Bobbys snickered again. One whispered to another, "Sharles!" and the other said, "Oh, my gosh!"

Emily went on quickly. "And then there are two Bobbys. If anybody wants to vote for a Bobby he must be sure to put on the last name."

"You can call me Bob," Bobby Cobb said loudly.

"No siree! I'll be Bob! I'm the oldest."

"I'm the biggest! And I can throw you when we wrestle."

"Like heck you can!"

"Aw, I'm the champion and you know it!"

Kalil spoke unexpectedly in a clear voice. "We can wrestle."

They turned and looked at him.

"In a pig's eye!" said Bobby Cobb, his voice heavy with scorn.

"Syrians can't wrestle!"

"We can," Kalil repeated.

"Come on outdoors and prove it then."

Emily was appalled. Bobby Cobb was so much bigger, and both Americans so much brawnier than the Syrians that she was afraid it would be a most unequal contest.

"Oughtn't we to get the officers elected first—" she began, but to her surprise, her grandfather waved her to silence.

"Shucks! Let's have a wrestling match! And the winner can be president. What say?"

"Ya! Sure! The winner can be president," the Bobbys yelled jubilantly.

"I'll referee," said Grandpa Webster. "I used to wrestle in the army."

"Did you, my grandpa?" Kalil asked with interest, and again the Bobbys snickered.

"Oh dear!" Emily thought painfully. "Can we ever make a success of this club?"

Her grandfather continued to talk placidly, as he brought out his overcoat, cap and rubbers. "Yep! I was fuller of tricks than a dog is of fleas."

"What was your weight?" Bobby Cobb wanted to know.

"I was light. But I spread dust on the backs of plenty of bigger men. 'The bigger they come, the harder they fall,' I used to say."

"Hey, that's good!" cried Bobby Sibley, taking a poke at the strapping Bobby Cobb who said, "Oh, yeh?" and batted him.

With the Bobbys tusseling, Kalil and Yusef silent, Layla dancing excitedly and Grandpa Webster marching in the rear, they went out to the snowy back yard. Emily followed apprehensively.

Grandpa Webster propped himself against a tree, a look of pleased importance on his face. He spat.

"Let's get it all clear," he said. "The rules'll be catch as catch can. No gougin'! No bitin'! No—" he chuckled—"no spittin' in the other fellow's eye! But any holt is fair." His eyes, under their bushy brows, moved appraisingly over his quartette of small warriors. "Who's taking on who first?"

Four pairs of eyes looked around uncertainly.

"We'll start off with Kalil and Bobby Sibley," Grandpa Webster decided.

The two faced each other for a moment, Kalil

watchful, Bobby grinning self-consciously. Then Kalil reached out and grasped Bobby by the wrist, throwing himself against him at about mid-waist. Bobby dropped violently, and in a second Kalil had his shoulders pinned. He looked toward Grandpa Webster.

"Well," Grandpa Webster said, "that's that!"

Kalil got up. Bobby Sibley got up too, looking puzzled.

Bobby Cobb said slowly, looking at Kalil, "You lucky stiff!" But Bobby Sibley gazed at Kalil with new respect.

Grandpa Webster motioned to Bobby Cobb and Yusef. "Next!"

This match was even briefer. Bobby Cobb, plainly panting to re-establish native prestige, catapulted into Yusef like a barrel going down hill. Yusef landed on the ground with a thud, Bobby on top of him.

"And that's that!" Grandpa Webster said again. "All right then! The winners take each other on. Kalil! Bobby Cobb!"

They stepped forward and squared off.

For a couple of moments they stalked around like roosters. Bobby Cobb pranced like a heavy Plymouth Rock making up his mind to attack a rival. Kalil pranced also, but gracefully, like a leghorn or—Emily thought—better still, like a spirited bantam.

What struck her even more was that he seemed to

prance with a surprising purpose. Bobby Cobb blundered around hoping for nothing, it seemed, except the opportunity to fling his superior weight against his enemy. Emily knew nothing of wrestling and so could not know what Kalil had in mind. But it certainly seemed to be no clumsy accidental crash of bodies.

Three times Bobby Cobb rushed his light-footed opponent. The first time Kalil simply stepped aside with a little look of puzzlement. When Bobby Cobb rushed a second time, Kalil stepped aside again, put out a quick experimental hand which hooked in one of Bobby's armpits and almost threw him headlong.

"I dare you to try that again!" Bobby yelled and made his third rush, plainly prepared to capture Kalil's hand if Kalil tried the trick again.

Kalil didn't. He simply stepped aside and as Bobby plunged with his awkward Plymouth Rock stagger he caught Bobby's wrist in both his own hands. What followed then was beyond Emily. She knew only that Kalil twisted, Bobby toppled over Kalil's shoulder, fell headlong, grunted, and was rolling when Kalil landed on him.

There was a great thrashing of arms and legs. There was a great noise as Bobby Cobb loosed a small-boy bellow of rage and Kalil—giving tongue for the first time—sounded a shrill excited cry of triumph.

There was more thrashing of arms and legs, more cries, increasingly confident from Kalil, more bellows, now full of despair from Bobby and then, to Emily's amazement, it was over.

Not a wrestler, she could not have told the obviously skilled tactics by which Kalil had so surprisingly got his bulkier rival pinned. But there was no question about his being pinned. He lay there as flat as a pancake with Kalil flat on his chest.

White-faced, bright-eyed, exultant, Kalil scowled down into Bobby Cobb's face and growled through gleaming teeth, "You got enough?"

Red-faced, amazed but suddenly grinning, Bobby Cobb yelled, "Mister, I certainly have! How'd you do it?"

Answer came not from Kalil but from Grandpa Webster's voice exploding on the side lines.

"How'd he do it?" cried Grandpa Webster. "He put the nicest double wrist-lock on you that I ever saw. By Jingo, I couldn't have done better myself when I was twenty!"

Kalil released his hold and leaped to his feet. All triumph vanished from his face. He helped Bobby up and began to brush him off with apologetic phrases.

Bobby Cobb broke in. "Hey, Charley! Don't apologize for licking me! Teach me how to do it."

Kalil smiled widely. "Of course!"

"If you show me that, boy, I'll betcha I can throw even guys in the Sixth Grade."

"Show me, too, Charley!" Bobby Sibley cried. "Say, who taught you to wrestle anyway?"

"Mr. Jed."

"Where is he?"

"He's gone away."

"Did he teach you, too, Joe?"

Yusef did not answer and Grandpa Webster nudged him. "How about it, Joe? Did Mr. Jed teach you too?"

"Oh, yes, Grandpa!"

"He taught both of us," Kalil said. "And we would like very much to teach you."

"Next meeting then," said Grandpa Webster. "My stomach is flapping against my backbone."

Emily fled to the kitchen almost bursting with joy. Pouring cider, slicing cake, with Layla working deftly beside her, she heard a fraternal clamor in the dining room. "Sure, Charley!" "Lookee here, Joe!"

Her grandfather remarked that the two Bobbys ought to call him Grandpa as Charley and Joe did. She went in with a plate of sandwiches.

"And Charley and Joe are to call me Emily, as the Bobbys do. No more 'ma'ams.'"

"All right, ma'am," said Kalil and bounced with laughter. He was himself again—merry, lively, dramatic, gesticulating with both hands.

"Bless Mr. Jed, whoever he is!" Emily thought.

While they ate they completed the elections, by the broom-straw method. Bobby Sibley became treasurer and immediately demanded dues.

"Dues?" repeated Kalil, puzzled.

"Money. Cash. Spondulix. If I'm going to be treasurer, I want something in the treasury, boy. Shell out now, everyone!"

"Does it cost money to belong to a club?" Kalil sounded anxious.

"Darn right it does! A penny at every meeting."

Grandpa Webster nodded. "That's right, boys. And I've got a proposition. I want to belong to this club, but it's turned into a wrestling club, and I'm too old to wrestle. So how will it be if I pay the dues? I mean everybody's dues."

"Gee, Grandpa! That would be all right!" Treasurer Sibley said, wide-eyed.

"Here you are then!" Grandpa Webster took out his purse and laid down seven pennies.

Refreshments were lavish. Frightened by Bobby Sibley's keen interest in the subject, Emily had outdone herself. But none of her efforts equaled the *baklawa* cake. Made of uncounted paper-thin layers, filled with honey and chopped nuts, it was as mysterious as it was delectable.

"Say," asked Bobby Sibley, chasing the last crumb with his tongue, "does your mother make this often?"

"Always on holidays," Kalil said politely. "Won't you please come and have some?"

"See you on the Fourth of July!"

"We'll see 'em a week from today! And Charley won't be the champ much longer after he shows us that trick."

"We'll all be champs."

Suddenly Bobby Cobb shot up, his red face shining beneath his red-gold hair.

"Hey, kids! That's the name for our club. We're the Wrestling Champs!"

"We're the Wrestling Champs!" "Hooray for the Wrestling Champs!" A cheer echoed against the ceiling of the little dining room.

It still seemed to echo after the boys had gone racing down the snowy path together, calling out plans, in noisy concord.

"Grandpa," said Emily thoughtfully. "Did you know that Kalil and Yusef could wrestle?"

A smile spread slowly over Grandpa Webster's face, round and innocent beneath the skull cap.

"Well now, maybe I did!" he said. "And I certainly take my hat off to that Mr. Jed."

17
Supper with Miss Fowler

BY THE TIME THE COLLEGE crowd left at the end of
Christmas vacation, Emily was too busy to miss
them. She had scarcely seen them in the handful of
days that intervened; Don, she had not seen at all. The
momentum inspired by the highly successful Wrestling
Champs had pushed her into another project.

She was teaching English one day a week to Mrs.

Mohanna and Mrs. Tabbit.

It had come about because she went to return the *baklawa* cake pan and found Mrs. Mohanna alone. Her husband and children, her interpreters, were gone, and yet she was bursting to express her feelings. With her bright eyes pleading to be understood, her small hands gesturing, she rushed to pick up Layla's doll, the perfume, the picture books and puzzles. (The skates and mittens were significantly absent.) She ran her fingers up and down an imaginary piano and kept saying "God Bless" and "Thanks" and "God Bless" again.

When she rushed to the kitchen Emily, using sign language herself, took the long-handled coffee pot out of her hands. Mrs. Mohanna understood and laughed. She seized Emily girlishly by the hand and they ran outside, up the snowy street to Mrs. Tabbit's house.

Emily had never been in Yusef's home before. It was a little more pretentious than Kalil's. The lamp hanging from the ceiling was made of brass with a dangling chain. There were easy chairs and pictures on the walls.

Mr. Tabbit was not at home, and neither was Yusef. But there was an assortment of younger children to whom Mrs. Tabbit—a short fat woman with a merry face—spoke volubly in Arabic. They said haltingly but politely that their mother was full of thanks and that their brother had liked the skates. Mrs. Tabbit herself ventured a few English phrases, but they were obviously her entire vocabulary.

Mrs. Tabbit, too, ran to the kitchen, and Emily didn't know her well enough to protest, which amused Mrs. Mohanna who twinkled at her. The children went out to play, and while the three women drank sweet, dark, foamy coffee out of tiny cups they tried to talk.

It was interesting, Emily observed, to see how much they could communicate in spite of the barrier of language. Mrs. Tabbit showed Emily her embroidery work, and Mrs. Mohanna ran home to get hers. They admired Emily's watch bracelet but she didn't know how to tell them it came from her grandfather. They admired the locket and she said, "Mother," pointing to each of them and rocking a baby and nodding and then at herself, shaking her head. After a puzzled moment they cried together, "Imma!" "Imma!" and Emily repeated "Mother! Mother!" and they said "Mother," jubilantly.

Then and there Emily decided to teach them English. Here was another thing she could do, right in her own home without neglecting her grandfather. She would get a small blackboard and some chalk—

When she told him her idea, Grandpa Webster

began to laugh. "By Jingo, you're your grandmother all over again! She taught school in a parlor, too."

"I remember," Emily said. It had been the first school in Deep Valley, 'way back in the fifties.

"And your mother would be all het up about this!" he added, looking wise.

The Syrians were slower to accept the idea. Emily was rebuffed at first, with excessive politeness, but nevertheless rebuffed, when she took it to Little Syria. Mr. Mohanna of the poetic speech and huge mustache, and prosperous Mr. Tabbit who wore a gold watch chain, were alike dubious of the proposition, and the women were suddenly shy.

But Emily pointed out how much help the women could be to their children with school work and to their husbands in business if they learned a little English. She told of the pleasant time they had had drinking coffee together.

"I want them to come to my house now."

She spoke eloquently, and she was plainly a popular figure. She won. They settled upon Wednesday as a good day for the classes, and the following Wednesday the women arrived, smiling, gay scarves over their heads, and Emily, like her grandmother, taught school in a parlor.

Or, rather, in a dining room, for Grandpa Webster wouldn't have been left out for the world. She set the blackboard up near his easy chair. He helped with the lessons, and afterwards, when they had coffee, he taught the women to say "coffee," "sugar," "cream," and "doughnuts" with much laughter.

They were fascinated by the little house. Mrs. Mohanna touched the piano and said, "Layla? Layla?" Mrs. Tabbit admired the antimacassars which Emily's grandmother had crocheted for her chairs.

The next week they asked if they might bring Mrs. Scundar. The following week it was Mrs. Mahluff. They were learning quickly, and their gratitude was touching. They never came empty-handed; in spite of Emily's protests they brought pastries and embroidered belts and pieces of handmade lace.

No wonder they were happy about it, Emily thought! They had been like caged birds. Their husbands learned English at business where they did very well, she had discovered. Some of those who had come ten years before and started out as peddlers, now owned their own stores. The children learned the new language at school, but the women had no chance to learn.

"This class should include all the women in the settlement. But I couldn't handle that in my small house. The public schools ought to take it over."

She broached the matter to her grandfather. "Don't you suppose the schools could be persuaded to start

English classes for the Syrians?"

"No harm in trying, and we've got that contraption there." He nodded at the telephone.

Emily laughed. "I'll call Miss Fowler."

At first she thought she would ask Miss Fowler to supper. The plan required a leisurely talking over. But she still had that shrinking from bringing outsiders into the little house. Instead she asked if she might bring a picnic supper to Miss Fowler's apartment. She told briefly what her scheme was.

Miss Fowler was enthusiastic. "You have a wonderful idea, Emily. Two wonderful ideas, for I'd love a picnic supper. Bring enough for three, though. I know another teacher who would be interested in working up Americanization classes."

"When may I come?"

"Tomorrow night? I'll make the coffee."

Elatedly, Emily put beans to soak. Miss Fowler came from Boston; she ought to like baked beans. They would keep hot, too, in a crockery jar. The next day she baked them, according to her grandmother's recipe, and baked brown bread and made cole slaw. She baked an apple pie and fixed the basket daintily with a lunch cloth and napkins on top.

She sat with her grandfather while he ate his bread and milk, talking about the great plan. She had changed to the new rose-colored wool, and now she put on the brown velvet hat with the rose underneath, and her coat and furs; and picked up the basket.

"You look like Little Red Riding Hood," he chuckled as she started away.

The basket was heavy, but Emily was too happy to mind. She walked briskly over the dark slough. She was bursting with her plan. And it was fun to be taking a picnic to Miss Fowler's. She had come to be fond of the little apartment, so warmly inviting with its fire, its books and magazines, and the pictures which always beckoned her thoughts to far-away places.

When Miss Fowler drew her hospitably into the living room, Emily saw a card table set up before the fire.

"I thought we'd have our picnic here," Miss Fowler said. A tall man came in with an armful of wood.

"Emily, you know Mr. Wakeman."

"Why, of course!" She looked up into friendly brown eyes.

He put down the wood, dusted himself off, and they shook hands.

"You look like Little Red Riding Hood, Miss Emily."

"That's just what my grandfather said."

He lifted the basket. "This is heavy. Did you walk?"

"Oh, yes!"

"And she lives all the way across the slough!"

When Emily's wraps were hung in the closet, they all went to the kitchen with the basket.

"I hope things are still hot," said Emily. "That coffee smells good, Miss Fowler."

"So does this," observed Mr. Wakeman, sniffing at the pie.

"You've even brought a lunch cloth and napkins!" Miss Fowler spread them on the card table, and Emily set out the baked beans and brown bread, the butter in its print of strawberry leaves, the cole slaw.

As soon as they were seated Miss Fowler said, "Start right in on your big idea, Emily. This can't be a late party, for Jed and I teach tomorrow."

Jed! Emily put down her fork. She looked across the table at the large, handsome young man who was serving himself to beans with pleased concentration.

"Do you, by any chance, wrestle?"

He looked up, smiling. "Yes."

"Are you, by any chance, Mr. Jed?"

"Some people call me that. You can just drop off the mister."

Emily stared at him radiantly. "Oh! Oh! I don't know what to say! I don't know how to tell you what that meant to Kalil and Yusef—the day we started the Wrestling Champs—that's our club!" She was too confused to talk intelligibly.

"Kalil told me that he won," Jed Wakeman said.

"Oh, yes! He won! And it changed everything for them. The American boys looked at them with different eyes . . ." She broke off. "But they said Mr. Jed had gone away."

"Why, yes! I was away for Christmas. But they told me all about it when I came back."

"All about what?" Miss Fowler said. "I want to hear." So Emily told the story, bubbling over with her excitement and the happy memory of Kalil's great triumph. She told about her grandfather acting as referee, and how Kalil and Yusef had been renamed Charley and Joe, and about the name of the club, the Wrestling Champs. All three were laughing.

"To think of you being Mr. Jed!" Emily ended.

"Well, you didn't know that I was Mr. Jed, but I've known for some time that you were Emily. The boys told me about the Wrestling Champs, and Layla told me about her music lessons and, of course, the women try out their English on me."

"Wait till Grandpa hears!" Emily said.

The baked beans were a great success. Jed Wakeman ate like Bobby Sibley, Emily thought. She didn't eat much. She was too busy talking.

"What are the women like, Emily?"

"They're sweet. So warm-hearted and hospitable!

And they're very religious. Their religion is the center of their lives. They get respect and obedience from their children. They do beautiful embroidery and crocheting. And their cooking!" She turned to Jed. "Have you tasted *baklawa?*"

"Yes. It's heavenly. But it can't compete with this pie."

"They deserve to be helped." Emily looked as she looked on the debating platform, alert and eager.

"The men need help, too," said Jed. "They need some simple classes in American history and government to help them in getting their Americanization papers."

"That's their greatest ambition," said Emily, "to get their Americanization papers. They love America. They adore it. It's hard to understand when you see their difficulties and humiliations here. The new world must be a lot better than the old one."

"Freedom is pretty important," Jed said soberly.

Miss Fowler said that many of the larger cities had such classes for the foreign born. They met in the evening.

"The government finances them, I believe. But the application has to be approved by the school authorities. I'm sure Miss Bangeter will like the idea, and Mr. Hunt, the Superintendent of Schools. I'll talk to them tomorrow."

"I'll talk to Mr. Sibley if you want me to," Emily cried. "He's very influential."

"Leave something for me," said Jed.

"You've done enough already!" She looked at him with shining eyes. "How did *you* come to be interested in the Syrians?" she asked.

He laughed. "Why, it's because of the Syrians I'm here. I'm a southerner."

"I could tell that from the way you talk."

"Louisiana. Tulane University. I want to take my Master's in sociology after I've taught a year or two. I heard about the Syrian colony here. It's a particularly interesting one. Deep Valley, of course, is a bit of New England transplanted to the middle west, and in the heart of it is this alien growth. I thought I'd like to do a thesis on the reactions of the two groups. I was especially interested to see just what the New Englanders were doing to help."

"I'm afraid you found they weren't doing anything," Emily said.

"Well!" answered Jed. "One of them was!"

Everything he said seemed complimentary, somehow, although he wasn't gallant in the artificial sense. But plainly he liked her, and she liked him.

When the dishes were washed and he had helped Emily into her coat, he went for his own.

"I'll carry that basket home," he said.

"It was a lovely supper, Emily," Miss Fowler declared, smiling. "And I think we've accomplished quite a lot."

They walked home across a starlit slough, Jed carrying the basket and holding her arm, looming very tall and big above her. They were still talking about Syrians. He knew where they came from. It was the Lebanon district, he said. She told him about Mr. Meecham.

"I want to interview that old gentleman."

"He likes the Syrians, Grandpa said."

When they turned in at the gate he stopped and looked up the path to the little house. Light from the lamp her grandfather had left in the window streamed across the snow.

"So this is the Hull House of Deep Valley!" Jed said.

Emily looked up quickly. "Why do you say that?"

"Well, it is, isn't it? Jane Addams invited the poor and the lonely and the strange right into her house in order to help them, and you're doing the same."

Sensing something tense in her silence, he said in a puzzled tone, "You've read *Twenty Years at Hull House,* haven't you?"

"Yes. My oration, when I graduated, was about Jane Addams and Hull House."

"And you never saw the similarity between what

she did and what you're doing?"

"Not till this moment. But I've often thought I would like to do what she did, if I could only go to college."

"And now you're doing it without going to college!" he replied.

On the porch he took off his hat. "I'd like to come to call if I may."

"Of course. My grandfather will be so delighted to meet Mr. Jed."

"When may I come?"

"Saturday night?"

"Thank you very much."

"That Jed Wakeman is *nice*," Emily remarked aloud when she reached her own room. He was, she thought, such a happy normal person, so—outgiving.

Her eyes chanced to fall on Don's picture inspecting her disdainfully. She took it up and changed it from the front row of pictures to the back. As she did so she wished she could put him that easily into the background of her life.

She turned away smiling. "Just wait till I tell Grandpa that he's going to meet Mr. Jed!"

18
Mr. Jed

EMILY HAD A WARM FEELING of pleasure about the request to call.

Don had always just dropped in, indifferent to her convenience. Cab had only taken her to dances. There was a flattering formality, an indication of a genuine wish to get acquainted, about Jed Wakeman's overture. It gratified her.

The ungratifying thought occurred that he might be coming just to talk about the Syrians.

"What makes me have ideas like that?" she asked herself. "There's a side of my nature that's always trying to pull me down—the way Don does. Well, I won't allow it! He asked to call because he likes me. And I like him. And I'm glad he's coming."

She wondered whether it was usual for a girl to serve refreshments on such an occasion. Annette would make fudge, probably, or something in the chafing dish. But she had no chafing dish, and she couldn't bear to think of taking Jed into the kitchen with its old range and oil stove and the wash basin with the roller towel hanging beside it.

"He *does* like to eat, though," she remembered.

She decided to have freshly baked cookies in the jar, and then wait for the inspiration of the moment.

Arranging the little parlor on Saturday evening, she felt the familiar qualms, but she suppressed them. She had subscribed to the *Atlantic Monthly* and to *Theatre Magazine* after seeing them at Miss Fowler's apartment, and now she laid the newest issues on the parlor table. She put music on the piano rack. She shook down the stove and added fresh coals so that the fire would be glowing when Jed came in.

Observing these preparations, Grandpa Webster put on a clean collar. He was jubilant about the visit.

"What's he like, Emmy? Big, I'll bet."

"Yes, he is."

"Shoulders like an ox, I'll bet."

"Yes, he has big shoulders."

"That's the way wrestlers are built. I've known plenty of 'em, thrown 'em, too. I'll tell him some stories!" He chuckled in anticipation.

Emily secretly hoped that he wouldn't tell too many. But she was glad her grandfather was staying up. She liked to have her home be like other girls' homes. If she had a father and mother, and a young man called, they would certainly wish to meet him, and her grandfather stood in their place.

"Of course, I'd just as soon he didn't stay up too late," she admitted, smiling into her mirror as she took a last-minute peek. She was wearing the rose-colored dress again, but she had added big gold earrings that had been her grandmother's. She sat down to wait.

At eight o'clock exactly the old doorbell chimed, and Emily opened the door. The tall young teacher almost touched the lintel, although his hat was in his hand. He handed Emily a green-wrapped parcel, obviously flowers, and she gave him her slow shy smile. She introduced him to her grandfather and went to the kitchen.

"I never had flowers given to me before," she thought, arranging yellow roses in her grandmother's

Parian vase. She carried them into the parlor.

Jed was straddling a dining room chair, smiling over the old man's account of Kalil's triumph.

"Cutest double wrist-lock you ever saw! I couldn't have done better myself when I was twenty."

"Charley is a bright boy," said Jed. He stood up when Emily came in, and she took her usual rocker. Grandpa Webster talked on with Jed listening and laughing. Jed seemed to be having a very good time, but Emily began to wish her grandfather would remember that it was past his bedtime.

At last he stood up, shaking Jed's hand warmly. "Come to a meeting of the Wrestling Champs, why don't you?"

"I'd love to, if I may." Jed glanced at Emily.

"Of course."

"Come to our Lincoln's Birthday meeting. We're going to have flags and a decorated cake. And I'm going to tell them about Abe. Emmy and I have been studying him all winter, and besides I feel as though I knew him because I fought in his war."

Jed leaned forward. "So did my grandfather."

"He did? By Jingo!" Grandpa Webster beamed. "What was his regiment?"

"I'm ashamed to say I don't know. But he was under Beauregard."

Emily's heart sank. But her grandfather rallied gallantly. "Those Johnny Rebs were darned good fighters!

I met a few at Gettysburg. Tell you what we'll do . . ."
He studied Jed from under his bushy brows. Emily
saw that he liked the big, gay, self-possessed young
man but she did not dream how much until he completed his sentence. "Tell you what we'll do," he repeated. "After I've told the Champs my side of the
Civil War, you can tell them your grandfather's side."

And having made this magnificent gesture,
Grandpa Webster went to bed.

When the door had closed behind him, Jed said,
"What a soldier!"

He looked around the softly lamplit room. "And
what a treasure of a little house! It's more like the
homes down south than most of the Deep Valley
homes I've been in."

Emily was too astonished to reply.

"It's so full of old things. Isn't that a Boston rocker
you're sitting in?"

She jumped up. "Why, I don't know! It's one of the
things my grandmother's family brought from New
Hampshire in their covered wagon. I've always loved
it."

"No wonder!" he replied. He ran his hand along
the landscape on the chair's top rail. "I don't believe
they made those stencil decorations after 1840. My
mother could tell you. She knows all about such
things. I've picked up a little from her."

"If you like old things," said Emily, "you must

come and see the parlor."

He walked around it, smiling tenderly, examining the carving on the sofa and side chairs, pausing before the secretary, lifting the objects in the what-not carefully in his big fingers. He smiled down at the wax flowers.

"These are delightful."

"My grandmother made them. I've kept everything the way she left it for Grandpa's sake. I've often wished I could bring in some modern things."

"You could, of course. For myself, I like to mix old and new. But so many houses here have nothing old at all. And a house with nothing old in it seems—unseasoned." He gave the parlor a last circling glance. "How my mother would love this room!"

"Tell me about your family," Emily said when they were sitting beside the stove again.

"It's a short story," he replied, "because there are only three of us, and we're very good friends. My Dad and mother were at special pains to make a friend of me, I suppose, because I didn't have brothers or sisters. We've always had a lot of people around—writers and artists. Dad is a writer, and mother an artist. And I was always included in the circle."

It accounted, Emily thought, for his self-confidence. She did not think he would be awed by anyone or at a loss in any situation.

"Where did the wrestling come in?"

"College." He grinned. "I can qualify for membership in the Wrestling Champs. I was middle-weight champion my last two years, urged to go into professional wrestling. But I liked sociology better. Now how about you? First, you're a schoolgirl in a hair ribbon; then, a pretty young lady at a dance, and now an earnest student of sociology."

Emily laughed, coloring. "Speaking of sociology," she said, "what's the news of our Americanization class?"

"Miss Bangeter likes the idea. Not that you've answered my question! And so does Mr. Hunt. But it will have to come up before the school board."

"Oh, dear!" exclaimed Emily.

"What's the matter with that?"

"Mr. Whitlock is president, and he doesn't like Syrians."

"Don't worry. No reasonable person could object to such classes. I went to see old Mr. Meecham. He's a character! And he'll come to the school board meeting."

"So will Mr. Sibley, I'm sure. And Miss Cobb is very much interested. When will it be?"

"The last of the month. I'll keep you informed."

They talked about Jed's debating team. It couldn't come up to last year's, he said. They talked about northern winters. Jed liked them, especially the sleighbells. "No one had prepared me for how jolly the sleighbells are!"

"Have you learned to skate?"

"I'm still bad. But will you go skating some night?"

"I'd like to."

They talked so long that Emily went to the kitchen and made cocoa, Jed following her, continuing to talk. He ate seventeen cookies and said they were delicious.

Putting on his overcoat, he apologized for the length of his call. "Please forgive me. I was having too good a time. How about that skating now?"

They decided on Wednesday night. He was at the door when he turned and looked toward the coal stove.

"Don't stoves like that need coal at night?"

"Why, yes! They do."

"I'll put it on for you."

"It isn't necessary. Thank you, but I do it all the time. Grandpa had a bad cold at Christmas."

"He's certainly a soldier!" said Jed, walking toward the stove. He picked up the full scuttle which always stood in readiness, and the coal went rattling in.

February, although so short on the calendar, always seemed long to Emily. Snow kept on falling, although there was so much of it already. She grew tired of shoveling paths, of dumping coal into the heater and taking out ashes. No amount of cream could keep her hands soft! But February, this year, was nicer than usual.

She and Jed went skating often. Arms crossed and hands clasped, they glided down the pond, smiling at the stars, drinking in the icy air, enjoying the gay clamor around.

Sometimes he appeared after school, wearing his mackinaw, his skates over his shoulders, and she would hurry for her skates, and her jacket, and fur hat and muff, and they would stay on the pond while the snow put on its twilight gown of blue.

One day Jed said, "Did you ever read Thoreau's *Walden*?"

"We read some of it in school."

"I used to love the part about Walden Pond in winter—because I'd never seen snow, I suppose. He told about cutting out a chunk of ice and kneeling down to drink and looking into 'the quiet parlor of the fishes.'"

"How nice!" cried Emily. "It sounds so cozy!"

On Valentine's Day the boy from Cook's Book Store brought her a leather-bound copy of *Walden*. On the fly-leaf Jed had written, "But your parlor is cozier!"

Before Valentine's Day he had attended the Lincoln's

Birthday meeting of the Wrestling Champs. Judge Hodges attended too. The dining room was brave with flags; the cake was decorated; and Jed brought Grandpa Webster a lithograph of Abraham Lincoln. North and South honored the martyred president in perfect amity.

Jed attended all the meetings after that, and with the same assurance he started calling for Emily after the meetings of the Browning Club. Alice Morrison was teasing, and Miss Fowler's black eyes had the matchmaker's sparkle.

"Jed's so nice, Emily! The whole high school likes him. When he came, he started calling the women teachers by their first names, with that courteous 'Miss' prefixed, of course. Miss Bangeter was startled at first but now she's Miss Caroline to all of us. He's made us all friendlier; he's such a friendly person!"

Emily's blue eyes shone in their thickets of lashes. "Yes, he is," she said.

Another dance came along, and Cab invited Emily. Then Jed invited her, and was disappointed when he found she was going with Cab. He came to the dance alone and took so many dances that Cab—in the midst of the party—shook Emily's hand in mock farewell.

"Good-by, Emily! That's the way it always is. Just when I get me a girl lined up, someone steps in and takes her away."

But Emily knew he didn't really mind. She and Cab were just friends, as she had told Aunt Sophie.

Jed danced smoothly and serenely. Both tall, they looked well in the mirrors of the Elks Club Hall. She was wearing the white and blue gown, and Jed loved it.

"You have distinction, Emily. And that fine old jewelry is exactly right for you."

"Distinction!" Emily thought. What a beautiful word! She liked it better than if he had said she was pretty.

Peter Pan with the great Maude Adams came to town and there was a rush for tickets. Jed got two in the parquet, and they had a very good time, for both of them loved the theatre.

Uncle Chester and Aunt Sophie were there and Emily introduced Jed. The next day Aunt Sophie telephoned.

"Your uncle and I thought your young man was charming."

"I like him myself," Emily said. "What's the news from Annette?"

"Oh, parties as usual! Mostly with Don. She and Don are getting awfully thick."

To Emily's chagrin her heart still twisted.

But she had hardly thought about Don. With Jed added to the Browning Club, music and dancing lessons, the Wrestling Champs and the English class she was very busy.

"How do you do it?" Jed asked.

"Oh, Miss Fowler loaned me Arnold Bennett's book, *How to Live on Twenty-four Hours a Day*." But then, because she could really talk with Jed, she grew serious.

"I filled my winter up in a sort of desperation. I just couldn't seem to face it that I wasn't going to college."

They were having cocoa in front of the coal stove after a skating expedition. Jed looked at her with a puzzled expression.

"What made you feel so badly about not going to college?"

"I love to learn."

"But you certainly haven't stopped learning."

"I'd like to be—a really cultured person."

"Well, you're certainly on the way to being. And Emily—it's a good thing for the Syrians of Deep Valley that you didn't go to college."

Her eyes filled with tears.

Jed reached over and patted her hand. He got up.

"Speaking of Syrians, that board meeting's coming up Friday night. May I call for you? Miss Bangeter has asked me to present our case, but if I run into difficulties I'll turn to you like Jerry Sibley did before the St. John game."

19
Webster Talks a Few

"YOU'RE NOT EXPECTING trouble up there tonight, are you?" Grandpa Webster asked on the evening of the school board meeting.

"Not really! Of course, Mr. Whitlock doesn't like the Syrians. He's been bad-humored about the whole thing." Emily laughed. "Jed says that if he's hard to handle he's going to call on me. Grandpa, where do I get my gift of gab?"

"From your mother," he answered promptly. "By Jingo, she could talk your head off when she was interested. Not about recipes or patterns or what Mrs. So-and-So said to somebody else, but politics—that kind of stuff. You should have heard her argue with your Uncle Chester."

Putting on a fresh shirt waist, Emily eyed her mother's picture. She picked it up and studied the posed and stilted figure. She did not look like her mother, although they both had curly hair, but there was something hauntingly familiar in her face.

"Maybe I'll have to talk somebody's head off tonight," Emily told her, smiling.

It was snowing. Jed stamped on the porch and came in covered with white snow. "See here! When does this let up?" he asked.

"There are pussies on the pussy willows," Emily reassured him, buttoning her coat.

"And I fed some juncos this morning," Grandpa Webster said. "Going north. Too warm for 'em here. Well, good luck, children! Don't let old Whitlock talk you down!"

"No one can talk Emily down," said Jed, and they went out into the white haze. He held her arm closely as they crossed the windy slough and climbed Walnut Hill to the high school.

"I should have hired a cutter," he said. "I've been

meaning to take you cutter-riding behind some sleigh-bells. *There's* a handsome cutter!"

A team of white horses drew it, and a coachman held the reins.

"It's Mr. Meecham," Emily said.

"Good! That's one for our side."

The school board met in the Faculty Conference Room, just beyond Mr. Hunt's office. The members sat around three sides of a long baize-covered table—Mr. Hunt and Miss Bangeter at the ends and Mr. Whitlock in the middle with his back to the wall. He looked as pompous as he had on Commencement night, and kept smoothing his mutton-chop whiskers, first on the right side and then on the left, with a commanding finger.

The sponsors of the plan for Americanization classes sat against the opposite wall—Gwendolyn Fowler, Miss Cobb, Mr. Sibley, Mr. Meecham. Mr. Meecham's beard was even longer and whiter than Emily had remembered it, and his expression more bitter. But he smiled when he shook her hand.

"I've seen you down my way," he remarked. Although he was so seldom glimpsed outside his high iron fence, Mr. Meecham was said to know all that went on among his Syrians.

Emily and Jed seated themselves with the sponsors and, after routine business, Mr. Whitlock stood up. He told his colleagues that a group of citizens wished to discuss a scheme which he considered very ill-advised.

"But we will listen, of course," he said. He nodded brusquely toward Jed. "Proceed, Mr. Wakeman!"

Jed acknowledged the ungracious introduction with unperturbed affability. He bowed.

"Mr. President, Miss Bangeter, Mr. Hunt, and members of the school board," he began in his pleasant soft voice, and settling his tall body in an easy pose he discussed the proposed classes briefly. They had been operated successfully elsewhere; they were financed by the federal government; they would be held in the evenings, at the high school, and the subjects would be English, United States history and government.

"The idea is to help new arrivals to adjust themselves and to prepare them for the examinations they are required to pass before they can be admitted to citizenship."

He smiled at Mr. Whitlock. "I'm referring, of course, to the Syrians. And some of the rest of you are so much more familiar with them than I am, that I'm going to yield the floor." He turned to Mr. Meecham.

The old man rose to his feet. He was almost as tall as Jed, and he made a strange figure with his piercing angry eyes, his flowing beard and his old-fashioned suit of rusty black.

"I came here," he said, "to vouch for the Syrians.

I have known them for over twenty years. They are honest and hard-working; they have done very well in Deep Valley under tremendous handicaps of prejudice and bigotry. I think it would be desirable and expedient in every way to offer them the opportunities which Mr. Wakeman has outlined. But I don't expect this board to do it. I learned long ago not to expect anything from Deep Valley where the Syrians are concerned."

Whereupon Mr. Meecham sat down, glaring.

Mr. Sibley spoke next. He said much of what Mr. Meecham had said but in tactful phrases. Miss Cobb added only that she approved the plan. She had demurred to Emily that she was not an orator. But Emily had explained that her value lay in her presence, because of the high esteem in which she was held. Last, Miss Fowler expressed the willingness of the high school faculty to assist in the project.

Jed rose again. "That's the story, Mr. Whitlock."

Mr. Whitlock rose.

"Before the vote is taken," he said, speaking slowly and smoothing back his whiskers, "I should like to make a few points. I agreed absolutely with one thing Mr. Wakeman said. We who have lived in Deep Valley for many years do indeed know the Syrians better than he does."

Emily flushed.

"We are not, as Mr. Wakeman seems to think,

unaware of their presence. We know them very well—too well, some of us think." He smiled wryly at a fellow member of the board of whose opinions he seemed to be certain. "A lot of us believe they should be kept in their place or they will cause trouble. We don't believe in pampering them. I don't mind going on record as holding those views."

He stroked his whiskers in silence for a moment.

"I believe in America for the Americans," he said then explosively. "I believe that immigration should be restricted. *Restricted,*" he repeated, pounding the table. And he began to pour out figures about the alarming increase in population. The flow of statistics, Emily observed, was impressing several board members. They scribbled them down and began to look worried.

"*So,*" Mr. Whitlock ended on a loud note, "I am opposed to the whole business." And he called for a vote.

Jed rose. "Before we vote, Mr. Whitlock, Emily Webster would like to have a word."

Emily sprang to her feet. She was trembling with indignation at what he had said about Jed. She stood with her curly head high, her cheeks crimson, looking at her audience. The facts she had previously marshaled were not pertinent at all, after Mr. Whitlock's absurd but obviously effective attack on unrestricted immigration.

She began slowly. "Mr. Whitlock, Miss Bangeter, Mr. Hunt, and members of the board . . ." The recitation of names gave her time to collect her thoughts.

"Perhaps," she continued, "immigration *should* be restricted. I don't suppose we can take the time to argue that here, for it hasn't very much bearing on this evening's business. Our immigration laws allowed some Syrians to come to Deep Valley. The question we must decide is how we are going to treat them."

She paused. "Over the winter I've come to know them pretty well. Not so well as their friend, Mr. Meecham, knows them." She smiled at the old man. "And not so well as Mr. Wakeman knows them. But better than most Deep Valley people do. Deep Valley is, we are all aware, a beautiful town and a very fine town for most of us to live in. But it hasn't treated the Syrians well. It's never taken the trouble to get acquainted with them. So I would like very much to tell you a little about them."

Then she told—in the manner of one telling a story—of her association with the rejected immigrants on Mr. Meecham's rejected land.

She began with Kalil and Yusef and the frogs' legs and went on to the game of Crack the Whip in which Kalil had been hurt so maliciously. She told of taking him home, and of the warm hospitality she had received—the coffee, figs and raisins, the excitement, the pleasure, the blessings on her head.

She told of her Christmas visit and the tender ritual of the donkey. She told of the children coming laden with gifts on the holiday and of the Wrestling Champs. She described the wrestling match in complete detail, squeezing out its humor. Everyone at the table was laughing; even Mr. Whitlock laughed reluctantly when Bobby Cobb went over Kalil's shoulder and Kalil and Yusef were rechristened "Charley" and "Joe."

Emily turned in a smiling aside. "Here, by the way, is Mr. Jed."

She told of her visit to the women when their interpreters were not at home, of their eager responsiveness when they talked in sign language together. She told of the English class held in her own dining room and of her pupils' loving gratitude.

"But they're crowding me out of my house," she added with laughing affection.

She leaned forward. "I ought to be talking about what we want this board to do for the Syrians. But I can only talk about what we ought to let them do for us: share their gaiety and warmth and generosity and kindness with the rest of Deep Valley."

She sat down, her lips quivering.

Mr. Whitlock stood up. He brushed his whiskers back, first on the right side and then on the left.

"That was quite a speech, Emily. I remember that

you did well on your Commencement oration." He glanced around the table. "Shall we take a vote?"

The vote was taken, Jed glowing down at Emily. It was counted. Mr. Whitlock rose a last time.

"It has been decided," he said with unsmiling face. "It has been *unanimously* decided," he began again, and at his solemn emphasis on the word "unanimous" Emily caught her breath in despairing premonition of defeat, "that the school board of Deep Valley shall petition the federal government to give financial support to Americanization classes in our city."

He was plainly going to say more, but before the words could come out a joyful Babel interrupted. Mr. Hunt cried "Hurrah!" Miss Bangeter, casting off dignity for once, caught Emily to her queenly bosom. Miss Fowler had started for Emily, but when Miss Bangeter got there first, she hugged Miss Cobb who hugged her in return. Mr. Sibley patted as much of Emily's back as was not covered by Miss Bangeter's embrace and Mr. Meecham leaned so close that his beard tickled her ear.

"Emily," he said. "When you're down in Little Syria again, come in and have a dish of tea."

And that was not all. Mr. Whitlock, continuing to smooth his mutton-chop whiskers, first on the right side, then on the left, smiled. As smiles go in this world, it wasn't much. Jed said later that he had seen bigger on a cat. But as Mr. Whitlock's smiles went, it was tremendous.

"Emily," he announced when the turmoil had subsided so that he could be heard. "I'm not wrong often, and maybe time will prove that my first opinion on this matter was right. But you convinced me. I'll admit it. I told Mrs. Whitlock on Commencement night that you could charm a woodpecker away from a telegraph pole. Now I'm going to tell her that you're even better than I thought. And I know she'll agree."

Jed exulted all the way home. "You were wonderful, Emily! I always regretted that I never heard you debate. Well, tonight I found out what everyone has been talking about."

He looked down at her radiantly through the still thickly falling snow. "What makes it so unbelievable is that you're not ordinarily much of a talker. In fact, you're the most restfully quiet girl I know."

Emily smiled up at him happily. "I'm so glad it came out as it did! I was pretty personal."

"It was the only way to get them." They turned in at the gate and plowed up a drifted path to the little porch. "By George! *That* time Webster talked a few!"

He was gazing down at her triumphantly. The light from the lamp in the parlor poured out upon her face—flushed, shy, happy, snow clinging to the disheveled curly hair. Jed Wakeman leaned down suddenly, took her cheeks between his hands and kissed her.

Emily swayed toward him in speechless surprise. She drew away, her eyes like stars, and turned the knob of the door.

"Good night," she whispered.

"Good night," he answered. As she closed the door quickly she heard him jump off the porch and go briskly down the snowy path.

20

Don Comes to Call

THE NEXT TIME HE brought her home, Jed didn't kiss her good night, nor the next, nor the next—

For the first time in her life Emily wished urgently for a confidante. She wanted to talk with some girl she could trust—or with her mother.

"It would be wonderful to talk to you," she said, staring at her mother's picture with her hand clasped around the locket. "The whole thing is so—puzzling."

She wondered about it continually as she went her daily round. Had he been offended at her response? Or had the kiss been a casual gesture? But he didn't seem the kind to be casual with a girl of her kind. Perhaps he was like Cab Edwards, afraid to get serious.

"After all, he's going back to college next year. He may not want to fall in love."

And when she went that far in her thoughts it sounded absurd. Was she the same Emily Webster who had been so humble and adoring with Don? Could it be she seriously thought it possible that anyone so desirable as Jed Wakeman could be in love with her? The truth was that she did.

Something else puzzled her—her continued interest in Don. Jed, in two months, had come to fill her life so that she couldn't bear to think of his ever going out of it. Yet Don's picture, when she caught a glimpse of it at the back of her chest, the brown and gold volume of Browning, still had magic. When Don's name came into the conversation or when she thought of him, she felt a little inward shiver.

"Can you be in love with two men at once?" she wondered. That was another thing she wished she could ask her mother.

Gradually the snows were melting. There were days of wild rain-filled wind, swaying the trees, pommeling the windows of the little house. When they ended, the world was as cold as jelly. But the green shoots of the bulbs were up. Fat robin redbreasts were scouting in the bare trees, and down in the slough the blue-winged teals were back, and the mallards; she heard them quacking in the night.

There would be more snow, of course. But that didn't matter when you knew the pasque flower was in bloom.

"Probably we have some pasque flowers right on our own lot," she said to Jed.

They climbed the slope which was mushily green with patches of snow on the north side of the trees. And sure enough, among the matted leaves, they found three pasque flowers looking up in pale surprise.

"Let's not pick them," Emily said.

They turned and looked down to the roof of the little house.

"This seemed like a long way from home when I was a little girl. I used to bring picnics up here."

"Alone?"

"Oh, yes! Unless I brought a doll along."

She had never, she realized, talked about herself with Don. Don had never thought of her or her problems. Jed liked to hear about her childhood and her growing up. Little by little she had told him almost all there was to tell—about her parents, and her grandmother; her differentness in school; even the great pain of not being able to go to college. But she had not told him about Don.

Woodrow Wilson had been inaugurated president of the United States. Jed liked him. He actually preferred him to Teddy.

Easter was approaching. Over at Aunt Sophie's, Miss Mix was making Emily new clothes—a smoke-blue silk with lace frills around the wrists, and a navy blue suit with a cutaway coat and side-draped skirt. Emily bought a new white blouse and a blue straw hat with flowers. It fitted her head so closely that she hardly needed hatpins.

She took these purchases to Aunt Sophie's to try on with the suit, and she was pleased with her reflection in the tier-glass. Her dark-lashed blue eyes looked alive and happy, as though she were expecting something wonderful to happen.

"You look very up to date," Aunt Sophie said approvingly. "It's too bad Easter comes so early. It will be too cold for suits. But you can wear your new hat."

For Aunt Sophie, Easter meant two things—hats and Annette's return. But in spite of the fact that she had heard so much about it, Emily forgot the day that the crowd was coming home.

One morning she thought, "I believe the University crowd got in last night," and a little later she heard light steps on the porch, the door pushed open and there was Annette smiling below a green tam.

Emily pulled her in happily and kissed her. As soon as Emily had taken her coat, Annette began to dance about.

"See something new?"

"No. I've seen that shirt waist before . . ."

"Yes! But look what's on it!"

Beneath Annette's sorority pin was a second small jeweled emblem.

"It's Don's fraternity pin! Do you know what it means?"

"It means you're engaged, doesn't it? Or practically."

"That's exactly what it means! Engaged—practically!"

"Well!" thought Emily, staring above Annette's head as she hugged her. "That settles that!" Annette was engaged to Don, so she would have to put him out of her mind. She was glad of it. She heard herself saying to Annette, "That's wonderful, Annette! I'm so pleased!"

"I knew you would be. That's why I was anxious to tell you. Not everyone likes Don. Some people think he shows off. They think he's putting on when he is really just being himself. But you always appreciated him."

"Yes, I did," said Emily slowly. "What do Aunt Sophie and Uncle Chester think?"

"They're not too happy about it. Of course, the Walkers are very well-fixed people. But Don has moods. You know that, Em! And Papa and Mamma have seen him when he was pretty glum. But they'll get to like him. He's so nice when he *is* nice! I'm terribly in love."

They sat down by the fire, holding hands.

"When are you going to get married?"

"Heaven knows! He's going to Yale, you know. But I may not finish college. I may stay right here in Deep Valley next year and keep you company." Her tone changed. "You're looking awfully well, Em!"

"Oh, I feel marvelously. I wish Grandpa were better. He doesn't seem to have the strength he used to have."

"Well, that's natural at his age! Getting back to you, you do look marvelously. Still going out with Cab?"

"Sometimes."

"Mamma said she saw you at *Peter Pan* with that new good-looking high school teacher."

Emily smiled.

"Is he nice? Nicer than Cab?"

"Annette, I've told you that Cab and I are just friends. And Jed . . ."

"Jed?"

"Jed Wakeman. He's a very nice person whom I thoroughly enjoy."

Annette pounced at her, ruffling Emily's curly hair. "You're as close-mouthed as ever, I see. I'm having the crowd tomorrow. Can you come?"

"I'm terribly sorry. I have a date." Amused pride at being included so casually in a man-and-girl party was drowned out by her relief in not having to see Don. And yet she ought to see him—get over him completely—get adjusted to the fact that he was engaged to Annette.

"Oh dear!" Annette was saying. "What are you doing?"

"Well, you won't understand, but Jed and I are going calling—down in Little Syria."

"Whatever is the charm down there?"

"We have friends there."

"Friends?"

"Yes, friends," answered Emily with a prick of irritation. "Jed and Gwen Fowler and I have been working up some Americanization courses. Jed is working toward his sociology Master's."

Annette jumped up. "Oh, I understand!" she said. "You *do* have a crush on this Jed. I think it's awfully exciting, Em."

"We're just friends," Emily insisted.

"Just friends! That's what you say about Cab. And yet instead of being with your own crowd you go trailing off to Little Syria with him on Easter day. Well, my party is a supper. Can't you come after your Syrian expedition—and bring him?"

"Perhaps I can," said Emily slowly. Perhaps she ought to go. But she didn't want to take Jed—not yet—not until she had had a chance to settle her feelings about Don. "If you don't mind, I won't bring Jed this time. It would—it would be nice just to be with the old crowd."

"I know just how you feel!" Annette said.

Emily had asked Jed for Easter dinner, and before going to church she set the table with her grandmother's damask and the Haviland dishes, and smiled to herself to think that once she had been afraid to have Gwen Fowler to supper. Jed had removed completely the old sensitiveness about her house. She was entertaining the Browning Club for their final meeting next week—without a qualm.

How Jed had built up her confidence—in her house, herself, everything!

"Don always tried to pull me down. He liked to make me feel inferior."

Uncle Chester drove her and her grandfather to church. It was indeed too cold for suits, but the church bobbed with new hats.

Across the aisle she glimpsed square military shoulders, and her heart quivered in the old familiar way.

"That's just an involuntary reaction! It's just force of habit! Anyhow, I'll get over it," she thought.

At the end of the service Annette darted over to Don.

"They'll probably walk home together," Aunt Sophie said. "Would you like us to take you and Grandpa on?"

"Yes, I would," Emily said. "I have company coming for dinner."

"Anyone I know?" Aunt Sophie asked coyly.

"Jed Wakeman."

Aunt Sophie squeezed her arm. "All this romancing!" she said. "What do you think about Annette and Don? We hope it won't last. Thank goodness, he has three more years in college!"

Jed, coming from the Episcopal church, brought daffodils for the table and he praised the chicken dinner. He tried to persuade Grandpa Webster to go along with them to Little Syria.

"Easter is the most important holiday among the Syrians, Mr. Webster. Yusef has a new suit and Kalil has a new shirt and tie. He says the men go from house to house wishing everyone Happy Easter."

"Only instead of 'Happy Easter,'" said Emily, "they say 'Christ is risen!'"

"Emily," said Jed, "how could I ever write my thesis without you?"

"Well, you kids can tell me all about it," Grandpa Webster replied. "The Judge is coming over. We thought we'd have a little chess."

The melting snows, which left woodpiles, chicken houses and shabby houses bare, made Little Syria even less attractive than it had been in the winter. But the sun had come out; song sparrows were singing. And like the Syrian men, Emily and Jed went from house to house calling.

The rigorously observed Lenten season was over. "Christ is risen!" everyone said joyously to everyone else. And the wives passed Easter sweet cakes which were buttery, like doughnuts, and spicy. Kahiks, they were called.

There were bowls of beautifully colored eggs—purple, yellow, scarlet, and eggs colored by onion skins, a rich brown. The Syrians challenged one another to break eggs. One would hold his egg forward and another would joke, "A little more room, please! I can't get to it." They hit them tip to tip, each one trying not to break his own. The winner went on to challenge another winner until there was one final winner. He proved to be Mr. Tabbit.

"Now, he'll save his egg," Kalil explained to Jed and Emily. "The strongest egg is always saved, sometimes for years. We have an orange-colored egg we have saved for three years because it was the strongest."

At every house Jed and Emily were offered coffee, in little cups on a tray. They were offered pastries, candies, figs and raisins, and there was rose water for the children. Emily loved watching Jed. He was having such a good time. And he was just as charming with the humble people of Little Syria as he was with majestic Miss Bangeter.

Leaving the Mohannas, they passed the Bobbys entering.

"Charley said they would have *baklawa*," Bobby Sibley called.

"Did you know that Mr. Sibley took the Wrestling Champs on a hike and picnic yesterday?" asked Jed.

"Oh, Jed!" said Emily. "What you did when you taught Kalil to wrestle!"

She had already broken their casual engagement for the evening. Jed had been most understanding of her wish to be with her crowd.

"I believe he's the most unselfish person I ever knew," Emily thought.

The Syrians had sent Grandpa Webster sweet cakes, and Emily gave them to him with his supper. Then she changed to the new silk dress and her pearl earrings and went across the slough to Annette's.

"Alone!" she thought. "No Jim Baxter!" She joked

with herself to hold down an inward trepidation about seeing Don again. Now, at least, she was sure of her self-possession. She couldn't imagine ever losing that precious confidence which Jed had helped her to gain.

"I'll see Annette and Don together, and that will end my feeling for him; then maybe I'll fall in love with Jed. Maybe I'm in love with him already?"

It was a typical Sunday night party. The chafing dish was on the table. Annette, in an organdy apron, was pretending to make rarebit which Minnie dashed out from the kitchen to supervise. Gladys was banging the piano and different groups formed behind her to sing "When It's Apple Blossom Time in Normandy" and "Oh, You Beautiful Doll" and, of course, "The Sweetheart of Sigma Chi." Emily left her wraps in Annette's room and came in smiling. She knew that she looked well in the smoke-blue dress and the pearl earrings. And Jed had told her that she had distinction! She greeted the girls affectionately and Gladys jumped up from the piano.

"What's this I hear about you and the high school faculty?"

She found herself extremely happy to be there, and she was at ease, even when Don came to greet her. He took her hand in his long, slender brown fingers, smiling his most vivid smile.

"I'm awfully happy about you and Annette," Emily said.

"Think I'm good enough for her?"

"I feel like Aunt Sophie does about Annette."

"Oh, well then! I have to improve fast."

Jim Baxter was there. Testing her new skills, Emily went over to her burly Nemesis and asked about his chances for the first team next year. To her amused amazement he seemed embarrassed but enormously pleased and launched into an explanation of the competition that he faced from the other players.

Fred Muller came up to ask about her dancing. "Have you learned the Boston yet?"

The evening was fun, but at ten o'clock Emily began to think about home.

Aunt Sophie didn't have to mention Jim Baxter tonight. Don spoke so quickly that he must have been waiting for this moment.

"I'll walk over with you, Emily."

"Oh, please don't! I wouldn't like to take you away from the party."

"I'll come back!" he said, turning to smile at Annette, who called, "Don't steal him, Em!"

They started over the slough, which sounded like spring with a quack of ducks now and then. The day had grown progressively milder and the evening had the softness of spring. You could hear the sound of melting snow running and trickling.

He told her about the Masquers production of *Arms and the Man,* and about the Junior Ball which was coming up next week. It was late this year; they had held it off until after Lent. He was taking Annette, he said, and it was costing him a pretty penny.

"Flowers and a carriage and all that sort of thing. The J.B. counts up."

At the door Emily held out her hand but he didn't take it.

"I need to rest before the journey back. Do you have any cookies, Emily?"

"But the party is expecting you."

"And it won't be a thing without me; will it?" he asked, and followed her inside. The lamplight shone on Jed's daffodils. Don walked over to touch them.

"They're certainly hot house; aren't they?" She nodded. "I didn't think the spring had come that far along."

Although she didn't ask him to, he took off his coat. She took off her own and they sat down. She didn't go in by the fire. She sat in the parlor, pleased to think that she could sit in her parlor with Don and not feel embarrassed now. She loved it all, even the wax flowers. She sat in what Jed called the "lady's chair" and Don sat on the sofa.

He took out his pipe and filled it, and a cloud gathered over his brow as he tamped the tobacco into the bowl of the pipe.

"Do you know, Emily," he said, "I've never forgotten my visits to this house last summer."

"Is that so?"

"They were different from other calls on other girls. That locust tree with you underneath it! It stands out like a cameo."

"Me in a hair ribbon," she said.

"Yes." He looked up quickly. "Lord, how you've changed! I heard before I saw you that you had turned into a stunner."

Emily laughed.

"But you *are!*"

She seemed to be listening to a conversation which two other people were making. Don Walker was flattering some girl, and she didn't even care.

Suddenly she thought, "But he shouldn't be flattering a girl. Even me. He's engaged to Annette." She said abruptly. "You're very lucky, Don, to have persuaded Annette to take that pin."

He flushed. "I note, Miss Webster, that you're changing the subject."

"I know you have to hurry back, and I want you to know I'm happy about your engagement."

"It isn't exactly an engagement."

"Well, practically," she said and rose. "I really think you had better go back now."

He emptied his pipe and put it in his pocket, stood up and pulled on his coat, looking tragic. Emily wanted to laugh.

He couldn't bear it, she thought, because she wasn't tortured by his engagement. He was probably in love with Annette, and he was most certainly not in love with her. But it was more than he could bear to have her take the matter so calmly.

She was smiling so perceptively that he asked with annoyance, "May I know the joke?"

"There isn't any joke."

"I meant to tell you, speaking of this so-called engagement, to read your Browning. Remember 'The Lost Duchess?'" He quoted:

"Had you, with these the same, but brought a mind!
Some women do so . . . "

Emily interrupted.

"Don," she said. "Would you mind going home?"

He pulled his soft hat violently down over his forehead. "I suppose you think that I'm a cad."

"I just don't think about you. Good-by," Emily said, and closed the door firmly behind him.

21

Under the Locust Tree Again

GRANDPA WEBSTER LOOKED UP at Emily from beneath his bushy brows.

"Emmy," he asked. "Is Jed courting you?"

They were sitting at dinner on a day in early May. Emily had just come from the telephone to say casually that it was Jed; he wanted her to go to hear the Minneapolis Symphony Orchestra which was coming to Deep Valley—when her grandfather interrupted with his astonishing question.

"Why, Grandpa!" Emily cried. "What makes you say a thing like that?"

"Well," he answered defiantly, "it looks that way to me. It's flowers, flowers, flowers! And candy, candy, candy! And books! And shows! And a picture of Abraham Lincoln for me, although he's a rebel and he admits it. By Jingo, I know courting when I see it! I went courting once myself."

Emily sat and stared at him. She didn't know whether to laugh or to cry. "Why, Grandpa!" she protested again. "I thought you liked Jed."

"I didn't say I didn't, did I?"

"No, not exactly. But . . ."

"I only asked a simple question," said Grandpa Webster crossly. "Is he courting you, or isn't he?"

Emily looked through the bay window at the slough which was one golden sheet of marigolds.

"I don't know," she replied.

"You mean he hasn't popped the question?"

She shook her head. "But Grandpa, supposing he did pop the question? What would you do if you were me?"

He looked important. "Why, grab him! Grab him!"

"You would?"

"Certainly, I would! They don't come any better than Jed."

"But, Grandpa, just a minute ago you were saying . . ."

"I know! I know! I just wanted to know how things stood. But you're hard to suit if you don't take Jed. Your mother would have liked him! Your grandmother would have liked him! And I like him!"

Emily jumped up. Her eyes were shining. "Don't say any more! He hasn't asked me, and maybe he doesn't intend to."

"You're old enough," said her grandfather. "You're a year older than your grandmother was."

"I know, Grandpa. But maybe Jed doesn't."

"What do you suppose is holding him up?"

Emily laughed and started to clear the table. She wondered herself.

She continued to wonder as May progressed. They saw each other almost every day. He helped her and her grandfather with their spring raking and burning. He helped them with the gardening. He kept old shoes and an old coat in the woodshed and came over after school to shovel.

"Is it too early to set out tomato plants, Grandpa Webster?"

"I judge not."

"Then I'll bring some tomorrow."

He set them out, whistling like the blackbirds in the slough, and set Emily to work cutting paper collars for them—to keep the cutworms off.

"Jed's a pretty good gardener," Grandpa Webster said.

Jed wanted Emily to come to the high school whenever his team debated. Miss Bangeter, Gwen Fowler and the rest looked at them approvingly. He wanted her to go with him on research trips to Little Syria. They took tea with Mr. Meecham, and afterward they climbed the hill beyond the settlement and brought home violets and white boughs of blooming wild plum which were dizzily sweet, but no sweeter than the homeward walk at twilight with birds singing in the newly leaved trees.

"We're certainly congenial," Emily thought, her brows drawn together. "We're very well suited to each other—at least, he's well suited to me."

He was always so happy, and she was sometimes depressed, although not so often as she used to be. And he was so completely unselfconscious, so untroubled by perplexities and doubts of the sort which had always beset her. But they beset her less and less. He was always confident, without being at all vain, and he was building that same confidence in her.

"He'd be perfect for me," she thought. "But he'd be perfect for anyone. Would *I* be right for *him*?"

He had never, since that night when she talked to the school board, acted loverlike. When they walked he held her arm in a firm protective clasp. And she thought he felt what she did when their hands touched. But she couldn't be sure.

Grandpa Webster looked at her hopefully every morning, but she had no news.

He became less intent on the problem as Decoration Day approached. He began to examine the snowball bush. Tulips were in bloom all around the house. Lilacs were out, flooding the dooryard with fragrance. But nothing would do except snowballs for an old soldier's chest on Decoration Day.

"Take a look at this bush, Emmy! Aren't those buds slower'n time?"

She brought down his uniform and pressed it. He shined his medal, and his shoes. The Mayor came to call, and the question came up again as to whether the Civil War soldiers would march or ride in the parade. The Mayor, Uncle Chester, Jed and Emily all strongly urged riding, but Grandpa and the Judge opposed it. Grandpa Webster was emphatic.

"Let those Spanish American cubs think we're too old to march? Not on your tintype! If the South acted up again, the Judge and I'd be handier with our muskets than they would. Of course, the Judge didn't get the practise at Nashville that we got at Gettysburg."

He told the Wrestling Champs about the First Minnesota's famous charge until they knew the story by heart. Bobby Sibley never failed to say: "My Uncle Aaron was there; wasn't he, Grandpa Webster?"

"You bet he was! He was a friend of mine."

The Wrestling Champs decided to decorate Uncle Aaron's grave. They went further and voted to spend the money in the treasury for the project. Kalil favored an artificial wreath; he showed them with his hands how big it ought to be, gigantic, with trailing ribbons. Grandpa Webster was touched.

"I think Aaron would like it better, though, if you kept out enough for all-day suckers."

Several times, with all her tact, Emily brought up the question of the marching. "It's going to be hot this year, Grandpa. It's hot already. More like June than May."

"Shucks! We're just going to march past the reviewing stand. It wouldn't hurt a baby. Emmy, you pressed my uniform, didn't you?"

"Oh yes, Grandpa! And you shined the medal. Don't you remember?"

"That's right. Have you gone up to the cemetery yet to clean up the graves?"

"Not yet. I go the day before, you know."

"And this year," put in Jed, "I'm going with her. You can be sure there'll be a good job done. I'll come straight from school, Emily."

"Don't hurry," she smiled. "It will be cooler to work in the late afternoon."

She was ready when he reached the little house at four, wearing a workaday sailor suit and a ribbon in her hair. She had cut the flowers—snowballs, which had bloomed at last, iris, painted daisies, the last of the lilacs. The ends of the bouquets were wrapped in wet paper.

Jed carried the pail in which she had placed gardening tools and three empty quart jars.

"What are they for?" he asked as they walked across the slough.

"To hold the bouquets. We sink them in the graves and fill them with water."

"How many graves are there?"

"Three. My grandmother, father and mother."

The sun was glittering on the Indian paintbrush which colored the meadows of Cemetery Hill. All the way up the long road they met people descending with empty pails and hands.

"Everybody's up tidying graves for tomorrow," Emily said.

But when they passed through the tall arched gate the cemetery was empty. It was green and quiet with late afternoon sunshine touching the crosses and angels.

Emily led him to the Webster plot and showed him the graves—her grandmother's with the clasped hands, her father's with the open book, her mother's with the cherub.

"You sit on that bench and talk to me," said Jed. "There isn't work enough for two."

He dropped to the grass and began to rake and clip with swift efficiency. She looked at his broad shoulders as he bent over the graves.

"Jed," she said, "I'm so much happier than I was a year ago."

"What was the matter then?" he asked.

"It was just before I graduated. I felt lonely because I had six tickets, and no one to give them to but Grandpa. And I wished my father and mother could see me graduate, and I felt badly because I couldn't go to college. I'm so much happier now."

"Your mother would be glad of that," he answered gently.

"She's closer to me, too," said Emily. "Last year she was just that stiff picture on my bureau—I've shown it to you. But now . . .

"She got this locket for her graduation, and I wore it for mine. And I've found out that she liked the sort of work I've been doing with the Syrians. And when Kalil sold me the frogs' legs, and I wanted a recipe, hers was there!"

"Do you look like her?"

"I have her laugh, Grandpa says. She was awfully full of fun, and so am I when I have a chance . . ." Emily stopped. "I can't explain it, but she's been close to me all winter."

Jed was digging holes for the jars now, spading earth out briskly. "Do you think she'd approve of me?" he asked.

Emily's heart tightened. "Why—yes! As a matter of fact, Grandpa said the other day that she would like you."

"He did?"

"Yes." Emily's laugh, which was said to be her mother's, came suddenly. "He said she would have liked you, and my grandmother would have liked you, and *he* liked you."

"What was the argument about? Don't *you* like me?" He turned abruptly, brushing away a fallen lock of hair with a dirty hand so that dirt streaked his cheek. His brown eyes were questioning.

"Of course I do," said Emily. She more than liked him, she thought. She wished she could push that hair back, and touch his dirty cheek, and put her arms around him.

He went back to the digging. "Let's plant more things up here," he said. "I like plants better than cut flowers on a grave."

"So do I. Grandpa likes an old-fashioned bleeding heart."

"Let's plant an old-fashioned bleeding heart then."

He sunk the jars and went to the pump for water and filled them. As Emily arranged the flowers, he asked more questions about the family history.

"You know all this. Grandpa's told it to you."

"But I like to hear it again. I want to get acquainted with your people, and I want you to meet mine. You'll love my father and mother, Emily."

"I'm sure I will," she said. Her heart tightened again.

They were silent going down hill in the sunset. The past seemed to fill the valley like a mist. Her grandmother's school in a parlor, her father falling in the quarry, her mother buried in her wedding dress—they were all things she had been telling to Jed. And she saw last Decoration Day with the flags along the street, and the crowds, and the jaunty fife and drum corps leading the old soldiers:

"When Johnny comes marching home again,
Hurrah! Hurrah!"

"I hope that marching won't be too much for Grandpa tomorrow," she thought.

The moment seemed significant somehow, as

though it marked an end and a beginning.

"You were kind to go with me," she said, crossing the slough where the frogs were croaking and the marsh hens were cackling and the bitterns were making that noise like her own dooryard pump. "And you did all the work! Won't you come in for supper?"

"Thanks! I'd love to! Your grandfather will be in high feather."

But to their surprise Grandpa Webster had retired. He put his head, clothed in a nightcap, through his bedroom door.

"I thought I'd get a good night's rest on account of tomorrow," he said.

"Did you have any supper?" Emily asked.

"Yep! Bread and milk."

"Do you feel all right, Grandpa?"

"Fit as a fiddle," he replied.

She fried bacon for herself and Jed, and made tea, and opened choke-cherry jelly. They ate in the bay window. The sky was colored by the afterglow.

"Let's go outside," she said when the dishes were washed. And they went out to the bench beneath the honey locust.

The sky changed from rose to peach color and then to gray. The air grew cooler, and the evening star came out.

"Kalil says every person has a star of his own. You

have one and I have one and Grandpa has—I was sitting on this bench when Kalil first came with the frogs' legs."

And when Don came, she added in her thoughts. Don! That spoiled child! Jed was a man. Someone to respect, to look up to. Big and warm and protective and loving. Her feeling for him seemed to soar like that last bird against the evening sky. She spoke quickly.

"I took Layla to Miss Cobb last week. Did I tell you? Miss Cobb loved her, and she said she'd give her lessons if I should ever go away . . ."

Her hand was lying on the bench, and he took it. She thought swiftly that it must be rough. She rubbed and rubbed cream into her hands, but after she and Grandpa took the stove down, they had started making the garden—

Jed didn't seem to mind it being rough. He put it to his lips, and then suddenly he had taken her into his arms and was saying over and over, "Oh, Emily, I love you so!"

"I love you, too!" cried Emily.

She began to cry for she knew that now she would never be lonely again.

After a time they talked. It was dark by then. Fireflies were blossoming and fading all around them. Across the slough they could see the lights of Deep Valley.

"Why didn't you tell me sooner?" she asked.

"You're so young. And I knew how much you wanted to go to college. And you know, Emily, your grandfather won't live many more years. It may be so you *can* go to college."

"But I don't want to!" she cried. "As long as Grandpa is alive I want to be right here in Deep Valley. I want to learn right here, the way I have been learning. And I want to work with the Syrians.

"And after we're married. I won't stop learning. I'll learn with you. I'll be learning all my life."

Jed took her hand and kissed it again.

When he had gone she ran into the house. She pounded on her grandfather's bedroom door. "Grandpa! Grandpa!"

"What is it?" he asked sleepily.

"I just wanted you to know. I'm engaged to marry Jed."

"Well!" he answered. She could hear him sit up in bed. She could hear his satisfied chuckle. "That's good news, Emmy! I told you he was courting."

"He was!" Emily said. "Oh, Grandpa! He was!"

Maud Hart Lovelace and Her World

Maud Hart Lovelace in her 1910 high school graduation photo

MAUD HART LOVELACE was born in 1892 in Mankato, Minnesota. She always believed she was born to be a writer. From the time she could hold a pencil, she was writing diaries, poems, plays, and stories. When Maud was ten, her father had a booklet of her poetry printed, and by age eighteen, she had sold her first short story, for $10, to the *Los Angeles Times*.

The Hart family left Mankato shortly after Maud's high school graduation in 1910. They settled in Minneapolis, where Maud attended the University of Minnesota. In 1914 she sailed for Europe and spent the months leading up to the outbreak of World War I in England. In 1917 she married Delos W. Lovelace, a newspaper reporter and popular writer of short stories. They had one daughter, Merian.

In 1926 her first novel, *The Black Angels*, was published. Five more historical novels followed. Maud wrote two of them, *One Stayed at Welcome* and *Gentlemen from England*, in collaboration with her husband.

With the publication of *Betsy-Tacy* in 1940, she began the successful series known as the Betsy-Tacy books, which were based on the lives of Maud (Betsy) and her best friend, Bick (Tacy). The stories of her childhood in Mankato (the fictionalized Deep Valley), small-town life, family traditions, and enduring friendships continue to capture the hearts of her fans.

Maud died on March 11, 1980, in Claremont, California, and as she requested, she was returned to her beloved Mankato and is buried in Glenwood Cemetery. Her legacy lives on in the books she created and in her legion of fans, many of whom are members of the Betsy-Tacy Society, a national organization based in Mankato, Minnesota.

—Based on *Maud Hart Lovelace's Deep Valley*
by Julie A. Schrader. Copyright © 2002
by Julie A. Schrader. Published by
Minnesota Heritage Publishing.

The Betsy-Tacy Society
P.O. Box 94
Mankato, MN 56002–0094
www.betsy-tacysociety.org

The Maud Hart Lovelace Society
277 Hamline Avenue South
St. Paul, MN 55105
www.maudhartlovelacesociety.com

About
Emily of Deep Valley

Marguerite Marsh

*"Tall and rangy in ankle-length skirts, her curly
hair woven into a braid which was turned up with
a ribbon. . . . Emily wasn't plain, exactly, but her
face was serious. She was shy and quiet, although
her blue eyes, set in a thicket of lashes under heavy
brows, often glinted with fun."*

—From Emily of Deep Valley

"IN MANY WAYS, that book [*Emily of Deep Valley*] told a true story," Maud Hart Lovelace wrote in a letter in 1973. The story of Emily Webster is very much the story of Maud's friend Marguerite Marsh. Like she did with the rest of her Betsy-Tacy books, Maud based the characters and places in *Emily of Deep Valley* closely on the people and places she knew.

In this book we see Deep Valley not through Betsy's eyes but through Emily's. Just as Emily's childhood is very different from Betsy's, so was Marguerite's different from Maud's. Marguerite was a member of Maud's crowd of friends but didn't appear as a character in the main Betsy-Tacy books. The reason for this may have been that Marguerite didn't participate in as many of the social activities as the rest of the Crowd did. She lived with her grandfather on the edge of town and had much more responsibility growing up than others her age. Marguerite suffered many tragedies in her life, and she always coped admirably. The similarities between Marguerite and the character of Emily make it apparent

John Q. A. Marsh

"Cyrus Webster was clean shaven but his heavy eyebrows bristled with martial grimness."
—From Emily of Deep Valley

that Marguerite's story must have seemed very romantic to Maud. It's a great tale of coming of age and learning to deal with what life gives you by turning disappointments into new and wonderful opportunities.

The character of Grandpa Cyrus Webster is based on Marguerite's grandfather John Quincy Adams Marsh. Born in 1826 in Chesterfield, New Hampshire, John was a schoolteacher for several years before going into the mercantile business. His brother, George (Uncle Chester), had come to Mankato in 1853 and opened the first general store. Mankato, established in 1852 along the banks of the Minnesota River, held many new opportunities. George sent for John, who arrived in Mankato by steamboat in May 1854, bringing merchandise purchased in Boston and St. Louis. George and John Marsh operated the general store until they sold it in 1858.

The Marsh brothers had been awarded a contract to carry mail between St. Paul and Mankato once a week, but this was soon increased to twice a week and finally daily. The mail contract allowed the Marsh brothers to preempt one section of land for every twenty miles of the route. This resulted in the acquisition of considerable real estate. John Marsh served as Blue Earth County treasurer in 1855 and served as supervisor, trustee, and clerk of Mankato in its early years. John was instrumental in starting the Creamery Packaging Manufacturing Co., the first butter-tub factory in Mankato.

John Marsh and Sarah Jane Hanna were married on December 29, 1859, in Mankato. Sarah and her family had settled in Mankato in 1853. She taught the first school in Mankato during the summer of 1853 with twenty-three students. Maud refers to this when Emily visits the grave of her grandmother and reads her tombstone:

"Emily Clarke Webster. Born 1835, died 1904." . . .
Emily remembered her well. She was something of a personage in Deep Valley, for she had been its first school teacher. Far back in the fifties, when the town was less than a year old . . .

John and Sarah had two children: Charles (Marguerite's father) and Lizzie. Charles and his wife, Alice, were married in Mankato in 1885. Their first child was a son who died before Marguerite was born. Marguerite Elizabeth Marsh was born in Mankato on July 4, 1890.

Although John Marsh had accumulated a considerable amount of property, he suffered a financial setback in the early 1890s because of debts accumulated by his son. Unfortunately, Charles Marsh was not a successful businessman. According to the accounts in the Mankato *Free Press*, John had co-signed many bank notes that Charles could not repay. That might have been the reason that Alice took her two-year-old daughter Marguerite and moved back to her home state of Pennsylvania. Alice died there in 1901, and eleven-year-old Marguerite returned to Mankato to live with her grandparents. Marguerite was thirteen years old when her grandmother, Sarah Hanna Marsh, died on May 18, 1904. Her father, Charles, died soon after. She was left alone to care for her aging grandfather.

John, Sarah, and Marguerite lived in a modest home at 115 West Front Street (now South Riverfront Drive) atop a hillside on the west edge of town. The Marsh home faced north and was surrounded by a white picket fence.

Emily followed the faded white picket fence surrounding her grandfather's acre to the sagging gate which was always ajar. The sloping yard wasn't well kept. The grass was filled with dandelions; and the lilacs and snowball bushes needed pruning. The snowballs, though, were in bloom. The little house huddled against a low hill. It was old and weather-beaten. With its gables trimmed with scroll work and topped by absurd little towers, it looked like a dingy, fussy old lady, shrunken by age.

Emily's bedroom looked over the slough, which extended back into the sheltered valley that the town called Little Syria. From her windows she could see the humble rooftops of the Syrians.

The Marshes' house was on the west side of the slough, which separated them from the little settlement known as Tinkcomville. This addition was developed by James Ray Tinkcom (Mr. Meecham). Tinkcom's story is exactly as Maud describes in *Emily of Deep Valley*. The land he developed failed to sell because of its distance from the center of Mankato. Finally, in the 1890s, Tinkcom sold several lots to Syrian immigrants, and soon other Syrians settled in the little valley that became known as Tinkcomville. One family opened a general store selling groceries, shoes, and dry goods, and it later expanded into a thriving farm seed business. The high water table

James Ray Tinkcom

*"Mr. Meecham's beard
was even longer and
whiter than Emily had
remembered it."*
—*From* Emily
of Deep Valley

in the land below James Avenue helped the Lebanese cultivate large, bountiful gardens. They also raised chickens, cows, and pigs. Today this slough is much smaller than it was in Maud's day. In the late 1940s much of the slough was drained and a high school was built.

The story of *Emily of Deep Valley* begins with two important events: high school graduation and Decoration Day.

Decoration Day (now known as Memorial Day) was celebrated much differently at the turn of the century than it is today. The entire town joined in this patriotic holiday, celebrating with a parade and special ceremonies honoring fallen and surviving soldiers. The *Free Press* reported on May 31, 1909: "The thirty automobiles that were in line accommodated all of the patriotic organizations, Company 'H' and the Twentieth Century Band being the only ones in the procession that marched. The procession entered the opera house where streamers and flags were waving in profusion from the balconies and boxes." In *Emily of Deep Valley,* Maud writes, "And the white horse of memory was replaced by an automobile. Yet Decoration Day was always the same."

Maud Hart Lovelace's Deep Valley by Julie A. Schrader

Mankato High School, ca. 1910—Deep Valley High School

Maud appears to have based Grandpa Webster's experiences on those of Captain Clark Keysor (Cap' Klein), as John Marsh was not a Civil War veteran. General James H. Baker, a veteran of the Dakota Conflict and the Civil War, was the basis for the character of Judge Hodges. In 1952 Maud wrote, "Old Cap' Keysor and General Baker used to visit the various grades on Decoration Day to tell us about the Civil War and the Sioux uprising." These stories and the Decoration Day celebrations left a deep impression on Maud.

As was customary on Decoration Day, families honored and remembered their loved ones with visits to the cemetery. Maud uses Emily's cemetery visit to describe her family members' backgrounds, most of which are very similar to Marguerite's family members' with the exception of her father's.

For Marguerite (and Emily), the week before graduation was filled with excitement and preparations. As in *Emily of Deep Valley*, *One Night Only* was the four-act class play performed by Marguerite's senior class in 1909. Between acts, the class papers were read, including the Class Newspaper, the Class Prophecy, and the Class Will, and the evening closed with the Class Song, written by Eleanor Johnson (Winona Root).

Marguerite was vice president of the Debating Club and one of three students chosen to represent Mankato High School in debating contests with other schools. The two other students were James Baker (E. Lloyd Harrington) and George Pass. She graduated from Mankato High School on June 4, 1909. The class of 1909, with fifty-one members, was then the largest senior class to graduate from the high school. Other members of the Crowd to graduate with the class of 1909 were Clayton Burmeister (Phil Brandish), Thomas Fox (Tom Slade), Mary Eleanor Johnson (Winona Root), Charles Ernest Jones (Pin Jones), Earl King (Squirrelly), Mamie Skuse (Mamie Dodd), and Marion Willard (Carney Sibley).

The high school commencement exercises were always held at the opera house in order to accommodate attendance, with each student receiving six tickets to distribute among family and friends. The Mankato *Free Press* reported: "The curtain rose bringing to view the graduating class seated on the stage completely surrounded with stars and stripes as a background and canopy, while above suspended was the class year in green and red, the senior colors."

The story has Emily struggling with her feelings of displacement and loneliness after she graduates from high school and all of her friends leave for college in the fall. No doubt Marguerite struggled with the very same feelings. Maud herself may have had some of them even though she went to college the fall after her high school graduation. Maud went to the University of Minnesota but took time off after suffering an appendicitis attack. She also struggled to find her place, and that story is told in a conversation between Betsy and Emily: "That 'lost year' gave me a chance to do some thinking. I got acquainted with myself, I found myself, out there in California. . . . But I changed. I–I began to see the pattern. It did me good to get away from my friends. Do you see what I mean?"

Searching deep inside herself, Emily comes to the conclusion that she has to "muster her wits and stand in her own defense." In doing so, she finds that learning can go on with or without college. Emily begins her "program of self-improvement" by taking dance lessons, practicing the piano, and starting the Browning Study Club. She and her grandfather befriend two Syrian boys, and Emily begins a boys' club to help them make friends. Soon Emily is helping the Syrians with language and civics classes in her home and working with Jed Wakeman and others to convince the school board to offer "Americanization" classes for immigrants.

Jed Wakeman is very impressed with and supportive of Emily. He points out the similarities between Jane Addams's Hull House and what Emily is doing for the Syrians. This realization had never occurred to her. Social work was something she wanted to do if she went to college. She never dreamed she could do it on her own. As a romance begins to develop between Emily and Jed, she still holds feelings for Don Walker. Don's behavior has made her feel unworthy and dependent on him and finally leads her to a most empowering rejection of him:

"I suppose you think that I'm a cad."

"I just don't think about you. Good-by," Emily *said, and closed the door firmly behind him.*

That scene from *Emily of Deep Valley* poignantly illustrates Alexander Graham Bell's famous line: "When one door closes, another opens; but we often look so long and so regretfully upon the closed door that we do not see the one which has opened for us."

When the door closes on Emily's high school years, she thinks she has been left behind, but instead she steps through a new door and finds opportunities and happiness she never expected.

The Rest of Marguerite's Story

After high school, Marguerite continued to live with and care for her grandfather. She served as the secretary for the Mankato High School alumni association, and she was active in the First Presbyterian Church. Her grandfather John Marsh died December 26, 1915, and was buried beside his wife and daughter in Glenwood Cemetery. His only survivor was his granddaughter, Marguerite.

In the fall of 1916, Marguerite enrolled at the University of Wisconsin in Madison and studied home eco-

Marguerite Marsh, 1913

nomics. When war was declared in 1917, the YMCA immediately volunteered its support. Marguerite enlisted in the YMCA in November 1917 and served sixteen months with the 82nd Division in France. She was one of thirteen thousand YMCA workers who served in France during World War I. Marguerite was assigned to a YMCA café at Tours, France, and later was in charge of a canteen at Gondrecourt, with the First Army school. The YMCA also operated a recreational room where free entertainment was provided for the soldiers, including moving picture shows three times a week. Marguerite returned to New York with the 82nd Division aboard the transport ship *Sierra* on May 21, 1919.

In 1921 Marguerite enrolled in a hospital training course at the Presbyterian Hospital in connection with Columbia University in New York. She married Myron Wilcox in New York in May 1923. Myron was most likely the inspiration for Maud's character Jed Wakeman in *Emily of Deep Valley*. The couple moved to Cedar Falls, Iowa, where Myron had taken a teaching position as a professor of psychology.

Back in Mankato, the house where the Marsh family had lived was torn down; Oscar and Katherine Schmidt of Schmidt Saddlery Co. built an elegant house on the property in 1923. The two-and-a-half-story neoclassical-style house was designed by Henry C. Gerlach Jr., the brother of Midge Gerlach (Tib). Constructed of red brick, the house had fourteen rooms and a large gathering hall and took nearly two years to complete. The house remained in the Schmidt family until 1958, when the YMCA acquired it for office space. The house was torn down in 1988 to make room for a new facility.

Marguerite gave birth to a son, John Marsh Wilcox, on January 31, 1925. Just two weeks later, Marguerite died in Iowa City, Iowa. She is buried near her grandparents in Glenwood Cemetery in Mankato. From her obituary in the Mankato *Free Press*: "There are lives made stronger by adversity. For Marguerite Marsh, one after another the home ties of her girlhood were broken by death. Through it all, she preserved her brave faith, the sweet poise of character that carried her through to a fine womanhood in a happy home of her own."

Dr. Myron Wilcox, Professor of Education at the University of Northern Iowa, retired in 1960 and died in 1969. Marguerite and Myron's son, John, was a solar physicist at Stanford University and helped design and build the Stanford Solar Observatory. He died while swimming in the Sea of Cortez near Puerto Penasco, Mexico, in 1983. The observatory now carries his name: Wilcox Solar Observatory.

Emily of Deep Valley was published in 1950, twenty-five years after Marguerite's death.

—Based on *Maud Hart Lovelace's Deep Valley*
by Julie A. Schrader. Copyright © 2002
by Julie A. Schrader. Published by
Minnesota Heritage Publishing.

About Illustrator
Vera Neville

Vera Neville

VERA NEVILLE was born in Detroit, Michigan, on April 2, 1904. A year later, her family moved to Interlaken, New Jersey, where her father worked as a real estate developer. As a young girl, Vera took ballet, piano, and horseback riding lessons. She spent summers on her grandmother's farm in Canada, where she fell in love with animals and began to craft little drawings of horses, cats, and mice.

The Neville family returned to Detroit in 1916, and Vera began to study art in earnest, taking lessons from Paul Honoré, an American artist known for colorful murals. After high school graduation, Vera moved to New York City and began her studies at the Art Students League. At the League, Vera sharpened her skills and talent, training under renowned American artists George Bridgman and Cecilia Beaux.

In 1928 Vera married fellow artist William B. Hamaker, and they settled in Greenwich Village. Vera first began working in fashion illustration and advertising art but later found steady employment as a children's book and magazine illustrator. Her first children's book, *The Meddlesome Mouse*, which she both wrote and illustrated, was published in 1931.

Over the next thirteen years, Vera illustrated many children's books, including the comical *Lazy Liza Lizard* by Marie Curtis Rains; *The Lonely Little Pig*, a collection of animal tales; and *Highway Past Her Door* by Mary Wolfe Thompson, a young adult romance. Vera wrote and illustrated two books of her own, *Little Bo* and *Safety for Sandy*. She also drew the pictures for stories in children's magazines, such as *Child Life* and *Story Parade*, as well as Christmas cards for the American Artists Group. Her illustrations of animals and children were delightful and lifelike, full of motion and detail.

In 1944, the Thomas Y. Crowell Company, publisher of the Betsy-Tacy books, needed a new illustrator for the high school series featuring Betsy and Tacy, which Maud Hart Lovelace had begun to write. Lois Lenski, the artist of the first four Betsy-Tacy books, declined to illustrate the new longer books as she preferred to work on stories for younger readers. Lenski mentioned Vera Neville as a possible artist for the forthcoming series. Vera was hired in 1945 to illustrate *Heaven to Betsy*, the first Betsy-Tacy high school story.

Vera's illustrations of teenage Betsy and her friends

were authentic to the 1900s era. She studied photographs of Maud Hart Lovelace and her friends to create the lovable pictures of Betsy, Tacy, Tib, Carney, Joe, Cab, and all of the other characters in the books. Vera researched fashion, furnishings, and household items to make her illustrations as realistic as possible. Readers fell in love with Vera's charming and sometimes comical, sometimes heartbreaking depictions of Betsy Ray. The high school stories proved to be as popular as the younger Betsy-Tacy books, and Maud wrote a new one each year.

Vera Neville and Maud Hart Lovelace continued their partnership for ten years, which included the four Betsy-Tacy high school books, the Deep Valley books (*Carney's House Party, Emily of Deep Valley,* and *Winona's Pony Cart*), and the stories of Betsy's adult years, *Betsy and the Great World* and *Betsy's Wedding.* At the same time, Vera drew the pictures for several more children's books, including *A Lion for Patsy* by Miriam Mason and *Two Hundred Pennies* by Catherine Woolley.

Vera illustrated one more children's book, *Pigtail Pioneer,* in 1956 and then retired from the publishing world. She settled in Michigan and worked in her father's real estate business. She passed away in March 1979.

Vera Neville's remarkable artwork lives on in the

Betsy-Tacy books as new generations of readers become acquainted with Betsy and her friends.

—Teresa Gibson

Sources: Patricia Neville Downe;
Lilly Erickson; Elizabeth Riley,
Keynote Speech, 1997 Betsy-Tacy Convention;
Archives of the American Artists Group,
Smithsonian Institution

THE BETSY-TACY SERIES BEGIN

BETSY-TACY
ISBN 978-0-06-440096-1 (paperback)

Set in 1897, book number one is the classic, much-loved tale of the five-year-old Betsy, who finds a friend when a little girl named Tacy moves in across the street.

BETSY-TACY AND TIB
Foreword by Ann M. Martin
ISBN 978-0-06-440097-8 (paperback)

Now eight years old, Betsy and Tacy continue their adventures with the addition of the pint-sized, golden-haired Tib, a welcome third.

BETSY AND TACY GO OVER THE BIG HILL
Foreword by Judy Blume
ISBN 978-0-06-440099-2 (paperback)

The girls turn 10 in this book and, while venturing further away from home for the first time, meet a real Syrian Princess who lives in the Slough.

BETSY AND TACY GO DOWNTOWN
Foreword by Johanna Hurwitz
ISBN 978-0-06-440098-5 (paperback)

The girls, now 12, venture into downtown Deep Valley, where Betsy is introduced to the librarian Miss Sparrow, and the girls see their first automobile, and learn about the world of theater.

THE BETSY-TACY HIGH SCHOOL YEARS AND BEYOND

HEAVEN TO BETSY AND BETSY IN SPITE OF HERSELF

Foreword by Laura Lippman

ISBN 978-0-06-179469-8 (paperback)

Heaven to Betsy: In the first of the high school books, Betsy is 14 and a freshman at Deep Valley High. Boys become very important—especially one Joe Willard, a new boy in town.

Betsy in Spite of Herself: It's Betsy's sophomore year and she takes a glamorous trip to Milwaukee to visit Tib.

BETSY WAS A JUNIOR AND BETSY AND JOE

Foreword by Meg Cabot

ISBN 978-0-06-179472-8 (paperback)

Betsy Was a Junior: Julia returns from college and brings back the idea of sororities, which Betsy (unwisely) introduces to Deep Valley High.

Betsy and Joe: Betsy's senior year arrives and finally she is going with Joe! That is, until Tony (her freshman crush) suddenly changes his brotherly manner to a more romantic one.

BETSY AND THE GREAT WORLD AND BETSY'S WEDDING

Foreword by Anna Quindlen

ISBN 978-0-06-179513-8 (paperback)

Betsy and the Great World: Betsy sets off for a year-long tour of Europe to start her writing career and put some distance between herself and Joe.

Besty's Wedding: Betsy returns home as WWI is sweeping across Europe . . . will she and Joe finally find happiness?

THE DEEP VALLEY BOOKS

EMILY OF DEEP VALLEY

Foreword by Mitali Perkins

ISBN 978-0-06-200330-0 (paperback)

Maud Hart Lovelace's only young adult stand-alone novel, *Emily of Deep Valley* is considered by fans of her beloved Betsy-Tacy series to be one of the author's finest works.

"I never grow tired of cheering for Emily, and neither will a new generation of readers." —Mitali Perkins, author of *Secret Keeper* and *Bamboo People*

CARNEY'S HOUSE PARTY AND WINONA'S PONY CART

Foreword by Melissa Wiley

ISBN 978-0-06-200329-4 (paperback)

Carney's House Party: In the summer of 1911, Caroline "Carney" Sibley is home from college, and looking forward to hosting a month-long house party. Romance is in the air with the return of high school sweetheart, Larry Humphrey, for whom she's pined many years.

Winona's Pony Cart: More than anything the world, Winona Root wants a pony fo her eighth birthday. She's wishing so hard that she's sure she'll get one—at least, tha what she tells her friends Betsy, Tacy, and Tib…